Cherished

Kim Cash Tate

Recycling programs
for this product may
not exist in your area.

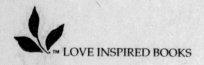 ™ LOVE INSPIRED BOOKS

ISBN-13: 978-0-373-78713-5

CHERISHED

Copyright © 2011 by Kimberly Cash Tate

www.LoveInspiredBooks.com

Printed in U.S.A.

For Emanuel and Nicole Lambert

Chapter One

Kelli London took her place on the piano bench and waited for her cue, grateful that her jittery hands were hidden from the crowd. She shouldn't have agreed to do this, but she loved her brother and had never seen him happier. How could she say no to singing at his wedding?

But it was the song Cedric had asked her to sing, one he'd heard only by chance. He had no idea what it meant to her. He didn't know that singing it would unleash memories of the last person she ever wanted to think about.

Laughter rose from the pews, and Kelli looked up, wondering what she'd missed.

"…and I'm sure Cedric wants me to get to the vows ASAP," Pastor Lyles was saying, "so they can get to that kiss they've been waiting for."

Kelli had only met the pastor once before, at her brother Lindell's wedding last fall, but it didn't take long to love his spirit and his style. A black man in his late fifties, he'd started Living Word Community

Church decades ago and watched it grow into a multi-
ethnic megachurch. At least a couple hundred members
were here today. Kelli guessed none of them thought
twice about the various hues and accents that had gathered to see this black couple wed. She loved that spirit
too.

Cedric was shaking his head with a shamefaced grin
as the pastor called him out. Cyd was smiling up at
him, gorgeous, beaming like the bright light she'd become in Cedric's life.

Pastor Lyles continued. "But I don't think he'll mind
one last song, and it's a special one, written by his sister."

Kelli drew a deep breath as Cedric and Cyd smiled
over at her, Lindell and Stephanie too—the flip side
of last fall. Then Stephanie and Lindell were the bride
and groom, and Cyd and Cedric were maid of honor
and best man, which was how they met. Kelli loved
the story, how Cyd turned forty on her younger sister's
wedding day, thinking she'd never marry herself. Now
here she was—a June bride. It was romantic that her
brothers would now be married to sisters, but it somehow added to her melancholy, that each of them had
found the love of his life.

Kelli gazed at the piano keys, and knowing they
had to, her fingers tapped the first notes. She fought to
stay in the moment, in the church. Her eyes swept Cyd
and Cedric, imagined the lyrics were just for them…

I will love you till the stars don't shine
And I will love you till the oceans run dry
I will love you till you know every why
I will, I will

of the heavy lifting." She smiled. "I kinda like having my brothers around again. Y'all are handy."

Cedric cocked his head, as if considering. "I kinda like having you around too."

"I know I do," Cyd said. "I'm so glad you decided to come."

"Thanks, Cyd, but I was thinking…" Kelli switched to lotus position. "You've got to be a tad overwhelmed. All these years, you've had this house to yourself. Then you got married a month ago, and Cedric moved in. And now, here I come."

"Are you kidding?" Cyd asked. "I bought this house eight years ago, *hoping* it'd be filled with other bodies." Clayton was a perfect location for her, since she was a professor at Washington University. "I just hate that it took so long. Come here." Cyd leaned across the bed, and Kelli met her halfway for a hug. "I really want you to consider this your home, for as long as you want to stay."

Kelli's eyes misted. "Okay." She'd gone back and forth about this move, especially when things progressed faster than anticipated. She'd thought it would take weeks to sublease her apartment—time to ponder further, time to change her mind. But an occupant surfaced quickly, and next thing she knew, all her belongings were on a highway headed north…along with her and her mixed feelings. But one thing was sure. She loved being here with Cyd and Cedric…and she loved that Stephanie and Lindell were only minutes away. Suddenly she giggled.

"What?" Cyd and Cedric asked.

"You *might* need some Spanx," Kelli said, imitating Stephanie's voice. "What a nut! I don't think I've laughed that hard in years."

"Ah, yes," Cyd said. "Only the privileged few get to experience Stephanie in all her nuttiness over the course of several hours."

The three women had taken turns driving Kelli's car from Austin, while the guys drove Cedric's with the moving trailer attached.

Kelli laughed again, remembering. "If you want to learn to cook gourmet meals for your husband but don't want to learn your way around the gym…*and* you want to pretend you still wear the same size, you might need some Spanx."

Cyd was laughing now. "If you're bound and determined to keep wiggling your rear end into those skinny jeans—"

"—even if it kills you—"

"—you might need some Spanx," they finished together.

"Oh, man," Kelli said, "remember this one? 'If you don't want everybody and their momma to see your sea billows roll…'"

Cedric had been eyeing the two of them with creased brow. "And here I thought you girls were having deep intellectual conversation in your car, like Lindell and me."

"Uh-huh," Cyd said. "Must've been too deep for words, 'cause from what I could see, whoever wasn't driving was asleep."

Cedric chuckled. "Exactly."

"Maybe we should've taken our cue from you and done the same," Kelli said, "but we couldn't stop talking."

Her eyes closed, and he was there. A shiver of remembrance danced down her arms. She could still see
that distant look in his eyes, could even hear him, that
tone of indifference that echoed forever in her head.
Kelli opened her eyes to capture another image—any
image—but he was everywhere now. And her heart allowed itself to be crushed all over again.

> *I will love you like an endless stream*
> *A million miles won't take your heart from me*
> *I will love you every breath you breathe*
> *I will, I will*

Almost to the bridge, Kelli could feel her emotions
cresting with the song. She closed her eyes again as
they took over, filling her voice, magnifying her range,
powering her through. She played the final chords with
the salt of tears on her lips and bowed her head at the
last note… and heard—*applause*? She looked out and
saw the guests on their feet and Cedric and Cyd fully
turned, facing her—Cyd wiping tears from her cheeks.
With her own anxiety about singing it, Kelli hadn't
given thought to whether people might actually like
the song.

She pulled a tissue from the box atop the piano,
dabbed her cheeks, and blew her nose, then muscled
a heart-heavy smile to acknowledge everyone's kindness. When she moved back to the front pew beside her
mother, only then did the guests stop clapping and sit.

"When did you write that?" her mother asked, patting her thigh. "That was beautiful."

"Thanks, Mom. I wrote it…a long time ago."

She turned her gaze to the ceremony, her heart beat-

ing a little faster still, puzzled by the response to the
song. It coaxed a different memory to the surface, and
as Cyd and Cedric exchanged vows, Kelli thought about
her long-ago dream of writing music that God would
somehow use. Then the better part of her brain kicked
in, reminding her that she'd left songwriting behind,
that she knew better than to dream.

That all those dreams had turned to dust.

"Kelli! Girrrl…"

Kelli looked up—midpivot in the Electric Slide—
and saw Stephanie threading her way through the line
dancers in her champagne-colored dress. Soon as the
song started, it seemed everybody left tables and min-
gled to claim a spot on the parquet floor. Kelli waved
her sister-in-law over.

"I've been looking for you." Stephanie scooted between Kelli and Devin, a nine-year-old cousin, as rows
of people sidestepped to the right. "I haven't had a
chance to tell you…girl, you *sang* that song. I had no
idea—hold up, am I doing this right?" She was headed
a different direction from everyone else. "Why am I
even out here? I hate this stupid dance."

Kelli laughed. "Back, Steph. We're going back."

"Oh." Stephanie checked Devin to get in sync, then
leaned her head Kelli's way again, her voice elevated.
"Anyway, I told Lindell I couldn't believe he didn't tell
me about that song, 'cause I would've had you sing it
at *our* wedding. And he said he'd never heard it…and
then I couldn't believe *that*."

"I know. Crazy, right? This way, Steph. Pivot left."

Stephanie was behind her now, and Kelli turned to

make sure she was following, but Devin had it under control.

Like a traffic cop, he moved his hands left, then right to direct her which way to go next. "And *pivot*," he announced, to the amusement of those around them.

Side by side with Stephanie again, Kelli continued. "Lindell and Cedric had already moved out of the house by the time I started writing songs in high school, so it was easy to kind of keep my music to myself." She shrugged. "Cedric overheard it because I didn't know he was there."

"Hmph," Stephanie said. "If I had that kind of talent, everybody would know about it. They'd have to tell me to be quiet."

The music switched, and they could hear people near the center of the floor cheering, "Go, Cyd! Go, Cedric! Go, Cyd! Go, Cedric!"

Kelli and Stephanie craned their necks, moving toward the action.

"Oh, goodness," Stephanie said, laughing. "Look at your brother. He's at it again."

Kelli laughed too, remembering Cedric and Cyd on the dance floor at Stephanie and Lindell's reception. Now the two had cut a wide swath in the middle of the floor with a different line dance, this one a little livelier.

Kelli and Stephanie worked their way to a spot in the inner circle.

"Have you seen this version?" Stephanie asked.

Kelli nodded. "But you know Cedric's gonna add his own twist."

Instead of a simple sidestep, Cedric led Cyd in bouncy moves to the left, with a slide before going right. And instead of a normal pivot, they did some kind of kick, kick, turn—with Cedric twirling Cyd into a two-step before moving back to the line dance, all of it seamless. The crowd was fired up.

After a couple of rounds, Cedric spotted Kelli and pulled her to the center.

"I don't know if you can hang with a twenty-five-year-old, big brother." Although Cedric was a fit forty-two, Kelli didn't miss an opportunity to tease him about his age. "I'd hate to embarrass you in front of your guests."

"Oh, you got jokes? We'll see about that, baby sis."

Cyd led the cheers this time as Kelli whipped some different moves on him. Cedric paused, then mimicked every last one to let her know she couldn't show him up. Lindell dragged Stephanie out there—literally—and Kelli was in stitches watching them try to copy what she and Cedric were doing. Soon everyone on the floor had joined in again, and then the music switched to Motown, which got its own cheers.

Cedric draped one arm around Kelli and the other around Cyd and led them off the floor. They stopped at the bridal party table, which had emptied of all but Dana, one of Cyd's bridesmaids.

"Why aren't you on the dance floor?" Cedric asked. "We need all the forty-and-over folk representing."

Dana glared at him. "Let's see how well you 'represent' with some heels on. My feet are killing me." Then she nodded toward the dance floor. "My husband left me. He's out there with the kids. And last I saw, Scott wasn't representing too well either. He looked almost as bad as Stephanie with that Electric Slide."

"I heard that, Dana," Stephanie said, walking up with Lindell. "I could learn the dumb dance if I cared to. And since you're trying to clown me, I might do it just to keep my black rhythm points. Can't have a white guy showing me up."

Dana got a kick out of that, laughing as auburn wisps fell about her face. "How about a white girl? Let's tell the deejay to play it again and see who's got it."

Stephanie eased into a seat. "Uh, no thanks. I always told you, you're one of those black white girls. You can go on the dance floor."

Dana eyed the dancers out there. "Well, pray for Mackenzie. I think the poor thing takes after Scott. Look at them."

Kelli's heart was smiling. Because she lived out of state, she didn't know these women well—not even her sisters-in-law—but from her brief interactions, including last night's rehearsal dinner, she could tell she would like them.

Cyd pulled out a chair and sat, her beautiful gown, passed down from her mother, swishing over the sides. "Ahh…think I can get away with sitting like this for maybe five minutes?"

Cedric massaged her shoulders. "You're good. The Jackson Five's got everybody occupied."

Dana touched Kelli's arm. "The bridal table was talking about you earlier."

"Me? Why?" Kelli took a seat.

"Are you kidding? That song. It was beautiful."

Kelli blushed. "Thank you."

"That's my little sister." Cedric beamed.

"Mine too!" Lindell said, giving her shoulder a squeeze. "So proud of you, girl." He looked at the others. "Just got her master's too, from UT–Austin."

"I heard," Dana said. "Is your degree in music?"

Kelli shook her head. "One's in communications and the other's in public relations."

"Wow, two?" Dana nodded. "That's awesome."

"Well…not really. Just means I didn't know what I wanted to do." Kelli didn't mind admitting it. "But I'm done being a professional student. I'm looking for a job now—"

"—in Texas." Cedric's tone made clear what he thought of that.

"What part of Texas?" Stephanie asked. "Are you trying to stay in Austin?"

"I've been looking at possibilities in Austin and Houston…and Dallas."

"Mostly Dallas, I'd bet," Cedric said. "That's where her boyfriend is." He looked around playfully. "Where is he anyway? I wanted to meet him, see if he measures up. What's his name? Miller?"

Kelli smirked at her big brother. "Miles. Miles Reed. He wanted to meet you all too, but he had a conflict."

"I'm sure we'll get another opportunity," Cedric said, "if I can get you to move back to St. Louis."

Cyd perked up. "Ooh, Kelli, I'd love that. Any chance?"

"I…doubt it." Kelli hedged to be polite; her mind had said a fast no. She hadn't lived in St. Louis since she left for college, and the distance had been good. Her mother had relocated to Little Rock to care for *her* mother, so Kelli had gone there on school breaks.

"How's the job market in Texas?" Cedric asked. "Improved any?"

Cedric knew the answer perfectly well. He was a VP at a head-hunting firm. He'd made some calls for her, but nothing had materialized.

"Not exactly," Kelli admitted. "I've been looking since early in the year, and, well…it's nearing the end of June."

Lindell rubbed his chin. "I'm thinking you can be unemployed in St. Louis just as well as in Austin."

Cedric gave a big nod to his brother. "*Better* than in Austin. In St. Louis, you can be unemployed *and* hang out with your brothers."

Cyd raised a hand. "And sisters. Don't forget about us."

"*All* of us," Dana said. "We'd love to plug you into Daughters' Fellowship."

"What's that?" Kelli asked.

"It started years ago with Dana, Phyllis, and me." Cyd pointed toward the dance floor at her other bridesmaid. "Real informal. We'd do potluck and talk about—sometimes *cry* about—what God was doing in our lives. Stephanie crashed the party last year." Cyd smiled at her younger sister. "It's evolved into kind of a Bible study/gabfest."

"Emphasis on gab," Cedric said. "Amazing how two hours can turn into five—every single time. You'd think you'd run out of things to talk about."

"Now, now, brother," Lindell said, "don't exaggerate. I think it was four and a half hours last time."

Cedric and Lindell shared a laugh as the women pounced.

"We're praying too, you know," Dana said. "Getting that fuel we need to be the best we can be."

"Lindell knows." Stephanie gave him the eye. "I left the house with an attitude before that last meeting. Came back changed. Didn't I?"

Lindell threw up his hands. "Hey, I'm not complaining. I might be the biggest DF fan at the table. Stephanie's not the same woman I married."

"What's that supposed to mean?"

"Babe, that's a good thing! I'm just sayin'."

Kelli laughed as Lindell backpedaled. For years her brothers had been busy with their careers, living the bachelor life. Hadn't occurred to them or her that they should live near one another, be a part of each other's lives. But now they were both settled down, with wives Kelli would love to know better. She'd always wanted sisters. And it was strange that she, Cyd, and Stephanie kind of looked alike—all of them tall with honey-brown skin and long brown hair.

And Daughters' Fellowship sounded great. Her own relationship with God wasn't where it should be. She'd known that for some time. Just wasn't sure how to get it back on the right track. The thought of getting together with these women, talking and learning from them, felt like water to her parched soul.

If only it were in another city…

Kelli sighed as she looked around the table at the laughter, the ribbing, the love. Did she really want to stay in Austin, away from all of this?

And what about Miles? They'd been dating almost a year. Although he'd graduated from UT–Austin last December and moved back to Dallas, the distance didn't seem so great with them both in Texas. Still, they were already several hours apart. Would a few more make a huge difference?

Kelli looked up as her mother stopped at their table.

"Hey, it's my gorgeous mother," Cedric said, placing an arm around her.

"No, it's *my* gorgeous mother," Lindell said, hugging her other side.

Francine London glowed with pride. "You boys are something else," she said. "And I didn't come to see y'all. I came to see how my daughters-in-law are doing."

"Oh, it's like that now?" Cedric asked. "I get married, and I get kicked to the curb?"

Francine laughed, keeping her arms around her sons' waists. "I'm wondering what's gonna happen when you all start having my grandchildren. I'm not gonna like being all the way in Little Rock."

"You need to move back too," Lindell said.

Francine dismissed it with a shake of the head. "Your grandmother's not doing well, can't get around, so we're better off staying put."

"Well, help us convince your daughter to move back," Cedric said. "We've been working on her."

Francine looked at Kelli, nodding. "I was thinking about that today, how nice it would be if you could be around your brothers and their wives. You know I'm big on family."

"Yes, I know, Mom." Kelli cut them off at the pass. "So...which one of you would be willing to let your little sister move in?"

Chapter Two

Brian Howard heard the extended applause, whistles, and chants for more—just as he'd heard in other cities—but he still couldn't believe it was happening. He had to be living someone else's life.

The fact that it was happening here made it even more surreal. His St. Louis life was lab science and experiments and hours upon hours of working mostly alone—the exact opposite of this huge outdoor concert with several Christian artists from different genres and a crowd of tens of thousands. This music artist life was supposed to be secondary, but moments like this made him wonder what God was up to. When he got the invitation—once he'd gotten past the shock—he hadn't been sure how he'd be received. But the roar now was almost deafening. He patted his heart twice and pointed upward to let the crowd know where the praise belonged.

"King of kings! Lord of lords!" he shouted into the microphone, echoing the name of the song he'd just done.

The crowd joined in the praise by roaring louder.

Brian looked out at the sea of people that had descended on downtown near the Arch on a Sunday afternoon. "Thank you, St. Louis! My home! I love you!" He pumped his fist and turned to leave the stage as they began chanting again. They were shouting the name of his signature song, the one he'd saved for last. He was surprised this crowd knew it.

At the back of the stage, Brian turned and cupped his ear. "You wanna hear what?"

"Out of This World," they yelled.

He took a few steps toward them. "I thought people were tired of that one."

"No!" they thundered.

Brian gave his trademark smile and cued the deejay with a glance. The thumping beat started, and the crowd went wild. He launched into the words as the dancers reappeared—four young women he'd told his manager he didn't want or need. But Harold had lobbied for them. With this bigger venue, he said, it was the perfect time to step up the "show" part of the performance. Brian wanted the focus on the message in the songs. He thought the women would unnecessarily distract—and he also thought the matter had been settled. But the dancers showed up today anyway, with choreographed steps to his songs.

He moved easily across the outdoor stage in faded blue jeans and a shirt, melding with the rhythm, the words, the energy. He loved this part, connecting with the people, imparting truth that would stay with them long after he was gone, words they'd repeat at home or in the car or at school. They might not even get the words right now, but he always prayed God would give

them understanding. That prayer had been answered
through countless e-mails, letters, and posts on Twitter
and his Facebook page about how his songs had led lis-
teners to the Bible. For him, that's what it was all about.

But music was also about business, a part he dis-
liked more and more. Or maybe it was the people with
whom he was doing business. He hadn't sorted it all
out, but with each passing week, that was the part that
was challenging him.

Maybe he wouldn't have to do anything. It was
a very real possibility that he'd be giving all this up
shortly to focus solely on a years-long ambition, a PhD
in biochemistry.

Brian came to his favorite part of the song, where
he rattled off the names of God. He'd never forget God
giving that to him over a bowl of cereal. The words
were strung together beautifully in his head, already
rhyming. He only had to write them down. He never
would have believed God was calling him to do this,
even on a secondary level, without moments like that,
one after another. Brian Howard, Christian rapper? He
hadn't even been a big rap fan. Yet here he was.

The dancers struck their last pose as the song ended.
Brian pumped his fist and took in the landscape of ex-
uberant faces.

*God, this is unbelievable, really unbelievable. Does
this have anything to do with my prayers? Are You
speaking through this?*

"St. Louis, you're awesome!" he said. "Thank you
for the love and the support. Keep living out of this
world, living for Christ."

He gave a final fist-pump and turned, making his
way through a black curtain at the back of the stage

and down a set of steps, the dancers following. A security guy met him in the restricted outdoor area, then his manager and a dozen other faces, familiar and unfamiliar. Someone passed him a bottled water, and he took a long swig as they ushered him to a tent area set up for the talent.

"Alien! That was the bomb!"

"You rocked the house, dude!"

Red-shirted workers gave him kudos, and he gratefully shook their hands. It had taken him awhile to get used to being called Alien, his rap name. It was another thing he felt God had given him. He'd been studying 1 Peter when he was struck by the apostle calling Christians "aliens and strangers in the world."

Harold put a hand on Brian's shoulder as they walked. "Man, I'm telling you, you're about to go to a whole new level. Did you see how that crowd responded? You've got the skills, but it's more than that. They *like* you." He pondered it, near giddy. "It's that clean-cut, boy-next-door look. I've got to hand it to you, that was the right call. I wanted edgy, but you knew the image that would work."

Brian glanced at his manager. "I'm just being me, Harold. That's all I can be. But it's not about me." He stepped inside the tent. "Did you see all those arms raised in worship when I was praying? Gave me goose bumps. That was awesome."

Harold pulled out his phone and started texting. "Yeah...that was something."

Brian stared at him a second, waiting for more. Seemed whenever he wanted to rejoice in the spiritual side of an event, Harold was focused on business. That was his job, but still...

"I'm already on this." Harold's fingers flew across the phone. "Trying to figure out how we can capitalize on what we saw today. This is gonna be bigger than we thought. The demographic is wide open."

"Don't get carried away," Brian said. "I told you, this is a summer of decision for me. I'm not making any new directional moves until I know for sure this is what God wants me to do."

"Uh-huh." Harold kept typing. "You'd be a fool to give this up. And to sit in a lab? Boy, you're crazy."

"Crazy or not, if I can't come up with any songs for this new album, that'll be a huge sign."

"I ain't worried," Harold mumbled.

Brian picked up his backpack and slung it over his shoulder. He wished he could say the same. The noise and activity of the other artists swirled around him. Beforehand he'd enjoyed meeting and talking to the others and praying in a circle with the sponsor organization. A local pastor, Dr. Mason Lyles, had led the prayer. Brian could see Dr. Lyles across the tent now—he'd hoped to get a chance to talk to the man before he left.

He pulled out his phone to check his messages and was surprised to see a text from Aaron, a grade-school friend.

In town for wkend. I know you're the man and all, but how about meeting a bro at Five Guys for dinner?

Brian smiled. He hadn't seen Aaron in more than a year. He sent a quick reply.

"Brian?"

He turned and saw Nicole, editor of a popular online gospel magazine. He'd sat down with her earlier for an interview, and she'd shadowed him the rest of the day. "Hey, Nicole," he said. "Been watching the performances?"

"Absolutely. You were amazing. I'd never heard you in person." Her eyes danced as she looked at him. "I hear you all are going out tonight."

Brian quirked his brow. "Nah, I'm actually headed to meet—"

Harold raised a finger at him, half listening to their conversation, half in his own on the phone. He brought the call to a close. "Actually," Harold said, phone tucked in his hand, "we're planning to grab a bite, then check out Club Stratus."

"All right, cool," Brian said. "Have a good time. I'll catch up with you tomorrow."

"Excuse us a minute," Harold told Nicole. He pulled Brian a few feet away. "You're going too."

Brian frowned. "You know I'm not into clubbing. Anyway, I've got plans."

Harold shook his head. "You got to."

"What do you mean—'got to'?"

"Look." Harold glanced over to make sure they were out of hearing range. "From the vibe I'm picking up, Nicole likes you. She's the one who asked what we were doing tonight and whether we could all hang out. Wouldn't hurt, if you know what I mean."

Brian couldn't believe what he was hearing. And yet…he could. "What *do* you mean, Harold?"

Harold leaned in closer. "Nicole's got one of the hottest online trade magazines. Imagine the kind of press she'll give you if you flatter her with some time tonight."

"You're serious."

Harold grew exasperated. "Yes, Brian, I am. Hop aboard the real world." He paused, letting a smile ease onto his face. "You should be jumping all over this. You're a hot-blooded male, aren't you?" He cast a glance Nicole's way. "*Look* at her."

Brian stared at him a moment, unsure what to do—not about tonight but about the weeks to come. Did he need to end it now? And *could* he end it, given they had a contract?

"I'll talk to her," Brian said finally.

"And say what? You'll go, right?"

Brian approached her. "I'm sorry, Nicole. My manager wasn't aware I had plans tonight. I appreciate all your time today, though. Can't wait to read the article." He gave her a smile.

"I hate to hear that," Nicole said. "I was looking forward to getting to know you a little better, but I understand. Maybe another time." She pulled out a business card and wrote a number on the back. "That's my personal cell. Call anytime."

As she passed Brian the card, her attention was diverted to someone behind him. "Dr. Lyles," she said, moving to greet him, "what a pleasure to meet you. Nicole Armor."

Brian stepped aside and watched them shake hands.

"Nice to meet you, Nicole," Dr. Lyles said.

When she had moved away, Dr. Lyles put his arm around the young guy standing with him. "Forgive the intrusion, but we're about to leave, and my grandson just had to meet Alien and get a picture with him."

"No intrusion at all," Brian said. "I was waiting for the chance to meet *you*." They shared a laugh. "Hey, man, what's your name?" Brian bent a little, putting an arm around him.

"Justin."

"How old are you?"

"Twelve. I know all the words to every song on your album. I even got one of your mix tapes and did a song at our family reunion."

"Whoa. And for a minute there, I thought you were shy." Brian exchanged a smile with Dr. Lyles. "You wouldn't want a T-shirt like mine, would you?"

Justin's eyes lit up. "Yeah!"

Brian looked to his left. "Nate!" He pointed at Justin and then at his own shirt. "Hook him up."

Nate gave the okay sign. "Come on over, fella. You can choose the color you want."

Dr. Lyles gripped Brian's hand. "Thank you, Alien. You made his day."

"Sir, please call me Brian. It's such a privilege to meet you."

"Privilege is mine," Dr. Lyles said. "I'm impressed with your work."

"Really?" Brian said. "You mean, you've listened?"

"Justin calls it keeping me hip…as if I weren't already." Dr. Lyles's eyes twinkled. "I admit he had to persuade me, because it's not exactly my genre. He kept saying, 'Grandpa, this is the same stuff you talk about on Sunday.' So I listened and got excited because not only could I follow what you were saying, I *loved* what you were saying. The bonus was I got to talk to Justin about things like what it means to live unashamed of the Gospel"—he grinned—"which never happened after one of my sermons." He put a hand to Brian's shoulder. "Keep doing what you're doing."

"Thank you, Dr. Lyles. Really…to hear you say that, to know you see worth in my music, is huge right now." Brian felt emotion rushing at him. His own childhood pastor had questioned what he was doing, even looked down on it. Out of respect for his grandmother, he had returned to the church he'd grown up in when he moved back after college. But he'd been struggling, especially this summer as he grappled with his future.

Dr. Lyles looked him in the eye. "Son, I'm not the only one who sees worth in what you're doing. I was out there during your performance. What a sight to see so many young people worshipping with you."

Brian could feel his insides churning. "Dr. Lyles," he said, "I know you're extremely busy, but is there any way we could set up a time to meet next week? I really feel like I need your counsel."

Dr. Lyles reached for his wallet and gave him a card. "Let's do it, son. I'd love to meet with you."

Brian laughed and took another bite of his burger.

"So I show up for this audition," Aaron was saying, "thinking I'm perfect for the role of the suave guy who tries to win the girl by offering the candy bar. But no. They think I'm perfect as the voice of the baby who steals her heart with the right brand of chocolate."

Brian laughed again. "But that's cool. At least you got a part. When does it air?"

"Next month sometime." Aaron sipped his Coke. "I guess it's cool. But I've gotten two commercials, and both times I'm not actually onscreen. I'm starting to get a complex."

"Just wait. You're at the humble beginnings stage,

but one day you'll be a one-name star like Denzel or Leonardo."

Aaron pointed two fingers at him. "Or Alien."

"Yeah, right. I'm more 'humble beginnings' than you are. You've got national television exposure"—Brian waggled his eyebrows—"even if we only see a cute baby face." He paused. "But you should've seen the crowd today. It was incredible. If I'd known you were in town, I would've told you about it so you could've come down."

Aaron gave him a look. "You know I've got mad love for you, but me and thousands of Christians? Not happening. Keep praying for me."

"I'm on it. One day…" He popped a fry into his mouth. "What brought you back from LA, anyway?"

"Cedric got married yesterday."

Brian swallowed hard. "Cedric? London?"

"Yeah, if you can believe it. Mr. Ladies' Man." Aaron dipped his own fry into a little cup of ketchup. "Seems really happy too. My mom and his mom are still close." He lifted his drink. "And, uh, I was wondering…has the statute of limitations run out on the no-dating-former-girlfriends-of-friends law? 'Cause your girl was there, looking finer than ever. I'm ready to make a move."

Brian's heart rate sped to a million beats a minute. "Did my name come up?"

"No. I learned my lesson years ago when I ran into her and asked if she'd talked to you. You never told me what happened, but clearly it didn't end on the positive."

Brian stared into the distance, past the faces of customers in the restaurant, seeing only one face in his mind. "I wonder if she's still in town." He only realized he'd spoken aloud when Aaron answered.

"Not sure. Why?"

"I don't know. I've tried to reach her over the years, but I can never get a hold of her. Knowing she might be here in St. Louis..." He looked at Aaron. "Do you have her number?"

"No, but wouldn't take much to get it."

Brian looked hopeful.

Aaron looked skeptical. "I'm asking again. Why? I don't think she wants to hear from you. You'll only upset her."

Brian sighed. Aaron was right. She'd definitely be upset. But that's why he wanted to talk to her, to ask her forgiveness. He hated the way things had ended between them. But maybe she'd be better off if he left her alone.

It saddened him, the thought that they might never speak again, that he'd never be able to apologize. But deep down, the sadness stemmed from more than that. He harbored the remotest hope that she might actually forgive him one day...that maybe they could even find their way back to a friendship...a ludicrous notion at best. But the truth was, he missed her still.

With all the uncertainty about his future, there was one thing about which he was painfully certain. He wouldn't be sharing it with Kelli.

Chapter Three

Kelli could feel herself being pulled from a deep sleep, but mind and body fought hard to hold tight. She felt like a deadweight, unable to move, muscles pleading for more time to rest and regenerate. She vaguely wondered what she'd done to aggravate them—when she found herself swatting something away from her face. She'd seen her share of critters in Texas, but what in the world was—?

She jerked upward, opening her eyes—to find Cyd's dog, Reese, pawing and licking her in the face. She blinked, gaining her bearings. She wasn't in Texas anymore.

"Hey, girl," she said, stroking the wavy-haired little dog. "Is this a special welcome or are you planning to do this every morning?"

Kelli checked the clock. Seven twenty. Sunlight was streaking through the mini-blinds. Felt weird to be waking up in Clayton. Although Kelli had grown up in the city of St. Louis, she'd gone to Clayton High as part of the school district's voluntary desegregation program. But she'd never imagined herself or anyone she knew living here. Seemed like another world.

She yawned, then suddenly reached for her cell phone, remembering she was supposed to call Miles last evening. The screen showed two texts and as many missed calls. She tapped his number, and he answered right away.

"What are you doing up so early? You must be on the golf course."

"Headed there. Dad and I decided to play a round." His voice—a little deep, a little Texas Southern—always drew her in. "So you made it safely? I thought you were gonna call."

"I was planning to, but I was so tired I must've fallen asleep." She smiled into the phone. "Glad to know you care."

"You already knew that."

She let his words warm her inside.

"I was hoping you'd call and say you changed your mind." He paused as if there was still hope. "I'm still not excited about you moving so far. It's already been forever since I've seen you. No telling how long we'll have to wait now."

"Forever, Miles? You were in Austin three weeks ago."

"Three weeks away from you is forever." His phone shifted, and Kelli heard his car door shut as he greeted his dad. He spoke back into the phone. "I thought we were working on getting closer, not farther apart."

"I know. I wish something had opened up in Dallas. I think I blanketed the whole town with résumés."

"Something might open up yet," he said. "I'm glad you get some time with your family, but I'm hoping St.

Louis is temporary. I'm looking forward to us living in the same city again."

Seemed Miles had stepped up talk of the future once he learned Kelli was moving.

"Well, they say if you've got a job, it's easier to find a job. If I gain some experience here, maybe somebody in Dallas will be willing to give me a shot."

"I can be patient about the job part but not the seeing you part. Let's make plans soon, either here or St. Louis. As long as we're together."

"Reese, where are you?" a voice called from downstairs.

Kelli covered the phone. "She's in here, Cyd!"

"I'll let you go," Miles said. "Dad's waiting for me. Call you tonight?"

She smiled. "You better."

Kelli clicked off as Cyd entered the room in her silk robe. "Oh no." She bent over, patting her thigh. "Reese, come."

The dark chocolate dog rolled over on her back, showing her patches of tan underneath, paws dangling in complete comfort as Kelli continued to stroke her.

"I'm totally enabling her disobedience but she's too cute."

Cyd gave Reese the eye. "She woke you up, didn't she? I'm sorry. She's normally in our room, but I guess she wanted to check out her new playmate down the hall."

"It's fine," Kelli said, legs still under the covers. She scratched behind Reese's ears. "Better be glad you're adorable." A yawn escaped. "What time do y'all leave for church?"

"I'm not sure today," Cyd said. "We normally go to

the nine o'clock, but with the road trip yesterday, eleven thirty's looking pretty good. Cedric's still asleep." Cyd paused. "Don't feel like you have to come with us. I know you're tired."

Kelli's bones issued a hearty amen. She could easily rest till noon. But before she could give it more thought, they heard slow steps moving down the hall, the hardwood creaking underneath. Cedric appeared, wearing wrinkled athletic shorts, a T-shirt, and a slouch that said he wanted back in bed. "Howdy."

Kelli exchanged an amused glance with Cyd. "You look terrible."

"I want to know one thing." Sleep coated Cedric's voice. "Whose idea was it to leave Austin in the middle of the night, drive fourteen hours straight, then unload a moving van?"

"Yours," Kelli and Cyd said.

And Cyd added, "While pumping your fist in the air and saying, 'Let's do this!'"

"And if I remember correctly," Kelli said, "you called Lindell a chump for suggesting we leave later and find a halfway point to stop overnight."

"I must've lost my mind." Cedric ambled over and collapsed across the foot of her bed. "I thought I was still your age."

Reese traded Kelli for Cedric, pouncing on him immediately.

Cyd sat beside him on the bed, massaging his back. "Poor baby. I'll get you some ibuprofen. You and Kelli should go back to bed. I wish I could. I got up to let Reese out, and now I'm wide awake."

Cedric looked at Kelli. "How are you feeling?"

"A little sore. Not too bad. You and Lindell did most

"I'm guessing Stephanie and Lindell won't be making the nine o'clock either," Cyd said.

"Oh!" Cedric sat up. "I *have* to go to the nine o'clock. Actually, I'm supposed to be at both. Scott and I are announcing the new ministry for young guys."

"Oh, I forgot too," Cyd said. "And I'm so excited. You and Scott are perfect for this."

Cedric sighed a little. "Yeah. We can certainly share from personal experience what *not* to do in life."

"And about God's grace, Cedric. It's awesome. Did you ever think you'd be talking to young men about God? And Scott…he thought God was through with him in public ministry, and not even a year later, here comes an opportunity."

Kelli stretched out on the bed again. "Is this the Scott who was in your wedding? Dana's husband?"

They both nodded.

"I guess I shouldn't ask…"

Cedric and Cyd looked at one another.

"It's okay, Kelli," Cyd said. "Scott confessed in front of the church, so it's not a secret. He had an affair last year."

"Wow. I never would've thought. He and Dana look so happy together."

"Trust me, they didn't look like that last fall," Cyd said. "They went through a whole lot. But again—God's grace. It's been incredible to watch."

"Wow," Kelli said again, thinking more about that word *grace* than about Scott.

"I'd better get rolling," Cedric said. He stood, yawning.

"I'm coming with you to the nine o'clock, babe," Cyd said. "I'll run downstairs and get you the ibuprofen."

Cyd left, with Reese trailing behind. On his way out, Cedric looked back. "You coming, Kel?"

"Umm…I don't know. Might shoot for next week."

He stepped back into the room. "You okay?"

"Just tired. Why?"

"I remember you used to bug me about going to church. You were so on fire for God. But you said you haven't been going to church at all in Austin."

Kelli felt a sudden sadness. What irony—Cedric asking her about church. As much as their mother had done for them, she hadn't raised them in church. It was her best friend, Brian, who'd invited her to go at the beginning of high school, and her whole world had changed. Lindell was away at college, but she got her mother to come now and then. Cedric, who was already working, always declined. She'd prayed for God to change his heart. Now here he was, on fire, involved in ministry. And she…

"I guess I kind of drifted during college," she said.

"I can understand that." He sat next to her. "I haven't had a chance to talk to you about the ways God changed my life. You know how I was." He gave a lopsided smile. "Cyd had a lot to do with where I am now, but as I think about it, Kelli, so did you. God used you to plant the seed a long time ago."

She tried to will them away, but tears started in her eyes.

Cedric put an arm around her and brought her close. "I've still got a lot to learn about God and how He works," he said, "but I think this move is about more than you being with your family again. This is about you and God."

Kelli knew he was right. She found it hard even to talk to God now.

"God's got a plan for you, Kel. Know how I know?"

She answered reluctantly. "How?"

"Because if He didn't have a plan, you'd still be in Austin staring at four walls, unemployed and by your lonesome. And I'm thinking He put the crazy idea in my head to drive through the night and get here so we could all go to Living Word today. Yep, I'm putting it on Him so I can feel better about suggesting that drive."

Kelli tried not to smile.

"So you have to get up and come, or my backache will have been for nothing." He raised his fist.

She blinked back tears. "What?"

"Fist bump."

"Fist bump?"

"You know the rallying cry. Let's do this!"

Kelli stared at it, then raised her own, a weak one, and tapped his fist with it.

Brian entered the main building of Living Word for his first Sunday of worship. For the past four weeks he'd met with Dr. Lyles on Tuesday mornings. Without planning to, he'd poured out so much of his heart on his first visit that the pastor invited him to return the following week. Now it was a standing appointment.

He had no doubt that this would be his new church home, although out-of-town concerts had prevented him from getting here the past month. But it was hard to break it to his grandmother. To her, church wasn't church unless it was held in that one building she'd been going to for fifty years. Over oatmeal this morning he said, "Grandma, come visit Living Word with me this one Sunday."

"Boy," she said, "only way I'm leaving Christ Temple is if they carry me out in a box."

The common areas were already filled with people when he arrived, and Brian was struck by many things—the multi-ethnic nature of the crowd, the young age, and the mostly casual dress. The church he'd grown up in was predominantly black, average age fifty, and you'd better be wearing a suit or a dressy dress and a hat. But the church he'd attended in college was more like this, so it was easy to feel at home in his khaki slacks and shirt.

He walked past several pockets of people, some drinking coffee in the café area, and went straight to the sanctuary where an usher handed him a program. Down a far right aisle, he chose a pew about halfway up and sat on the end. There were still fifteen minutes to go before the start of service, so he settled in and opened up his Bible.

Kelli had mixed emotions as she entered Living Word. Coming here for weddings was one thing, but now she felt strange, like an outsider with a sign taped to her back that read *Prodigal Daughter*. None of these people knew her—or that she hadn't been to church in seven years. But that's how she felt as she walked past them—that they were all watching, that they all knew her story.

Still, it felt good to be here with her family—special bonus running into Stephanie and Lindell in the parking lot. And it felt good to finally feel her feet turning back to the path where she knew they belonged.

She followed the others through the fellowship areas, stopping every few feet as they greeted people. Cyd and Stephanie had grown up in this church, and it had become home for Cedric and Lindell as well. They seemed to know everybody.

Inside the sanctuary, Kelli learned, the whole crew sat together in the same place, week after week—left of center, fourth pew from the front. Dana, Scott, and Phyllis were already there and moved down for the rest of them.

Kelli whispered to Stephanie, "Where's Phyllis's husband?"

"Oh, Hayes doesn't come."

She wondered why. Had he never gone to church? Or had something happened in his life that caused him to turn away, as with her?

The praise and worship team assembled on the platform. Kelli stood with the rest of the congregation, waiting for what had always been her favorite part of the service.

"We want to welcome you to Living Word this morning," the worship leader said as the band started playing some opening notes. "Some of you may be here each and every week. Others may not have been to a service in years. We want you to know it doesn't matter. God's arms are opened wide. Won't you run to Him? Run to His throne of grace."

Stephanie leaned over to Kelli. "Wonder what's up with Logan this morning. He normally just starts singing."

Kelli wondered if his welcome could be meant for her. But that would be too weird.

The band shifted to the first song, and the beautiful

arrangement captured her instantly. When she realized it was "Come, Thou Fount," her eyes closed, and the entire congregation disappeared. The opening words to the hymn always moved her, but never more than now.

Come, thou fount of every blessing,
Tune my heart to sing Thy grace;
Streams of mercy, never ceasing,
Call for songs of loudest praise...

Grace. Mercy. In her mind's eye, she saw a throne lifted high, her feet walking toward it. She joined her voice with the rest, every word filled with personal meaning.

Jesus sought me when a stranger,
Wandering from the fold of God...

Tears fell from her eyes. That's exactly what she'd felt like when she entered the building...a stranger. Had Jesus sought her? Had He led her here? The whole idea of it seemed too huge—could He care that much for her? All she knew was she felt welcomed suddenly... by God Himself.

She sang the last words as a prayer—*"Here's my heart, oh take and seal it, seal it for Thy courts above"*—then continued her own prayer straight through the next song, overcome. During the third, she was struck by an answer to an old prayer: she and her brothers were in church together, worshipping God.

She was drained by the time for announcements, a good sort of drained. She barely noticed that Cedric and Scott had gone forward to wait their turn to speak.

"Also, a reminder that choir rehearsal is canceled this Thursday night," someone was saying. "Our assistant worship pastor, Logan Duncan, will be a featured panelist at the Christian Songwriters Conference—"

Stephanie gasped and grabbed Kelli's hand.

Kelli looked at her and whispered, "What?"

"That's it."

"That's what?"

Stephanie bit her lip. "Can't tell you yet."

"Then why did you grab my hand?"

"'Cause it's about you. But I'm still processing."

"So please be in prayer for Logan," the woman continued, "with regard to that conference and all the wonderful things God is doing with this worship ministry."

Cedric and Scott took to the podium next. "Good morning," Cedric began.

"Good morning," sounded back from the congregation.

"I'm Cedric London, and Scott Elliott and I are excited to tell you about a new ministry forming at Living Word for guys between the ages of eighteen and twenty-five. If that's you, then you know this is an age when you're getting your bearings in the world and being tested regarding what you believe and choices you'll make." He cleared his throat. "I'm almost forty-three, only met Jesus this year, so I'm hoping to reach you all with some real talk about what's out there and why it doesn't compare with living for Him."

Scott stepped to the microphone. "Many of you know my story. I've been walking with the Lord since I was young, but I really messed up in my marriage. Cedric and I can't present perfect Christian lives to you guys, and we don't want to. Through speakers, frank discussion around the Bible, and some mixing it up with sports and other activities, we want to learn and grow together, hold each other accountable, and maybe discover what it means to be broken, imperfect vessels that God can somehow use."

The congregation took to their feet with applause, and it was obvious Cedric and Scott hadn't expected it. When the applause faded, they asked interested guys to sign up in the lobby so they'd have an idea of the number of people who might want to participate.

Pastor Lyles got up then and added his own comment. "I've known Scott for many years," he said, "and I've had the pleasure of getting to know Cedric over the past year. Often it's when you know you don't have it all together, when you know you've fallen short— that's when God can use you mightily." He smiled. "But that's another sermon."

Kelli listened closely to what the pastor was saying. She wanted to hear *that* sermon.

"Today," the pastor said, "we're continuing in the Gospel of Mark, but first we'll hear from the choir…"

Stephanie poked Kelli with her elbow. "I'm done processing. I think it'll work."

"What'll work?"

"I've got a plan for your life."

"Oh, is that all?"

Stephanie laughed from her belly without making a sound. "I'm serious. Tell you about it after service."

Kelli had an inkling what Stephanie might be up to, based on their road trip yesterday, and she also had an inkling what she'd say. No way.

Chapter Four

The second the service ended, Brian was up and out of the pew, trying to dodge past the others walking up the aisle. He was beside himself—he couldn't believe Cedric London was actually at Living Word. After talking to Aaron, he'd practically persuaded himself to give up the thought of finding Kelli. But seeing Cedric here— giving an announcement, no less—was instant motivation. He had to find him. Had to see if he'd be willing to give him Kelli's information.

With one service ending, another starting soon, and Bible studies held during both, the building was thick with people. "Excuse me, where are the ministry booths set up?" he asked a passerby.

The guy pointed. "Make a left and you'll see them down that hallway."

"Thanks."

Brian saw many church ministries represented, but one line stretched the farthest, filled mostly with young men. That's the one Brian headed toward, and he spied Cedric at the front, engaged in conversation. He hung back a minute, debating whether to get in line or wait to the side.

"Brian Howard? What's up, man?"

Brian turned to his right. "Lindell?" He was at Living Word, too? "Good to see you!"

They gripped hands and hugged.

"I thought I was seeing things," Lindell said. "It's been, what—five, six years?"

"Seven." Brian knew exactly. "High school graduation."

"That's right." Lindell nodded. "So what you been up to? Let's see, you were headed to Emory, right?"

"Good memory," Brian said.

"And you were a science geek like me, so let me guess. You ended up majoring in biochem."

Brian's eyes widened. "Yeah! That's wild."

"So what are you doing with it?" Lindell asked.

"Actually, I'm in the doctoral program at Wash U—"

"Awesome."

"—but I'm at a crossroads. Long story. So what about you? You must be done with your residency by now. Did you stick with internal medicine?"

Lindell nodded. "Joined a practice off of Ballas Road, and it's really been a blessing—"

"Flash from the past." Cedric had come up from behind and slapped hands with Brian. "I saw y'all over here and couldn't believe my eyes. What's happening, Brian? You at Living Word?"

"I'm new here. But I love it already." Brian felt a tinge of hope. Cedric and Lindell didn't seem to harbor ill feelings toward him. Maybe Kelli had kept the details of their breakup private. "That ministry you're starting sounds awesome."

"You should come," Cedric said. "You must be about at the top of our target age group. We're looking for ways to connect with these guys. If you have any ideas, I'd love to hear them."

"All right," Brian said. "I'll check it out."

"I'd better get back," Cedric said, taking a step toward the booth, "but it was good to see you, Brian. I'm sure I'll see you around."

"Cedric," Brian said, his heart in his throat, "can I ask the two of you a quick question first?"

"Sure."

"I've tried to get in touch with Kelli a couple of times over the years. Could you give me her number, maybe even her e-mail?" He was suddenly nervous, imagining their response. *After the way you hurt our sister, you must be crazy.*

Lindell had a funny look on his face. "Dude, you just missed her."

Brian stared.

"She's here now," Cedric added. "Just moved back. She's staying with my wife and me, and she came to church with us this morning."

Brian was stunned. Didn't know what to say or think. He was almost glad he'd missed her. Whenever he imagined getting in touch, it was by phone or e-mail. Could he bear seeing her face-to-face?

He searched for his next words. "Wow…could you give me her cell number or maybe your landline…if you have one."

"How about this?" Cedric said. He pulled his phone from his belt clip. "Why don't you give me your number, and I'll pass it to her." He started typing Brian's name into his contacts.

"Sounds good." What else could he say?

Brian's heart dragged all the way to his car. So close…and yet so far. Kelli would never call him. And once she found out he was at Living Word, she probably wouldn't return.

"Emergency session of Daughters' Fellowship is now called to order." Stephanie tapped the distressed oak table lightly with the butt of a butter knife.

A couple of butterflies twirled in Kelli's stomach. Her first DF meeting, and it was an "emergency session"—on her behalf.

"Cyd, can you pray?" Stephanie asked.

Cyd nodded and scooted her chair in. They were seated in the round, so she grabbed the hands closest to hers—Kelli's and Dana's—and the others followed suit. "Lord, I don't even know what this is about," she said, lifting her voice a hair above the chatter, "but You know. I pray You will lead our discussion and accomplish Your purposes. As always, we want nothing but Your will, in Jesus' name."

"Okay," Stephanie said, jumping right in, "I wanted us to get together because—wait." She whipped her head around as their server passed. "Ma'am, excuse me," she called, "we really need to order."

"Be right there," the woman said, hustling past. She'd told them that twice already.

Stephanie looked at her watch, then at Dana and Phyllis, the moms in their fellowship. "You guys need to be back at church in less than an hour."

"We should be fine," Phyllis said. She touched Dana's arm, a hint of intrigue in her eyes. "Feels like we're on a covert mission or something, doesn't it? Sneaking out of church and then sneaking back by 1300 hours in time to scoop up the kids."

"We're not *sneaking*," Dana said, scanning her menu.

"I know, but we're usually doing something at church while we wait for kids' church to let out." She giggled. "It's kind of fun. I feel like a renegade."

Stephanie gave her a look. "You don't get out much, do you?"

Phyllis returned the look. "Honey, hit me back four kids later and tell me if you're getting out much."

Cyd rapped her own knife lightly on the table. "Calling to order again. Can we get to the emergency? I'm dying to hear."

Stephanie leaned in. "Okay, here's the deal. At church—"

"Ladies, ready to order?"

"Aww," they all groaned, laughing.

The server threw up a hand, laughing with them. "I can come back later."

"No!" they chorused and laughed again.

She flipped her pen from behind her ear and jotted down their orders—blueberry, buttermilk, and buckwheat. When they were done and the server had gone, Stephanie hunkered back down.

"At church," she said, remembering exactly where she left off, "when they mentioned that Logan would be at the songwriters' conference next weekend, it hit me. Kelli needs to be there."

"I had a feeling that's where you were going," Kelli said. "But I have no idea why."

"Because you're a songwriter."

"I wrote a few songs years ago. That doesn't make me a songwriter."

"Do we have to go through this again?" Stephanie rolled her eyes away from Kelli. "Y'all, we were helping Kelli pack, and she found an old notepad at the bottom of a drawer with songs in it she'd written. I got her to sing some in the car on the way up here—had to twist her arm and promise my firstborn—and I couldn't believe how good they were."

"They're awesome," Cyd said. "I could feel those lyrics."

"I've only heard one," Phyllis said, "that wedding song. And that's all I needed to hear to know you've got something special. It gave me goose bumps."

"Thanks, you guys, but as I said, it's not that big a deal. Music was just…a hobby of mine for a while."

"But, Kelli," Dana said, "you obviously had a passion for it at one point, right?"

Kelli gave a reluctant nod. There was a time when she and that notepad were inseparable. She remembered Brian twisting her arm one day too, to get her to share her songs. Kelli planted herself back in the present.

"And you obviously have talent," Dana was saying. "It's not just your family that likes it; the whole church gave you a standing ovation." She sipped her coffee. "So, I'm curious. You never dreamed of doing anything with it?"

"That's exactly what I asked her," Stephanie said.

"Long time ago."

"What happened?" Phyllis asked.

Kelli shrugged. "Lots of things."

The table was quiet, just as the car had grown quiet when they reached a similar point. Kelli had been able to change the subject then, but given that this entire meeting was called on her behalf, she knew it wouldn't work this time.

"So, okay," Dana said, raking her hand through her auburn hair as if she were getting down to business, "you had a passion and a dream. Some things happened. But it doesn't change the fact that God's gifted you." She paused while a passing server refilled her coffee cup. "What if He wants to use it? What if your songs are meant to be heard?"

"There are a gazillion songwriters out there who want their songs to be heard, people much more talented than I am. And maybe one out of the gazillion gets a break."

"Yeah, but that doesn't matter," Cyd said.

Kelli frowned. "Why not?"

"If God wants to use your music, He'll use your music. He can show Himself strong by making you the one out of the gazillion."

What would it be like to have that kind of faith? Kelli stuck with reality. "Well, anyway," she said, "God's not interested in using my music."

"Why would you say that?" several voices blurted at once.

Kelli didn't have an easy answer. No way was she touching the truth. She stared at the table.

Cyd leaned forward. "Kelli, are you saying this because you've prayed and you just feel like God is leading you a different way? Because I could totally understand that."

"Don't have to pray about it, I just know. God's not looking to use me like that."

The women looked at one another with raised brows.

"Kelli, this doesn't sound right to me," Cyd said. "Is it because of something from the past? And now you think God can't use you? Because that's exactly what Scott went through, and you see what he's doing now."

"That's true," Dana said. "To be honest, I didn't think God could use him again either after what he did. An affair is so scandalous. I'm flat-out amazed by God's grace and mercy, maybe more than Scott."

Kelli reflected on that. Scott's story had really touched her. "I hope it's okay to ask, but what happened to the other woman? I'm assuming she was sorry. Do you know if God is using her now too?"

"Heather?" Dana rolled her eyes. "She wasn't sorry about anything. She tried to get Scott *back* in bed after they were caught."

"Um, before Dana gets worked up," Phyllis said, "I think we'll do a really fast detour and get back on topic. So…Kelli…the point was that there might be some parallels between your situation and Scott's, as far as his thinking God couldn't use him."

"I actually do see a parallel." She wasn't sure how much to say. "I did some things I regretted too, the summer before I went away to college, and I was so ashamed I basically distanced myself from God." She looked into their faces. "Today was the first time I'd been to church in years."

Surprise registered on their faces. "I didn't know," Cyd said.

Kelli continued. "I wasn't sure what to expect. I felt like it would take awhile to work my way back into God's good graces, but it was like"—she flung wide her arms—"He just embraced me." She shook her head. "And then listening to Cedric, Scott, and Pastor Lyles…

It's hard to believe, but I guess it's true. For whatever reason, God uses people who don't have it all together." She felt emotion welling. "So I'm not saying He won't ever use me. But in the area of music? No."

"Okay, ladies, here we go," the server said, helped by another who dished out half the plates. Kelli stared down at her pancakes, remembering the joy she'd once found in songwriting. She heard Phyllis praying over the meal and something about clarity and wisdom regarding Kelli's situation.

"Well, then," Stephanie said, pouring syrup over her pancakes, "seems to me this emergency session is right on time. You needed some intervention so you could stop leaning."

"Leaning?"

"Stephanie recognizes the signs well," Cyd said, "because she's our biggest leaner."

"Hey!"

Cyd cut into her stack. "It's from Proverbs 3," she said. "We made it a DF check. If one of us is trying to figure out what to do, we ask, 'Are you leaning on your own understanding, or are you trusting God and acknowledging Him?' If it's the latter, the psalmist says God will make your paths straight."

Kelli set her fork down. "I've never thought about it that way."

Stephanie pointed her fork at Kelli. "There you go. DF to the rescue. I say we acknowledge God by asking right here and now—*just to be sure*—if He has plans for your music." She lifted a forkful of pancakes. "And I don't think this conference is a coincidence. Might be a quick way to see how He directs your path."

"Why do you say that, Steph?" Phyllis took a bite of sausage.

"Registration closed months ago, remember? God would have to open a door just to get Kelli in. And if she gets in, she's got to deal with *real* feedback on her music, from industry people." She turned to Kelli. "If they're not feeling your music—hey, you won't hear another peep from me about it. We'll just take it that the door is closed, like you said."

Kelli's insides were getting jumpy. "Where's the conference being held?"

"It's in Indianapolis this year." Stephanie smiled. "After driving from Austin, a trip to Indy would be a piece of cake."

"Kelli," Cyd said, "we don't want to push you into doing anything you don't want to do. I think we're just sensing that deep down, the dream is still there. And you've stuffed it for reasons that might not even be valid. I think it's a great idea to pray and be sure... if you're willing."

Kelli could feel the stirring. There was no doubt— the dream was still there. But if she allowed herself to pursue it, only to find a closed door, the disappointment would be unbearable. If only it didn't hurt so much when dreams turned to dust.

Chapter Five

Heather Anderson, undeterred by her four-inch heels, wheeled her luggage across the main lobby of the Indianapolis Hilton. Her insides were a jangle of nervous anticipation. She couldn't believe she was here, couldn't believe she was about to see Ace Vincent again. He was all she could think about for the past month, ever since they'd met at The Razz, a hole-in-the-wall club in St. Louis's Loop. She just knew it was fate, his showing up to play for fun with friends in a local band, her happening by the same night. She might've been the only one who knew who he was—drummer and songwriter for No Return, a Dove Award-winning Christian rock band. The intimate venue allowed her access to him after the set, and they talked most of the night. Since then, they'd texted regularly and talked by phone a couple of times, the latest three days ago when Ace invited her here.

The lobby was bustling with people, most checking in for the conference, Heather supposed. She straightened her back and finger-fluffed her long blond mane as she glided by a group of guys huddled near the coffee bar, all of them checking her out. Probably wannabe songwriters. Heather understood. She was a wannabe recording artist.

She glanced around for the elevators, then headed toward them, double-checking her text messages for the room number. 2125. She hadn't been sure about this arrangement at first. Ace had said he'd get her a room when he invited her, then he texted later to say the hotel was sold out, and she could stay on the sleep sofa in his suite. She wondered if he'd planned it that way all along—not that she cared if he had.

A pair of elevator doors on the far left were open already, so she stepped in, pushed 21, and watched them close. The lift made the butterflies scramble all the more.

She didn't know which excited her more, time with Ace or the promise he'd made to introduce her to other recording artists who'd be at the conference. That night at the club, she'd told him her dream and asked if he had any advice.

He'd answered with a slow grin. "A singer, huh? Let me hear you." He nodded toward the stage. "Up there."

Heather smiled back at him. She could play this game. "Sure. If you and the band play for me."

His grin got bigger. "Let's go."

He called the band members back together, and they all decided on a song. Minutes later she was singing before the crowd—albeit a small one—with Ace on drums.

"That was awesome," she told him afterward, hugging his neck to thank him. "Well? What did you think?"

Ace looked her up and down, nodding. "You've got the goods, that's for sure. Didn't think you'd be able to belt it out like that. And Lord knows you look fine."

They stood just inches apart, and Heather could feel the heat between them.

She leaned a little closer. "So, do you ever hear of any artists needing a background vocalist?"

He shrugged. "From time to time."

"I know you meet tons of people, and you'll probably forget me by tomorrow, but can I give you my number in case you hear of anything?"

He closed the small gap between them, their shirts grazing. "There's no way I'd forget you by tomorrow."

He was right. The next day he texted just to say he was thinking about her, and from there they'd been in regular contact. She was thrilled when he invited her to the conference, offering to help connect her with others. She knew he had ulterior motives, but then, so did she. If she and Ace became romantically linked in the process, all the better. She'd dreamed of that too—being the special woman on the arm of an entertainment artist.

The elevator stopped, and Heather took a deep breath and let it out. A wall mirror hung nearby, and she checked herself, dabbing on powder and lip gloss. She pressed her lips together and deemed herself ready. Moving down the long hallway, she could feel her life switching into another gear, a higher gear, leaving behind the ordinary and even the disappointments. She was about to live her dreams.

Ace answered her knock in gray cotton shorts, a plain white undershirt, and bare feet. Wrestler stocky, he had sandy-colored hair that stood on end. "Hey, you." He took a step back so she could enter.

"Hey," she said, crossing the threshold.

He looped an arm around her waist and brought her near. She wasn't expecting their first kiss right there in the doorway, but she didn't mind it either.

He led her by hand further into the suite. "How was your drive?"

"Passed pretty quickly." Her smile felt shy. "Must've been the music I was listening to." She'd texted him at a bathroom break that she was rocking out to No Return's songs as she drove.

"That'll do it," he said. "Go on, have a seat." He left Heather by the sofa and walked to the kitchenette. He lifted a bottle. "I got some champagne to celebrate."

"What are we celebrating?"

He poured the bubbly into two water glasses and brought them over, his leg brushing hers as he sat. "The here and now. You and me." He handed her a glass. "I like to celebrate all of life's little moments. Here's to us."

Heather liked the sound of *us*. She clinked her glass with his and took a sip, then looked at her watch. "Should we be doing this? Don't we need to be downstairs for the banquet in about an hour?"

Though she wasn't officially registered, Ace had said he'd get her a badge with conference privileges.

"What if you get tipsy or something?" she asked.

"From champagne? Nah. Besides, we're not going to the dinner."

"We're not?"

"Waste of time. Rubber chicken and lemon cake, then a keynote speaker? Trust me. Room service will be a lot more fun." He downed the rest of his glass, leaned over for another kiss, then jumped up. He went and grabbed the bottle.

"But what about the networking part? I wanted to meet people like Monica Styles and Rick Richards. We're at least going down for the concert, right?"

He flopped a leg over one of hers as he sat, then kissed her again. "That depends."

"On?"

He poured more champagne into his glass. "On whether we're in the middle of something more interesting up here."

His nearness gave her goose bumps. "But we can save the something interesting for after the concert. I love Monica Styles."

"Monica and I will be on a panel together tomorrow morning. I'll make sure you get some time. Maybe you can sing a cappella for her. I know she'll love your voice."

"Ace, that would be awesome. A dream come true."

He smiled, his face a short breath from hers. "I'm all about making dreams come true."

Heather took another sip of her champagne, settling herself against him, starting to like his plan. They'd spend quality time together this evening, then she'd network hard tomorrow. How many conference attendees hoped to get a few minutes with Ace, glean a bit of his wisdom? And she had him all to herself…for just the first of many nights, if things went as she hoped.

Chapter Six

Kelli stared at the conference banner stretched across the east wing lobby. *Christian Songwriters Summit*, it said. The tagline brought the flutters—"What were you made to do?" She was teetering on the edge of something, in her heart at least, and she didn't know whether to run or see it through. But mostly she wanted to run.

"Uh, Kelli?" Stephanie called across the gap in the registration line. "Gonna join us?"

"Oh." Kelli glimpsed the line growing behind her as she moved closer to Stephanie and Cyd. They'd already checked into their rooms. Now the conference was about to begin. A steady buzz enlivened the area, the chatter of anticipation.

"Monica Styles is at the top of my list." Stephanie poked the singer's face on the conference brochure. "I've got to find a way to talk to her. I really want her to hear Kelli's songs."

Cyd nodded. "She's one of my faves. Can't you just hear her singing Kelli's wedding song?"

Kelli stared at them. "I don't know who's crazier—

me for letting you talk me into this, or you two for thinking something's going to come of it."

Stephanie lowered the brochure. "Kelli, I don't know what I'm going to do with you. Did we not pray to see if God would open a door?"

"Yeah." Kelli's expression said, *And?*

"Are we not here?"

They inched forward.

"Well, still...turned out all you had to do was call Pastor Lyles, then he made a call."

"Oh no, honey, let's examine that more closely," Stephanie said. "I called Logan, who told me to call Pastor Lyles. How interesting that the conference director, Rita Miller, is the pastor's personal friend, *and* he'd just done her a favor by serving as a reference for her son to get into seminary." She raised a single brow. "Do you not think God is working? Why not believe something amazing will come of this weekend?"

"I do," Kelli said. "I believe the three of us will have an amazing weekend getting to know each other even better. That was a huge draw for me. I always wanted a sister, and now I've got two."

"Aww," Cyd said. "Group hug." She gathered them both in an embrace. "I told Cedric that's why I really wanted to come. No matter what happens with the music, I'm thankful for the special time we'll have this weekend."

Stephanie smirked. "Don't indulge Kelli's low expectations. The sister thing is nice, but we're here for a purpose. And I got me a verse for the weekend."

Cyd showed her surprise. "Wow, you must be really into this. You're looking up Bible verses now?"

"Ha, ha. And yes, I'm totally into this. Kelli can

thank me when she takes off. Here's my verse—'All things are possible to him who believes.' So those are our marching orders. We're believing. Period."

Kelli had to smile. Stephanie was pulling her way outside her comfort zone, but bit by bit, she couldn't wait to see what would happen.

Cyd straightened and saluted. "Marching orders duly noted." She put an arm around Kelli. "That was my other reason for coming—to be this one's cheerleader."

A spot opened at the registration table, and the sisters walked up. "Hi," Stephanie said. "We've got three Londons—Kelli, Cyd, and Stephanie."

The young guy flipped to the Ls and scanned the computer printout. "Sorry, I don't see any Londons on the list."

"Our names were just added this week."

Stephanie leaned over the table. Kelli thought she might take over and search the pages herself.

"Here you are," he said. "Last page."

Kelli could see that their names had been handwritten.

The guy handed them a conference packet, name badges, and a bag full of assorted papers. "Registration was limited this year," he said. "Been closed for months, no exceptions. Guess you three were meant to be here." He clasped his hands. "Better thank your lucky stars."

They smiled and left the registration table, and Stephanie bowed her head toward theirs. "Hear that? Meant to be here." She winked. "I know who I'm thanking—and it ain't no star."

"We are so thrilled to welcome you to the twelfth annual Christian Songwriters Summit. I'm Rita Miller, and my husband, Jim, and I are honored to serve as your hosts this weekend."

Kelli scooched her chair around to face the stage fully, leaving the remains of her lemon cake. Dinner discussion had been lively—especially with Logan at their table—but till now, she hadn't thought much about the program itself. Seeing Rita piqued her interest. Kelli had noted the Millers' names for years in the writing credits of popular songs. She'd pictured Rita Caucasian—and she was—but for some reason, she'd also pictured her youngish. Rita looked to be in her sixties, her graying hair cut short, dressed in a solid-colored top, sensible black slacks, and flat shoes.

"...and we're excited," Rita was saying, "because this conference has become a launching pad for some pretty impressive careers." She looked down at a banquet table up front. "Monica Styles joins us for a special performance tonight"—cheers and applause rang through the ballroom—"and I still remember her smiling face when she came to the conference three years ago with a dream to break into this business as not only a songwriter, but a singer as well. Look what God did."

"Woooo!" Monica's fist flew up in the air, which got others going. She looked even cuter in person, a petite twenty-three-year-old with dark brown hair that fell in layers around her face and extended down her back. Kelli loved that Monica couldn't be pigeonholed. She was a young black woman who liked to blend many genres—pop, gospel, neo-soul, and even a little smooth jazz, all with lyrics that glorified God.

Rita laughed with them. "But before Monica's performance," she said, "you'll hear an inspiring keynote speech by one of our first conference attendees, Roger Sloan, who pitched songs and collected rejections for years—only to win a Dove Award last year!"

Rita waited for the applause to fade. "Our conference theme is not a slogan. We prayed long and hard for God to give us our focus this year, and we hope you ponder the question deep in your hearts—what were you made to do?" She looked out over the crowd. "Do you have a passion for writing music for God? Do you hear melodies and lyrics in your sleep? If you know exactly what I'm talking about, we want to encourage you. If this is what you're made to do, go for it! Don't give up. Before time began, God prepared good works for you to do, and if you're here, yours likely involve music. Believe that God will accomplish that good work through you."

Kelli felt a shiver—and not because Stephanie had elbowed her in the ribs. She had that feeling again, like she was on the edge of something.

"One final comment before I introduce Roger," Rita said. "We keep the conference small because we want to hear your heart and give you special time and attention for the two and a half days we're together. You show up eager to share thoughts and ideas—and of course, your music—and we're able and eager to oblige you. But"—she gave a grin—"we're not as small as we used to be, so there's one important guideline to keep in mind."

Kelli sat at full attention.

"I know it's tempting to stop one of our faculty or featured artists and ask him or her to listen to your songs, but time doesn't allow them to accommodate everyone, and it easily becomes overwhelming. We're asking you not to do that."

Stephanie was frowning.

"Thankfully, there's no need," Rita said. "We've got the Songwriters Showcase tonight and tomorrow night, which you've already signed up for—"

"What showcase?" Stephanie whispered, eyeing them both. "I didn't see where Kelli could sign up for that."

"—and we've got the ever-popular individual critiques." Rita lifted a white card in her hand. "If you submitted song demos for review, you should have received in your registration packet a note card with an appointment time. That's when you will receive a professional critique of the songs you submitted." She moved away from the podium. "Some of you have asked if it's too late to submit now. I'm afraid so. The deadline was one month ago, to give our team time to listen to and evaluate the songs."

"I can't believe this," Stephanie mumbled. She ducked her head past Kelli and hit Cyd on the arm. "Can you believe this? We missed out on all the good stuff. Kelli's songs can't be evaluated."

Kelli stared ahead. Much as she hated to admit it, a touch of excitement had eased into her heart about this weekend. But she should've known better. This was their answer, their confirmation that the door was shut where her music was concerned. She couldn't have submitted songs even if they'd allowed late submissions. She didn't have a demo.

"Well, as I said," Kelli offered, "I'm glad we get to spend time with each other this weekend."

Cyd patted her leg. "And you'll still learn lots. You

never know when you might be moved to delve into music again."

"There y'all go again," Stephanie said. "Low expectations."

Cyd made a face. "You're the one who said we missed out on all the good stuff."

"I was making an observation, not *camping* there. While you two were calling it a day, I was sending up a prayer for God to move this mountain."

Cyd raised a wary eyebrow. "When did you become Ms. Mighty Woman of God?"

"Hey, Logan." Stephanie had a teasing lilt in her voice as she called across the table. "Monica's performing in a few. You gonna dance? That'd be a real treat for the ladies."

Logan gave a smile that was calculating. "Remember, Stephanie. Once this weekend is over, I'll be seeing you week after week at church. Plenty of time to plot my revenge. You started all this."

Kelli chuckled. Somehow Logan the bachelor had landed at a table full of women, and they'd been giving him a hard time—naming people who'd be perfect for him or claiming him for themselves. He wasn't necessarily Kelli's type, but there was no question he was good-looking. She was dying to ask his ethnicity. Was he part Latino?

"I'll cut a rug with him," said a woman who'd introduced herself as Hattie Cooper, "but I want it to be a slow number." She looked twice his age, but she'd already told Logan he was a "handsome fella."

"I think we should hold an auction," said the woman

beside her. "A Dance with Logan. We could put some charity back in the black."

The table roared with laughter.

"Are you blushing over there?" Cyd asked. "I don't think I've ever seen you blush."

Logan looked elsewhere, trying his best to pay them no mind, but his face was the shade of tomatoes.

"Okay, Logan, we'll leave you alone," Miss Hattie said. "But one question first, and I'm serious. What's with the women at your church? Are they mostly old like me or married? Not a lot of singles?"

"Miss Hattie," Stephanie said, "there are at least two hundred single women at our church who'd marry him next Saturday if he asked."

Miss Hattie slugged Logan on the arm. "Well, son, why haven't you picked one?"

"Whoa! You've got some muscle," Logan said with a laugh. "Miss Hattie, I'm only thirty-one. And to be honest, I'm not really interested in marriage right now. My time is filled with the same thing most everyone else here's time is filled with—music. I guess you could say that's what I'm married to." He smiled. "But maybe one day, way down the road."

"All right, young man," she said, giving him the eye. "But don't forget to give me your e-mail so I can connect you with my granddaughter."

Kelli snickered when she caught Logan peeking at Stephanie, mouthing, *All your fault*. Seconds later her phone vibrated. She'd thought it funny that so many of them had set their phones on the table, tweeting or updating their Facebook statuses. She brought her phone close to see who was calling.

Miles. She'd avoided his calls all day while they

were traveling and checking in, but she couldn't delay much longer. She answered as she ducked out of the ballroom. "Hi."

"She lives."

"I'm sorry. It's been a busy day."

"Been on the job hunt?"

"Um…" Could she call it that? "Yeah. Taking different paths, trying to see which doors will open."

Several people had gathered outside the ballroom. Kelli moved farther away so he wouldn't ask where she was. "How'd your presentation go?"

"Way better than I expected. You were right. Preparation was key. I studied the material backward and forward and was able to answer all their questions. The team left excited about the kind of software we could develop for mobile access and management. And of course, my immediate supervisor was glad I made him look good."

"I had no doubt you'd knock it out of the park. You need to do something special to celebrate."

"I would, if you were here. As it is, my 'celebration' consists of a fund-raising dinner my parents are hosting for renovations of the children's museum. And by the way, I can't wait for them to meet you. I know they'll love you."

"I look forward to meeting them," she said, though she wondered what they'd think of her. From what she had gleaned, Miles's people were old money—or at least "older" than anything she'd ever glimpsed—and big into community prestige.

"I'd better get going," he said. "What are you doing tonight? Anything special?"

Kelli saw the lights dim in the ballroom. She hated

being secretive, but there was no way she could explain the conference without delving into aspects of her life she'd left untapped thus far with him. Maybe one day. But not right now. "Spending some time with my sisters-in-law. Kind of a girls' night out."

"Have fun," he said. "I'll talk to you later this weekend."

As Kelli worked her way back to the table, a familiar up-tempo beat fired up. Rita's voice boomed above the chart-topping song. "She needs no introduction here, does she?"

"No! Woo!" sounded from the crowd as people rose to their feet. Kelli stood between Cyd and Stephanie, her eyes on the stage.

"The incomparable, the electric, the young woman who'll set your heart on fire for God—Monica Styles!"

The special effects lighting went wild and Monica's voice filled the air before anyone could see her, moving many in the crowd to their tiptoes. A laser spotlight flashed various spots around the room, then landed on Monica as she took the stage. She had an infectious exuberance, bouncing with her dancers across the stage with lively moves that got the rest of them going.

Kelli rocked side to side and sang along, shaking her head as Stephanie mimicked Monica's raise-the-roof dance. Stephanie looked back at Logan and gestured for him to join in, but he stuck with a cool head bop, like Cyd.

"Hallelujah!" Monica said, the song fading beneath her voice. "Are y'all having a good time?"

Hoots and calls sounded all around. A concert vibe had replaced the conference vibe in the space of four minutes. Probably wasn't hard to do in a music-loving crowd.

"I'm so glad to be here tonight," Monica declared. "This conference blessed me in ways I couldn't have imagined, and I know it'll bless you too. Right now I'm excited to share one of my favorites from the album I'm working on... I'm hoping it becomes a favorite of yours too."

The music started pumping.

"And I've got a special surprise for you," she said above the beat. "My good friend is featured on this song. I think you may know him. His first album is still garnering lots of attention, and he's making a surprise appearance with me here tonight!" She stepped aside and extended her hand. "Show your love for Alien!"

The crowd roared as loud as it had for Monica. Kelli was clueless. She looked at Stephanie, thinking she would know who he was, but Stephanie shrugged.

Alien made his entrance onstage, rhyming on top of the music, easing into choreographed moves with Monica. Kelli loved the beat, nodded her head—then froze.

She took a couple of steps forward. *I must be seeing things. That can't be Brian.*

She'd already had one shock this week where he was concerned. When Cedric told her he'd seen Brian at Living Word, she'd thought he was joking. He had to call Lindell to prove it, which only meant it was true but she still couldn't believe it. When Cedric said Brian wanted her to call him, she thought *Brian* had to be joking. The thought made her skin crawl.

Like seeing him right now.

Brian, a Christian rapper? He was one of the few kids in high school who knew exactly what he wanted to be, a scientist. She couldn't count the number of times they'd visited the St. Louis Science Center together—his idea of Saturday fun. How had he ever gotten onto this path?

"Give Him your all," he said above the music.

"Give Him your all," the crowd answered back.

"Kelli, you okay?" Cyd touched her shoulder. "You look…weird."

Kelli kept staring forward, her ears filling with Brian's vocals.

"It's not about you, it's all about Him…"

He's got to be kidding.

"Kelli, what is it?" Cyd asked.

"That's Brian Howard. My old boyfriend."

"What?" Cyd turned. "Steph, Kelli knows him. He's her old boyfriend."

Stephanie moved closer. "The one Lindell and Cedric saw at church?"

Kelli nodded.

"They didn't say he was a rapper!"

Cyd looked at her sister. "Maybe because he wasn't rapping at church? I'm just guessing. How would they know if Brian didn't tell them?"

Applause rang out around them. Brian left the stage, and a slower song began, one Kelli recognized as one of Monica's popular worship songs. But she couldn't worship at the moment. She was still frozen in place, frozen inside.

Cyd and Stephanie gazed alternately between the stage and Kelli. "Why don't we go, Kelli?" Cyd finally asked.

Stephanie took her hand and pulled her. "Come on. You and Cyd were so big on sister time. Let's get a head start right now." She glanced at the stage. "We'll get a fresh start tomorrow, and hopefully Mr. Alien will have moved on to another planet."

Kelli followed them out, with the sick feeling that she and Brian were on a collision course. She'd run into him sooner or later, whether here or back in St. Louis...and she hadn't the slightest idea how she would handle it.

Chapter Seven

Heather lay in bed, mind racing, or maybe bouncing like a pinball, careening from one good thing to the next, or maybe skipping, as in a field of flowers with blue sky, not a cloud in sight, or maybe… Maybe her mind was just spinning from too much wine. She shook her head hard to clear it, but it still felt like a jumble—a good jumble. All of her thoughts right now—for once—were good.

She moved her leg closer to Ace's to play footsie. He'd drifted off more than a half hour ago, but she wanted him to wake up, keep her company. They'd had a few moments of conversation over dinner in the suite—prime rib, red potatoes, bottle of red wine—but it all seemed to be building to one thing, the bedroom. Now she was wide awake and wanted to really talk, get to know him better, find out more about his background, how he got in the business.

She turned to look at the clock—11:48—and sighed. First session would start tomorrow morning at eight, and she wanted to be her best self. Better try to get to sleep, just close her eyes and—

"Journey On" started playing, one of the songs recorded by Ace's band. She lifted her head to find his phone. It was on the nightstand but stopped after several seconds, then started up again. On the third go-round, he stirred, grabbed it.

"Yo." His voice was gravelly, his body unmoved. "Angela? Where are you?" He sat up suddenly. "You're what?"

Heather looked at him. Emergency?

"Listen, just close the door and put the key in the ignition. The alarm should stop." He paused. "All right. How far away are you?... No, no problem." He sighed. "I said it's no problem." He paused. "Love you too."

A ton of bricks landed on Heather's heart. She closed her eyes so she could keep skipping through that field.

Ace got out of bed. "Heather?"

Would it matter if he thought she was asleep?

"Heather!" He reached across the bed and shook her. "Sorry, you have to go."

"What?" She squinted. "What do you mean?"

"My girlfriend's on her way. She'll be here in less than an hour."

She sat up. "Your girlfriend? If she means that much, why am *I* here? And why is she coming at midnight, anyway?"

Ace expelled a long sigh, running his fingers through his spikes. "We've been having trust issues."

Wonder why.

"She knows Mallory Knight is here this weekend. We used to date. She said she wanted to surprise me, but I think she's checking up on me. Ooh, boy"—he rubbed the back of his neck—"if she hadn't had a problem with the car alarm when she stopped for gas, I wouldn't have known she was coming till she knocked at the door."

Heather was reeling. "Well, what am I supposed to do?"

"I can give you some money for another room. They've probably got some last-minute cancellations. But other than that, I don't know. I'm sorry."

Ten minutes later Heather was pulling her suitcase back down the long hallway. She just wanted to find a good place to cry. And lie down. Her head was still spinning, and she suddenly felt like vomiting.

She pushed the Down button for the elevator, then the Lobby button, and leaned against the wall, head drooping. When she got off, she wandered over to the registration desk, where a lone man was reading a book.

"Um, I need a room." Her voice was so slight she barely recognized it.

"Ma'am, we've been booked for months. There are several conferences in town."

"No cancellations?"

"I'm sorry. None."

Heather felt tears of despair rising. "Could you give me some numbers for other hotels around here?"

He hadn't moved, his finger poised as a bookmark. "I could, ma'am, but I'm hearing everything's sold out in the area. It's just one of those weekends."

Heather nodded and turned, staring into the distance. What was she supposed to do? She couldn't drive the several hours it would take to get home, not feeling like this. Even driving far enough to find a hotel with vacancies seemed too ambitious. She barely had strength to stand, and she felt like—

She turned back. "Where's your restroom?"

He looked up from the page. "Across the lobby, down that hall, ma'am."

Hand to her mouth, Heather hustled as fast as she could, pushed open the bathroom door, and entered the first stall, leaving her luggage just outside. The second she leaned her head over the toilet, she vomited, again and again. Sweat beaded her forehead, and she thought she would faint. She sank to the floor, but just as she did, her stomach heaved again and she moved her face over the toilet, emptying whatever was left of the food. She grabbed toilet paper and wiped her mouth, then more to wipe her forehead, shaking all the while. She flushed the toilet and sank against the beige wall.

Right here was a good place to cry.

The sobs that had been gathering in her chest spilled out. *Why? Why did this happen?* How could Ace just put her out like that? He'd *invited* her. He'd *slept* with her. She laughed into her sobs. None of that mattered to him. *She* didn't matter to him. She never mattered. She was the one who could walk into a room and grab all the attention, the one guys tripped over themselves to get to, the one who never had a problem finding someone to hook up with. But she was never the one who mattered.

She was the one who got kicked out of men's beds.

Heather pulled her knees to her chest, the scene from eight months ago vivid in her mind. She knew she'd entered forbidden territory, sleeping with a married man. But she and Scott had met in the choir, sung duets, had good conversations. He was unlike any man she'd known, a sincere man who actually wanted to live right—and she wanted a man like that, a special man, to want her.

She knew what she was doing—flirting in a non-flirtatious way, gaining his friendship. She felt special whenever she was with him, and she dared to imagine herself with him, really with him, the one he'd love and adore.

But the fantasy died the day Dana burst into the room and caught them in bed. Scott made his position clear. He loved and adored his wife. Heather needed to stop calling.

Now here she was once more, the dispensable one.

She felt sick again. Not a vomity sick but a cheap and filthy sick. How could she give herself to Ace, to Scott, to others, and receive nothing in return? Nothing but an aching loneliness. And a feeling of worthlessness.

Who *was* she, anyway? Just a tramp? She'd heard the whispers. When Scott confessed before the church, he didn't implicate her by name, but many in the choir suspected…and called her names under their breath. And maybe they were right. An empty laugh escaped. *Admit it, girl. Of course they were right.*

"You're beautiful, baby," her mother always said. "You've got the look men fantasize about. Use it to your advantage."

That's what her mother had done. Heather couldn't remember a time when her mother didn't have a man in her life to care for her in some way. She and Heather's dad had been married four years, but after their divorce Heather watched a parade of men move into and out of her mother's life. She'd never felt comfortable around those men or with her mother's lifestyle. No one ever said it outright, but it just seemed wrong, spending the night with different men. Definitely wrong that she'd basically left Heather to raise herself. Her mother was the last person she wanted to emulate…and yet… A new wave of tears emerged. Wasn't that exactly who she'd become?

Her head fell on her knees. Didn't her mother ever feel used herself? Didn't she ever feel absolutely empty? Because that's how Heather felt. She hugged her knees, trembling.

I can't live like this. I don't want to live like this. But what do I do? God, help me.

The tears flowed harder when she heard her own heart crying out. Who was she to ask for God's help? Tramp. Adulterer. Served her right, getting kicked out of that room after all she'd done. Why would God care about her?

God loves you, Heather. Don't ever forget that. He cares for you.

Heather lifted her head and looked around. The words were so clear, as was the voice. Logan.

She'd known she couldn't stay in the choir after all that happened. When she told Logan she was leaving—not just the choir, but the church too—he asked why, but she'd said she didn't want to talk about it. She wondered if he suspected, but if he did, he didn't let on. He simply left her with those words: "God loves you, Heather. Don't ever forget that. He cares for you."

She blew it off at the time. Who didn't know that? But now, right now, those words loomed like a life-line, and she wondered if she could grab hold of them. She wondered if they were true. She needed that talk with Logan.

Heather reached over and pulled the straps of her purse toward her, digging inside for her phone. She scrolled through the contacts. *Please be here.* It was— Logan's cell number. He gave it to every choir member and said to use it freely, always stressing that the choir was about more than singing; it was a ministry.

But how would he feel about ministry with an ex–choir member at one in the morning?

Heather rose and left the stall to wash her hands, splash her face, and think it through. She knew Logan well enough. Cool guy, approachable and friendly, but one could only get so close. At least that's how it seemed to Heather, maybe because he never regarded her like most guys, never gave her that extra glance or extended hug. But they'd worked closely together because she sang solos on songs he'd writ—

Heather's eyes almost popped out of her head. Logan was a songwriter. He'd mentioned going to this conference other years. What if he was here?

She sighed, sobering fast. Still, that didn't mean she could call him right now. And yet…*now* was when she needed that lifeline. She wouldn't have any peace until she talked to him. She just had to.

Heather picked up her phone again and called. She lost hope after a few rings, but then heard, "Hello?"

"Hi, uh, Logan? I'm sorry to wake you." She still didn't sound like herself. "This is Heather Anderson, from the choir?"

"Hey"—he cleared his throat—"Hey, Heather. What's going on? Is everything all right?"

The question almost made her cry again. "I just… no. Everything's not all right. Um, something you said to me awhile ago came to mind, and I have some questions about it. I'm wondering if you might be here at the Indianapolis Hilton."

"You're at the hotel?" he asked. "Yes, I'm here, but… you want to talk *now*? Can't it wait until—"

"I don't know what else to *do*…" She'd tried to hold back the tears, but her voice broke. "I got put out of the room I was staying in, and I'm down in the lobby bathroom…"

"It's all right," Logan said. "Listen, I'll meet you in the lobby in ten minutes. Okay?"

Heather gulped back tears. "Okay. Thank you, Logan."

Heather sat in the seating area off the lobby, staring at the floor. The sound of heels breezing through made her look up. A sharply dressed woman headed straight for the elevators. Had to be Ace's girlfriend. She hung her head again and, from the corner of her eye, caught someone else approaching.

She turned and saw Logan. For the quickest of seconds, her heart did the little skitter it always did when she saw him, as if surprised he was still as good-looking as last time. The dark features, close-cropped hair, and that Spanish swagger—that's what she called it, after learning his mother was from Madrid—were easily distracting. But the skitter never lasted long around Logan. He dealt too straight for that.

Heather stood, suddenly self-conscious with so much leg showing beneath her mini, not to mention the tight shirt. But she had greater concerns than that. "Logan. Thank you for…" Emotion choked her words.

He gave her a light hug. "Heather, come on, sit

down." His eyes swept her luggage as they sat on the sofa. "Tell me what's going on."

Now that he was here, she didn't know what to say, where to start. She took a deep breath. "When I left the choir, you said God loves me and cares for me. I need to know if it's true. *Really* true." She paused. "For someone like me."

He frowned. "Someone like you?"

She stared at the floor a few seconds before looking at him. "I'm not a good person, Logan. Did you think I joined the choir at Living Word because I wanted to worship?" She looked down briefly again. "I joined because you all were gaining national attention. That's why I came to Living Word to begin with. Someone told me I had a soulful voice…and lots of recording artists start in the church, so…" She shrugged.

Logan stayed quiet, listening.

Heather grabbed some toilet tissue she'd stuffed into her purse and blew her nose. "And I came here for the same reason, trying to jump-start a singing career… and I guess I was kind of looking for love too." She felt the tears starting up. "It took getting put out of a man's room for me to see how messed up my life is."

"Heather…" Logan shifted his knees more toward her, his brown eyes piercing. "Jesus wouldn't have had to die on the cross if our lives weren't messy. I thank God that He would love someone like *me*. None of us is 'good.'"

She blew her nose again. "Oh, Logan, you've never done anything near as bad as me."

Logan gave her a thin smile. "Sorry to burst your bubble, but I've done my share. Yet for some crazy reason, God loves us and cares for us anyway. And He forgives us. It's really true. That's why He sent His Son."

Heather had sat in church Sunday after Sunday hearing Pastor Lyles talk about Jesus. Yet only now could she really hear His voice. *Sin. Repentance. Forgiveness. Savior.* Didn't seem fair, really, that God should forgive her so easily. Or love her so easily. She'd always thought she had to earn someone's love…and even then it never worked, after all the trying. The tears spilled over.

Jesus, please forgive me. I'm sorry. I'm so sorry.

Logan took her hand. "Can I pray with you?"

She nodded, head lowered.

"God, I pray You give Heather a real understanding of Your love for her. Let her know how special she is to You, that You sent Jesus to die for her so she could live for You."

Logan let loose her hand, and Heather sat silent a moment, turning his prayer over in her head. "I'm not even sure what it means—and it's kind of scary—but I'm feeling like that's what I want, to live for Him." She played those words back for herself. "Huh. Almost laughable for somebody like me."

"Will you stop that?" His eyes showed kindness. "If that's what you want, God will lead you. Every step."

Her brow wrinkled. "Do you think God has plans for our lives?"

"Sure He does."

"I've always wanted to sing, but I wonder if His plan for me is totally different."

Logan shrugged. "Let's ask Him."

"Really?" Heather thought it amusing. "Just like that?"

"Just like that."

Logan prayed again. When he was done, Heather looked at her watch and jumped up. "You're going to be dead tired tomorrow—uh, today—because of me. I'm sorry."

Logan stood as well. "I'll be fine. Question is, what about you?" He glanced toward the registration desk. "Hotel's probably booked."

She nodded, remembering her predicament. "I'll figure something out. I can sleep in my car a couple of hours, and I'll be good to drive home. No big deal."

Logan seemed to be thinking. "Come on," he said. "You can have my bed. An old buddy of mine is staying on the same floor. I'll crash on his chaise."

"I can't put you out of your room like that. You've done too much already."

"You think God didn't have a plan for you this very night?"

The question rocked her. Could He have? Was it His plan for her to call Logan in the first place? "If it's God's plan for you to give me a place to rest for a few hours, then I really think you should keep the bed, and I can take the chaise."

"Nah, wouldn't look right."

"Who would know? It's the middle of the night."

"I always think worst-case scenario. All it takes is one person seeing you come in or out. I don't want anybody to get the wrong impression. No big deal, though."

"Yeah, for you, but when you wake up your friend…"

Logan smiled. "I'll relish every minute. He beat me bad in a game of spades before we went to bed."

Heather smiled too, and it felt good. "Deal."

She followed Logan, unable to believe he cared

about not only doing what was right, but what he thought would *look* right. They got to the bank of elevators, and the one on the far left was waiting. Heather took a breath, remembering the woman who'd stepped inside that same one earlier and gone up to Ace's room. She had been full of plans and dreams and anticipation…and desperately alone.

This woman was different. She had no idea what the plan for her life was now. The dreams and anticipation about the weekend were gone. But she had something that woman never had—hope and peace. And she wasn't quite sure what all it meant, but she knew it made all the difference. She had Jesus.

Chapter Eight

Brian rolled out of bed in his hotel room early Saturday morning with music on his mind. Nothing tangible—no beats or hooks—just the very real fear that if he didn't focus and come up with something, he'd be in trouble. His second album was due in a month—well, actually *this* month, but he'd gotten an extension. Songs should've been recorded by now. His industry buddies should be listening, giving feedback, helping him sift and weigh which ones to include. Instead, he had nothing.

It wasn't that he wasn't trying or praying hard, but every time he thought he had something, it sounded silly next time he listened. He didn't even have a guiding theme. He wasn't used to this. With his first album, the theme and the songs came quickly. Now, when expectations were higher, he was struggling.

He groaned as he brushed his teeth. In some ways it was easier to focus on problems with the album than the bigger picture. He'd been praying hard about that too. The last two years had been stressful as he attempted to navigate between biochemistry and the music ministry God kept growing. Problem was, if music became the priority, so long, PhD. His academic advisor had sat him down at the end of spring semester and reminded him that he was in a world-class research program that required intense dedication. If he couldn't commit in that way, he needed to rethink his plans. Given the three years he'd already invested, if he left the program, they could award him a master's degree.

The ultimatum—long time coming, he knew—hit him hard. He wasn't ready to abandon his dream of a doctorate in science, a dream long nurtured by his grandmother. And yet he couldn't deny the strong pull he felt toward ministry in music—not to mention the album hanging over his head. So he'd asked his advisor for the summer off to contemplate his future, which she reluctantly granted, taking his fellowship money to hire two undergraduates to assist in the lab.

Deep down Brian had felt he wouldn't return. With time to concentrate solely on music, things would jell. The album would get done early in the summer. Promotion and marketing for the October release would fall into place. And he would know for sure that he was doing what God wanted him to do. But two months into summer, nothing was jelling…and he couldn't be more confused.

He showered and dressed, his head beginning to ache as he examined his life every which way. One day at a time, he told himself finally. He'd get on the road and get home, devote the rest of the day to writing lyrics in the studio. He was packing his bag when his cell phone rang. He glanced at the caller ID and sighed. Definitely not in the mood.

"What's up, Harold?"

"Why did I have to hear from your grandmother that you went to Indianapolis to perform at a song-writers' conference? That's why you turned down the gig at Solomon's? Are you crazy? How much did they pay you for that?"

Brian looked out the window. "Monica asked me weeks ago if I'd appear with her, way before the Sol-omon's opportunity. Everything's not about money, Harold."

"That's debatable. It's certainly about strategy. You turned down an opportunity that would've put you be-fore a sizable crowd."

"I had to honor my promise. It was my decision to make."

"Your decisions affect me. I'm your manager. It's a win-win for both of us when you make smart, strate-gic choices that elevate your career. Bad enough you turned down so many opportunities during the fall and spring."

"I'm a grad student, Harold. I told you going into this thing that I wouldn't be able to tour all over the place. I did what I could, and I've been making up for it this summer."

"Not as much as you could be. Touring is how you—*we*—make money. What will you do this fall when the album comes out? Steal away to the lab again? You have a commitment to the label and to me to do every-thing you can to promote this album."

"I know." Brian squeezed his temples. This was what he'd been hearing from both sides—his academic ad-visor and Harold. He needed to be more committed.

"And speaking of the album," Harold was saying,

"I've been thinking seriously about this. You need to have one or two tracks that we can promote in the mainstream. They can be uplifting, motivating, all of that—"

"Just no Jesus."

"Right. I mean, no. What I'm saying is, people will know Jesus is the underlying source for the motivation, without you preaching it. I just know it would take off and take you to another level."

Brian crossed his arms, staring upward at the sky. "That would be fine, Harold, if that's what I was called to do. I'm unsure about a lot of things right now, but that's not one of them. I couldn't care less about rap. I care about the Gospel, and God's given me a vehicle through rap. When God's done using me that way— which could be, like, now—I'm back in the lab."

"I knew that'd be your initial reaction. Just think about it." He paused. "I also want you to think about changing labels. You only had a two-album deal with Revive. I can get you more money if you go secular. I just want you to pray about it."

Brian felt like his head would explode. Why did he even take Harold's call? "Yeah, I'll be praying, Harold. I've got to go."

He hung up, still staring out the window. His remark had been flippant, but with every passing second he knew how true it was. More than anything, he needed to keep praying. Keep pressing in. Things were plain weird right now. Between Harold and this dry spell, God had to be shifting things. Maybe He *was* through using him in Christian rap. He never promised that Brian would have more than one album.

Brian got his Bible out of his bag and sat at the desk. Suddenly he didn't want to rush to get on the road. He was desperate for God to lead him in some kind of way...although lately he always ended up at the "wait on God" verses, which never got him excited.

He was about to turn off his cell when it rang again. Monica's name lit up the screen.

"Hey," he said.

"Heyyy, tell me you're still here."

Brian could hear the smile in her voice. "I'm here. Why, what's up?"

"I wondered if we could have breakfast. I've got some time before the first session, and I'm about to order in the suite. My assistant, Laura, is up here too."

"Aw, sounds good—and I'm definitely hungry. But I'm over here stressing a little. 'Bout to jump into some quiet time, hopefully get some direction."

"About the album?"

"Album, school, plus Harold's trippin' as usual."

"You don't need direction about Harold. Stop being nice and let him go. It's long overdue."

"You're probably right. I guess I felt I had to be loyal because he took me on and got me my deal."

"But if you ask me, he was never straight up with you, saying he wanted to make a move to the Christian genre. You were his chance to get back in the game. But he's wanted you to go mainstream all along."

"He made that clear today. Wants me to leave Revive."

Monica sighed. "It won't hurt you to go without a manager, at least for a while. You'll have more freedom to figure out what you want to do without him pressuring you this way and that. It's one stress headache you can get rid of."

Brian nodded to himself. "I can always count on you to tell me like it is."

He and Monica had struck up an easy friendship from their first meeting a couple of years ago. They could kick around most any topic, but he especially liked having someone to talk to who understood the industry.

"Of course you can count on me." The smile rang in her voice again. "I understand not coming to breakfast, but you've at least got to stop by the conference before you go—oh! I've got an idea. It would be fun if you could sit in on some of the workshop this morning, share some of your wisdom with budding songwriters. You know, give back a little."

"Nice guilt trip."

"Seriously, I know they'd love to hear from you. When I attended, my favorite part was hearing from people who were doing what I wanted to do. Just think—one comment from you could motivate someone to keep trying."

"I don't know about that, but..." He actually did like sharing about music and the industry. "I don't mind stopping through," he said. "Don't know how long I'll be able to stay, though."

"Awesome."

They wrapped up the conversation, but when he meant for his thoughts to land on the Bible he'd opened up, they landed on Kelli instead. He could see her here, mixing it up with songwriters. That had been her passion. Had she ever pursued it? Was she still writing?

He heaved a sigh. Five days had passed since he'd seen Cedric and Lindell, and just as he'd expected, Kelli hadn't called. Being here only made him think of her all the more. How ironic that he'd be talking to songwriters today, when she was the first songwriter he'd ever known.

Lord, please help me get in touch with her. I want to talk to her. I...I miss her.

Kelli walked with Stephanie and Cyd into the first session of the morning, coffee in hand.

"Aww," Stephanie said, "I thought we were early. The first few rows are already taken." She cast a disapproving glance at Cyd. "You just had to stop in Starbucks. That line was ridiculous."

Cyd sipped her caffè mocha. "I'm not seeing the problem. There are scads of available seats."

"I wanted a clear path to the panelists so I could snag one of them to tell about Kelli's songs and see if they'd listen."

Kelli huddled closer to them. "But Rita said we can't do that."

"We can't shove demos in their faces," Stephanie said, "and we don't have one anyway. But what if I tell them how fabulous you are and they *ask* to listen? Rita didn't say you can't sing for them."

"Oh. Yeah. They don't have time to listen to a demo but an impromptu concert? No problem."

Stephanie arched an eyebrow. "*All* things are possible."

Kelli looked at Cyd, and they both shook their heads as Stephanie led them to the closest row available and planted herself on the aisle. They chatted with others around them as people trickled steadily into the room. None of the panelists had arrived yet.

Kelli wasn't sure what she thought about it all. Until

recently, her world was filled with résumés and query letters to public relations firms and corporate marketing departments. That was why she'd gone to graduate school. That was where she'd built her career. But for the past week, all she'd thought about was music. And here, all she'd talked about was music. Funny how it all seemed to coincide with her return to St. Louis—and to church. Was she to believe this was God? Or was she setting herself up for a giant fall?

And why was Brian popping up all over the place? She wouldn't let herself process what happened last night, refused to talk about it with Cyd and Stephanie. When he entered her thoughts, she kicked him back out—though, admittedly, she had to do it several times. Brian? In the music industry? Even now, she had to admonish herself not to go there. His life was his business and none of hers. She hated that he was still in St. Louis, at Living Word, no less. But she'd made up her mind. She wouldn't stop attending Living Word because of him. If she ran into him, she'd look past him. She'd do what she'd been doing the last seven years—pretend he didn't exist.

"What is *she* doing here?"

Stephanie was looking toward the back entrance, so Kelli turned as well. In fact, many were taking a gander at the woman with the sleeveless deep V-neck top and skinny jeans and the long flowing hair.

"Who is that?" Kelli asked.

"Heather," Cyd said.

"Hold up." Stephanie shifted to get a better look. "Why is Logan with her?"

Heather. Kelli remembered the name. The one who had the affair with Scott.

Heather's eyes connected with theirs...and fell. She whispered something to Logan and sat in the back.

Cyd turned back around. "So Heather's a songwriter?"

Stephanie shrugged. "Who knows? Opportunist more than anything."

Logan walked up from behind and whispered something to Cyd. She got up and followed him out of the room.

Stephanie stared after them. "What in the world?"

From a front entrance, Rita Miller walked in with her husband, followed by Monica Styles, Mallory Knight, and Ace Vincent. Everyone but Rita sat behind his or her nameplate at the front. Rita stood behind a lectern at the end of the table and waited as the room quieted.

"Good morning," she said, her smile bright. "I'm so excited about our first workshop session this morning. Typically we focus on the technical and creative aspects of songwriting, the business of songwriting, and so on, and that's all good. But this morning we're going to take a step back. We want to talk about the most important aspect of this ministry of songwriting—and it's not a pen, a piece of paper, or an instrument. It's the heart.

"Songs of worship begin with a heart of worship and a life of worship. So we're calling this session 'Heart of a Psalmist.' Our panelists are going to be open about their struggles in keeping a right heart in the midst of all the busyness and the disappointments and the successes. Temptations do come, and if we yield to them, we can be taken off track. If our focus is not ever and always on glorifying God—trust me—it's easy to lose our way."

Heads nodded around the room, Kelli's among them. She remembered when songwriting was as natural as breathing, back when her relationship with God was strong. In all these "off track" years, she hadn't heard a new melody or lyric in her head.

"Let me introduce our panel members," Rita was saying. "To my immediate left is my husband, Jim…"

Kelli turned as Cyd slipped back into her seat.

"…and there's Logan Duncan," Rita said, looking toward the back, "who apparently had lost his way."

The attendees chuckled as Logan gave a sheepish grin and took his place among the panelists.

Stephanie leaned toward Cyd. "What was that about?"

Cyd whispered, "Tell you later."

"Was it about Heather?"

"Later."

"…and lastly, Ace Vincent, drummer and songwriter for No Return," Rita said. "Thanks, all of you, for giving of your time for this conference."

The room applauded.

"Monica, I want to start with you," Rita said. "You told me something just now in the hallway and said you didn't mind sharing it with the group."

Monica nodded. "But I have to warn you, I didn't say I'd share it with a right heart—because it's still fresh, and I'm kinda mad!" She laughed at herself.

Kelli smiled. She liked the way Monica kept it real.

"Last night I told y'all during the concert that I was still working on my album." She took a breath, shaking her head. "I was supposed to be back in the studio next week to do the last song. Got a call *thirty minutes ago* that the song I *thought* I was doing was given to another artist, a secular artist. Excuse me?" Her hands flew up. "Is that legal? Can we sue? Those were my first—and second and third—thoughts." She expelled a sigh. "I had planned to write all the lyrics for the album, but *they* approached *me*, and I happened to love the song. Now they leave me in the lurch?" She paused and pasted on a smile. "'Heart of a Psalmist,' that's what we're talking about, right? It's times like these that really test me, and I know I have to keep my heart in the right place and trust—instead of going off on somebody."

Stephanie leaned over. "See, I like her, and she's better than me...'cause I would've gone off and *then* got my heart right."

Rita stood facing Monica. "Oh, that's terrible, and yet it's an excellent real-life illustration. Things will not always go as planned in this business. Sometimes it's just plain wrong. It's in those moments that we remember who we are as believers, and we have to ask ourselves how we will respond. *Will* we trust God? Will we believe that all things work together for good?" She looked back at Monica. "We'll be praying for that to be resolved, dear heart. God'll give you a song better than the one you had."

"Amen!" several people said.

Stephanie looked at Cyd and Kelli. "This is our opportunity. The girl needs a song. Kelli's got songs."

"Me and everyone else in the room, not to mention thousands more in the world."

"You know what, Kelli?" Stephanie asked. "Just go ahead and thank God I'm in your life, 'cause somebody needs some bold faith around here. You just watch. I'm believing I'll get Monica to listen to your songs."

Cyd was shushing her, so the three turned their attention back to the front.

"We've all heard tales of moral failure in this business—and by 'moral failure,' people usually mean an affair outside of marriage. But what about staying pure as singles? That's a heart issue, isn't it? Is it even possible to stay pure in this business?" She looked down the panel.

"We've got two good-looking single men right here—Logan and Ace. I don't know how that happened." Rita lifted her hands in an amused shrug. "Don't mean to make you squirm, guys, but you signed up, so I'm putting you on the spot. Let's start with Ace. You travel the country, play various venues. Tell us how you keep a right heart in the midst of that life."

Ace sat back in his seat. "I guess I'll admit it's not easy." He stroked his chin, half smiling. "People are attracted to what they perceive as fame and fortune, and—we can be real, right?—women throw themselves at us all the time. So, for me, it's important to surround myself with people who keep me accountable, like my band, and stay prayed up and in the Word."

Was it Kelli's imagination, or was Logan staring down the panel at Ace with a funny look?

"It also helps," Ace was saying, "to have a very special woman in your life, and mine is right there." He nodded toward the front row. "When I think about her, no one else really matters."

Kelli heard the back door open and turned around. Heather was heading out, but the door didn't close right away. She seemed to be holding it for someone else.

Brian.

Kelli felt the breath get sucked right out of her. Her head snapped back around, and she hoped he didn't see her.

"I love what you said, Ace," Rita was saying. "Accountability, prayer, Bible—perfect ingredients for maintaining a right heart." Her eyes lifted. "And lookie here, *another* good-looking single guy joining us. Come on up, Brian, or, uh, Alien." Rita smiled. "Monica told me you might be coming. We saved you a seat at the front."

From the corner of her eye, Kelli saw him pass. He took his seat at the end of the row, and someone brought him a handheld microphone.

"Brian, we're calling this session 'Heart of a Psalmist,'" Rita said, "and we're sharing how we need to keep a right heart in this business, which can be a struggle. I don't know how long you'll be able to stay with us, so I'll ask you now. Is this something you think about as an artist? Is it important for you to keep a right heart before God?"

"Absolutely," Brian said.

He turned to face the people in the room, and Kelli's heart reacted. The onstage Brian was a persona, someone she didn't know, from whom she could distance herself. But seeing him this close and hearing his speaking voice had an altogether different effect. She remembered how much a part of her he'd once been.

"I think about it all the time," he said. "It's a huge weight, trying to represent Jesus like I should, not just onstage, but always. I don't want to be a fraud or a hypocrite. You know?"

Really, Brian? Since when?

"So I'm constantly asking God to help me do the right things, make the right choices, be who He wants me to be."

Kelli's arms started to shake, and she held herself.

"One of my favorite prayers is from Psalm 24: Lord, give me 'clean hands and a pure heart.'"

Kelli looked up now, her every fiber trained on him, and it was as if he sensed it. His eyes connected with hers, and she could tell he was stunned. She saw him lower his microphone—and it was the last thing she saw. Kelli scooped up her things and grabbed her bag, leaning over to Cyd. "I'm stepping out. I need to be alone for a little bit."

She wanted to hold it together long enough to get out of the room, but the walk up the aisle seemed an eternity. She got to the door finally and opened it. Then she stood on the other side…and cried.

Chapter Nine

"I love that prayer, Brian," Monica said. "And I have to tell y'all, he really is the same person onstage and off. I'm one of his biggest fans, and it's mostly because he does have such a good heart."

Brian's stomach was in knots. "Thanks, Monica. I appreciate that." It was all he could do not to jump up and run out. He'd thought he was seeing things at first. But by the way she looked at him—and her quick departure—it was Kelli. If he missed this opportunity to talk to her, he'd go out of his mind. But he couldn't just leave. How would it look? He'd just gotten here.

"We've gotten some excellent nuggets so far." Rita acknowledged her panelists. "We'll hear from Logan and Mallory, then we'll open it up to questions." She gestured to Logan. "You lead a choir and a praise and worship team each Sunday, and they often sing songs you've written. How do you maintain an authentic heart of worship week after week so it doesn't become drudgery? And do you feel a responsibility to make sure your choir and worship teams do the same?"

"It can definitely start to feel like a job with all the related drudgery if I'm not careful…"

I can't do this. Not when Kelli's out there.

Brian walked over to Rita and leaned in, whispering, "I'm sorry. Something just came up, and I have to go. Can't promise, but I might be able to make it back for a later session."

"Sure, sure," Rita said, nodding. "It was a bonus to have you at all."

Once he started up the aisle, he was practically jogging. He pushed the door open, looking right and left. No one. Just conference rooms with doors ajar and faint voices wafting into the hall. He continued to a busier section of the hotel, gazing about all the while, then stopped near the Starbucks, sighing. He wouldn't find her. She'd gone up to her room. Why didn't he follow her immediately? How could he have hesitated one sec—

He would know the back of that head anywhere. In a cushioned chair angled away from foot traffic, head lowered… Kelli. Brian's stomach clenched. All these years he'd waited to talk to her, *wanted* to talk to her, but now he realized just how hard it would be.

"Excuse me."

Brian turned and saw a woman with two teenaged boys.

"We hate to bother you," the woman said, "but my sons just had to know… You wouldn't happen to be Alien, would you?"

"Yes, ma'am." He smiled as he shook their hands.

"Told you, Mom!" one of the guys said. "I knew it was you. I've got your CD and I've watched some of your online interviews."

"Wow, thanks, man. I appreciate the support. Tell me your names."

"Matt."

"Bobby."

"And I'm the mom." She smiled. "You might be surprised to know that a fortysomething white woman is into your music, but our whole family have become fans. Thank you for the way you're reaching young people in particular."

"Thanks so much. I'm blessed to be able to do it."

"Can we get a picture with you?" Bobby asked.

"Of course."

As the mom adjusted her camera, Brian glanced back to be sure Kelli hadn't left. He posed with the guys, shook their hands again, and said good-bye, then turned and took a big breath. The walk to her chair was a slow one.

"Kelli."

Startled, she looked up at him, then rolled her eyes. "Go away."

He walked in front of her. "Kelli, please." He saw her tears now and felt a stab of pain. "I just… Can we talk? Please?"

"No." She tried to walk away, but he grabbed her hand and pulled her toward him. She jerked it back. "What don't you understand?" she asked. "You asked, and I answered. I don't want to talk to you."

His eyes were pleading. "I do understand, Kelli. Believe me, I do. You have every reason to hate me. But that's why I want to talk to you." His cell phone made a vibrating sound on his hip, but he ignored it. "That's why I've tried to reach you over the years, just to have one conversation. Can you just give me—"

She lifted her hands to stop him. "We don't need another conversation. The last one…" She wiped a tear with a shaky hand. "The last one was enough to last a lifetime." She turned and walked away.

Brian stood there, the sting of tears starting in his own eyes. What was he supposed to do now? He didn't blame her. He hated what he'd done himself. *But how can I fix it, Lord, if she won't hear me out?*

He had to try again. He caught up in a few quick strides and stepped in front of her. Their eyes locked inches apart, and she was more beautiful than he ever thought she could be. A tear rolled from his eye. "Just a few minutes, Kel. We don't ever have to talk again, if that's what you want." He flicked another tear from his face. "Please, Kelli. Can we talk somewhere in private?"

Kelli wished he'd gone away the first time she'd asked. She wished he hadn't found her at all—and he wouldn't have if she'd thought to get a room key. The moment she stepped outside the conference room she realized she had nowhere to go.

He looked different. Taller. More muscular. Manly. But those eyes were the same, those big brown eyes with lashes a girl would kill for—eyes that still penetrated straight to her soul. She hated that she hadn't moved from his gaze. She couldn't possibly listen to him. Yet in the years since she'd last seen him, one question—one word—had kept her awake at night. *Why?* If she'd been aching to know, and he'd been aching to tell her, maybe they could both get closure… and move on.

She sighed and nodded slightly, averting her gaze. "Fine. Where should we go?"

He cast his eyes about. "I don't know how much privacy we can get down here. We could go to my room, if you don't mind. I have a little while before I need to check out."

"Fine." She started toward the elevator.

They rode up in silence, got off on the seventh floor. Kelli followed him into the room and eyed a packed bag near the door.

"You want to sit at the desk?" he asked, moving some things aside.

"No." Kelli stood at the foot of the king bed. "I'm here to listen to what you have to say, then I'm gone."

He sat on the edge of the bed, and his phone vibrated again.

"Don't you need to get that?"

"It'll wait."

"But you're a big star now, right? You'd better handle your business."

"That's what I'm trying to do, Kel."

She looked away.

Silence engulfed them.

Brian cleared his throat. "Kelli…first thing I want to say is I'm sorry…for the things I said and did, for hurting you, for—"

"Brian, I did not come up here to listen to some lame, empty apology."

"It's not empty, Kelli." He stared at his feet, then lifted his head. For a moment he just looked at her. "You were my world. You don't know how many times I've wished we could go back." His head fell again. "If only we'd never…"

"We talked about that, Brian." Kelli was starting to shiver. "We both regretted what happened." She remembered the tears they'd shed the day after.

Brian was hunched over, staring at his clasped hands. "We said our relationship would be different from others we knew, that we'd stay pure. I don't know, maybe because we were at my house... I guess I felt like I should've done more to stop us from getting carried away." He looked up at her. "I was really weighed down by it..."

"Then I told you I was pregnant."

"And my world just flipped," Brian said. "Totally flipped."

"And mine didn't?"

He lowered his head. "I know."

"As devastated as I was, the thing that held me together was believing you loved me."

He reached for her hand, emotion filling his brown eyes. "I *did* love you."

Kelli took her hand back and held herself. "Love could never have said the things you said. You accused me of sleeping with someone else."

"I didn't *accuse* you." He looked frustrated. "I was *asking*...but I knew even as I asked you, it was wrong. I was scared out of my mind, Kel. We'd only slept together once, and I couldn't understand why God would punish us like that, for one mistake. I felt like I'd ruined my life and yours. I was weak and looking for a way to run from it all."

"And that's exactly what you did."

Silence blanketed the room again.

Kelli stared down at him. "So that's your why?" she

asked finally. "You were scared and weak? So was I, and I had to deal with it by myself."

Tears fell from his eyes. "I'm so sorry, Kelli."

"I *wanted* us to keep that baby, *our* baby"—Kelli started weeping—"and I asked you if we could. And you were so *cold...*" She sank to the floor, overcome with the pain of her own decision. "And *I* was so scared and weak that I..."

Brian moved from the edge of the bed to the floor, their shoulders touching, and wept with her.

"I should've been there for you and for our baby," he said, his head hung low. "I was more than scared and weak. I was selfish, thinking about myself and my future, thinking about everything my grandmother had instilled in me and hoped for me. I betrayed everything I believed in." He paused. "I even betrayed everything I'd ever thought about my mother."

Kelli looked at him. "I don't know what you mean."

"She got pregnant at seventeen and never really got her life together. You know I had little respect for her, the way she left me in Grandma's care and did whatever she wanted. But after what I did, it hit me—at least she gave me a chance at life." Brian looked shaken. "I've asked God a thousand times to forgive me. And I don't know if you'll ever be able to forgive me, but"— he looked at her—"I've never stopped thinking about you, Kelli. I miss our friendship. I miss talking to you. I miss *you.*"

Kelli met his gaze. She could almost believe he was sincere. And for a strange, fleeting second, she wanted to forgive him, walk with him through the pain that remained. But every time she thought of that day...

She came to her feet, picked her purse up from the

floor, and shouldered it. "When I needed you most, Brian, you walked away. I've never felt pain like that in my life. I could never trust you again, not even as a friend." She turned to leave, then paused and turned back. "I know we'll probably run into one another. We're in the same city, at the same church. But I'd appreciate it if we didn't speak. It'll just be better that way."

Brian's jaw tightened as he stared into the distance. He nodded.

Kelli headed for the door.

"Kelli?"

She looked at him.

"I'm glad you're at the conference. So, you're still writing?"

"I'm only here because my sisters-in-law encouraged me to come. The last time I wrote a song…" It came again, the sadness. "Last time I wrote a song was the night before you left me."

She opened the door and walked out.

Chapter Ten

Heather sat in the lobby area, waiting for the work-shop to end. She would've been on the road to St. Louis already, had Logan not texted her.

You ok? the text said.

She hadn't been till she saw those words. Someone cared. Logan cared. She knew it was just his nature to minister, to be there for people. But it seemed between last night and now he had become a friend or, as he put it, a big brother in Christ. She'd teased him at break-fast this morning that he was good at his job, asking more than once how she was doing, whether she was rested enough to drive home, and whether he could pray with her. She'd told him what had happened the night before, and he knew Ace's comments in the workshop must've upset her.

Heather had texted back. i'm ok. leaving indy now rather than later.

Another message came. wait til wkshp ends. meet me in lobby.

She'd waited, all the while chastising herself. Why

had she gone to that workshop? She knew Ace would be there, but Logan had said he could do what Ace had promised—introduce her to some recording artists. She would meet Monica and others after the panel discussion. But instead, the only thing that happened—again—was she got her feelings hurt. She just wanted to go home and get away from everything related to music.

Her eyes followed a woman getting off the elevator, the one who'd been sitting with Cyd and Stephanie. She didn't know her name, but she remembered her from Stephanie's wedding. Old habit. She always took note of beautiful women, to size up the competition in any given place. But now she took note for a different reason. The woman looked upset, and Heather felt a little sorry for her, surprising herself. Since when did she care about another woman's problems?

Ah, finally. Logan approached from another direction with a smattering of conference attendees, Cyd among them. She and Logan had their heads together, but when Cyd saw the woman, she went to her. They headed back up the elevator.

Heather rose from her chair to meet Logan. "Hey. You didn't have to do the make-sure-Heather's-all-right thing. I'll be fine."

"Actually, I didn't ask you to wait to check on you— but I'm glad to hear you'll be fine. I'm on a different big brother mission." His smile held a hint of intrigue. "I was thinking it would be awesome if someone could disciple you, teach you how to study the Bible, pray with you, that kind of thing. Are there any women in your life who could do that?"

Heather gave a blank stare. "The people I know wondered why I went to church."

"Okay, so...no?"

"No."

"Good! I mean, not *good*, but I'm glad I'm on the right track. I asked Cyd if she'd be willing to disciple you."

Heather's eyes got wide. "You have no idea how wrong a track you're on. Cyd hates me."

Logan looked perplexed. "Why would you say that?"

"Did she say she'd do it?"

"She said she'd pray about it."

"See!"

"What's to see? Discipling someone is a big time commitment; I can see why she'd want to pray about it. Why do you think she hates you?"

Heather sighed and looked away. He obviously didn't know. She looked at him. "Logan, I'm the one Scott had the affair with."

Logan stared at her a few seconds, then looked away.

Heather sat back down. She'd thought she could avoid telling him, but there it was, out in the open. What must he think of her now? Ace was one thing, but a married man? Sadness welled up again. She'd already begun to like the thought of Logan as her big brother.

He sat beside her, elbows on his thighs. "I'm trying to figure out how I missed it," he said. "I remember the two of you staying after rehearsal to practice duets, but I never put it together, not even when Scott confessed."

"Well, Cyd didn't have to put it together. She was with Dana when we got caught."

His eyes said it all.

"I'm the last person Cyd would want to help. She

doesn't even speak to me. And frankly, I wouldn't blame you if you stopped talking to me, now that you know."

A tenderness entered his eyes. "So I'm supposed to think you're the worst person on earth? This might be a shocker, but there were two of you involved, and I actually still talk to Scott. Cyd does too."

"Scott's different. He was always a good guy. Everybody likes him. Me? Not so much."

"That was the old Heather."

Old Heather? Was there a new? She'd just committed her life to Jesus last night. Couldn't have changed that fast.

"Well," she said, "you're probably the only one who'd see it that way. Cyd sure won't."

"I'll be honest, Heather. I'm sure it's hard for Cyd to look past what happened. Dana's her best friend; you were the other woman. But knowing this, I'm even more encouraged by her response. She could've said no the moment I asked. I'm impressed that she's praying about it." He paused. "But how would you feel about learning from Cyd?"

"I don't know," Heather said. "It's kind of wild, given the circumstances. But she used to lead the singles' Bible study, and I heard she was a good teacher. And before…you know…she always made a point of speaking to me. I think I'd be open to it, if she's willing. That's a big *if*."

"I'll be praying," Logan said, getting to his feet. "I'm on the next panel, and break's almost over. You heading back?"

Heather nodded, standing also. "Thanks for everything, Logan."

"No problem." He gave her a quick hug. "Text to let me know you got home safely."

She nodded and watched him leave, certain she'd spend the entire drive home trying to understand all that had unfolded in the last twenty-four hours. She wasn't sure she ever would.

Chapter Eleven

Kelli was ready to go home. For the last thirty minutes she'd been curled in a fetal position on the bed, paralyzed all over again as she replayed the past, wishing she could go back and change it.

She'd known exactly what she was doing. Even as she'd lain there in that sterile room, shivering, afraid, alone, there were no illusions. She was there to dispense with the baby she and Brian had conceived…and with it, all vestiges of their relationship. She'd stared down the decision for three weeks. Could she go through with having the baby, knowing Brian didn't want him or her? Could she change her entire life plan? How would she tell her mother, Cedric, and Lindell?

Every day the pain grew greater. She'd loved Brian for almost four years—the first two as purely her best friend—and he'd left her…while part of him remained. She couldn't bear it. She needed all of it to go away— the problem, the pain, the memories.

She phoned a girlfriend from school to take her, an acquaintance really, one who wouldn't ask many questions. And she cried for days afterward, ashamed, pleading forgiveness, but asking herself why God should do it. Why would He forgive her when she knew better? It hadn't taken her long to realize she *had* been under an illusion. The pain and the memories would never go away.

Cyd sat beside her on the bed, stroking her back. "Kelli, I wish you'd tell me what's wrong. What did Brian say? Did he hurt you?"

Kelli sniffed. "Actually, he apologized for the past. But it only dredged everything back to the surface."

"Will it help to talk about it?"

"No." She'd never told anyone about the abortion. "I can't, Cyd."

"Just know I'm here if you ever feel the need—"

The card key slid into the lock and the door opened. "Hey! Are y'all in here?"

"We're here, Steph," Cyd called.

Stephanie let the door slam. "Well, why haven't you answered? I've been calling and texting and—" She stopped when she saw them. "What's wrong?"

"Kelli talked with Brian. Brought up old memories."

"Really?" Stephanie joined them on the bed. "I thought it was a puppy love thing, but you two must've been serious. I guess I should've known. He sure seemed like he'd do anything for you."

Kelli lifted her head and looked at Stephanie. "What are you talking about?"

"That's why I've been trying to reach you two." Stephanie plopped on the bed. "After the panel, I stood in line to talk to Monica. When it was my turn, I raved about you, said you found out about the conference late, didn't have time to submit a demo, and asked if she'd be willing to listen to you sing a couple of your songs."

"She said yes?" Cyd asked.

"No. She gave me that look—like *I hear this all the time*—and politely blew me off. But that's when God showed up. I *told* y'all to believe. I am *all about* believing all things are possible now. I admit, I might've doubted a lit—"

"Steph." Cyd gave her a look. "What happened?"

"Okay, okay. Brian came into the room again to talk to Rita. I introduced myself, told him I was Kelli's sister-in-law, what we were trying to do with her music, how Monica had declined—"

Kelli sat all the way up. "You didn't."

"Girl, yes, I did. And we just hit it off. I mean, sorry, sounds like you've got issues with him, but he is such a nice guy. So get this…" Stephanie shifted. "He said he wants your music heard more than anything. He went over, talked to Monica, came back, and said she'd listen. Can you believe it?"

Cyd's mouth dropped. "That's incredible. So what now?"

"Monica said we could meet in twenty minutes, which was ten minutes ago. Kelli, this is the chance of a lifetime. I'm so excited for you."

Kelli blew her nose. "I can't meet Monica in ten minutes. I don't even know if I want to. I'm not in the mood to sing." She curled back into her ball. "I just want to go home."

"Uh-uh." Stephanie pulled her back up by the arm. "I'm all for a good pity party, but now ain't the time. Remember our prayer in the pancake house? We asked God if He had plans for your music. We said show us if the door is open or closed. Right now, it's still open. We can at least see what she says."

Stephanie was right. Kelli had agreed to let God direct. She didn't want to retreat again. But… "I won't do it if Brian's there," she said.

"Brian left. He's on his way back to St. Louis."

Kelli sighed. At least the timing was good. Nothing Monica said could make her feel any worse. So what if her songs stank? There were much deeper things on her heart right now.

She swung her legs over the side of the bed. "That's what we're here for. As my brother would say, 'Let's do this.'"

Stephanie tried to look sympathetic. "Except he'd have a tad more enthusiasm."

Kelli clutched her old steno pad filled with songs as she, Cyd, and Stephanie walked into the ballroom. It was empty, with chandeliers overhead and tables pushed to the sides. Suddenly it hit her. Monica Styles would be listening to songs she'd written as a teenager, and she would pass judgment. Maybe Kelli couldn't feel any worse, but she sure felt stupid. She hadn't read any how-to handbooks before she'd written those songs. Hadn't been to a conference like this. She was just a young girl writing what was on her heart. An amateur. Maybe Monica would spare her by not laughing in her face.

"Let's pray real quick," Cyd said.

The three moved closer and grabbed hands.

"Father," Cyd began, "this is all about You and Your plans and purposes. Not Monica's and not even Kelli's. We're believing that You've given Kelli these songs, and we pray You will do exceeding abundantly with them, beyond what we could ask or think. Do it for Your glory, O God. In Jesus' name, amen."

Kelli exhaled as the door opened. A woman stepped in and held the door for Monica, who was on her cell phone.

The woman walked over to them, extending her hand. "Hi, I'm Laura, Monica's assistant."

The women introduced themselves, and they made small talk until Monica ended her call.

"Hey! How are y'all?" Monica asked, walking over to them.

They went to shake her hand, but Monica hugged them instead. "Good to meet you." She wore a big smile. "So y'all go way back with Brian, huh? Any friend of Brian is a friend of mine."

Kelli wasn't sure what to say, so she just smiled.

Stephanie stepped in. "Actually, Kelli's the one who's known Brian a long time. She's the songwriter I was telling you about."

"I know I sounded skeptical when you told me," Monica said. "Everybody knows a dope songwriter. But when *Brian* said she was dope, I had to listen. You might have the song I need!"

Kelli swallowed hard.

Monica was looking around. "Oh, good, there's the piano." She looked at Kelli. "Brian said you play."

"Cool," Kelli said. "I thought I'd have to sing a cap-pella."

"We know your time is limited," Stephanie said, "so maybe we should get started." She led the group to the piano. "How many songs would you like to hear?"

"Two or three are all I have time for." Monica paused

to read a text message, then lowered the phone. "And let me warn you, I'm blunt by nature, which I *try* to temper by grace." She put a hand to Kelli's shoulder. "If I don't like it, I'll tell you."

Kelli's heart pounded.

"Perfect," Stephanie said. "We want the straight-up truth." She looked at Kelli. "Ready?"

Kelli lifted the lid and sat at the piano, propping her steno pad on the stand. She'd skimmed through it before they left the room and chosen a few favorites. She was pretty sure she remembered how to play them—kind of like riding a bike. She was also pretty sure she remembered the words, but she wanted the pad in case her brain froze.

She went with a lively song first, one she called "Praise Him."

Monica leaned against the piano, nodding her head. In no time she'd caught on to the lyrics and began singing along. But about two-thirds of the way through, she raised her hand for Kelli to stop.

"I really like that," Monica said, "but I've got all the up-tempo songs I need on this album. The one I was about to record was a slow, worshipful type. Got any like that?"

Two came to mind, and Kelli chose the one she liked best.

Monica stared into the distance, listening, and looked at her phone when it rang—a tune that competed with Kelli's—but she didn't answer. Moments later, she raised her hand again and made a face. "It's cool, love the words, but the vibe isn't really me." She looked at her assistant. "We got time for one more?"

Laura gave an iffy nod. "You'll have to jet right after. Next panel's about to start."

Monica looked at Kelli. "Bring it, girl. Give me your best."

Kelli nodded, staring at the keys.

Stephanie leaned over and whispered, "Kel, think Cinderella. You tried to shove those other songs into the slipper, and they didn't fit. Choose the one that fits, and you know what I'm talking about. Sing that wedding song."

The jitters came instantly. It would be doubly hard to sing today, after seeing Brian. She closed her eyes. *Lord, help me. If You want me to sing it, You'll have to give me the strength.*

Taking a deep breath, she played the first notes.

After the first couple of bars, Monica glanced at her assistant and looked back down. When she shook her head, Kelli thought she was about to raise her hand again—and she did, this time in praise. She seemed lost in the song, and while she couldn't pick up all the words easily, she sang the repetitive parts of the chorus.

"I will love you…and I will love you…I will love you… *Yes!*"

Kelli peeked at Cyd and Stephanie, both of whom were about to jump out of their skin…and trying to hide it.

At the middle of the bridge, Monica shook her head again. "Stop. Just stop."

The room fell silent. Kelli was confused. Didn't she like it?

"We've got to call Roxie," Monica said to Laura. "She needs to hear this. Now."

"I agree," Laura said.

Monica pushed a button on her phone and waited. "Roxie, whatever you're doing, put it on pause. I got something for you...yes, you need to hear this...no, just listen. One second." She put the phone on the piano. "You mind starting from the top, Kelli?"

"Not at all." Kelli ran through the song again, this time to the finish, glad she could keep her composure.

Monica picked the phone back up and walked across the room, talking to Roxie, Laura beside her.

Kelli, Cyd, and Stephanie talked with their eyes.

Looks good, right? Cyd's eyes said.

What's Monica saying over there? Stephanie's said.

Kelli's were cautious. *I just don't know.*

Monica walked back over. "I can't begin to tell you how pumped I am," she said. "I like this song better than the one they took from me—ha! Thank You, Lord!"

"I'm speechless," Kelli said, shaking her head. "I can't believe you like it."

"Roxie loved it too—she's my manager. We need the production team to listen, but I know they'll love it. I'm just now realizing, though...you don't have a recording that I can pass along to them." She thought a moment. "If I had my MacBook, we could record it here at the conference and send it. Do y'all have one?"

The women looked at one another.

"We're still in PC world," Stephanie said, "but if that's all we need to do, it won't be a problem. When do you need it?"

Won't be a problem? What planet was Stephanie on?

"Like, yesterday," Monica said with a laugh. "If we can get everybody to sign off, we might be able to get in the studio, cut the song, and keep close to the same schedule we had. That would be awesome."

"Let's see," Stephanie said. "Today's Saturday. How about we get it to you by Monday?"

Kelli and Cyd shared a skeptical glance as Stephanie exchanged information with Monica and her assistant.

"We've gotta run, but I am *so* glad Brian told me about you. I've got to call and thank him." She turned back around again at the door. "And nobody said you could sing! Girl, you can go!"

Kelli smiled as they scurried out.

"Can you believe it?" Stephanie pumped her fist in the air, then hugged Kelli. "All things are possible, baby! Woo! I feel like *I'm* the songwriter, I'm so excited."

Kelli laughed, totally overwhelmed.

"More like the manager, the way you worked all that," Cyd said. She hugged Kelli herself. "Looks to me like the door is open, sweetie. Did God make it happen or what? I can't wait to tell Cedric."

"It doesn't even seem real." Kelli gazed at the piano again. "But let's not get too excited. Her production team might not like it."

Stephanie put her hands on her hips. "Will you believe for two seconds, please? Just two seconds. Try it."

Kelli pondered those words, knowing it was her main struggle. How could she believe God would want to bless her after what she'd done? Forgiveness was one thing; giving her the desires of her heart was something else.

"So, what's the plan with the demo, Steph?" Cyd asked. "How do we get that done by Monday?"

"I'm thinking it'll be fairly easy," she said. "I'm calling my new friend, Brian."

"No, you're not," Kelli said. "I don't want Brian's help."

"Hello? You're already benefiting from his help. I'll bet he's got a MacBook, and I'm also betting he won't mind if you use it to record this song and send it to Monica's people." She took out her phone. "I'm calling right now."

"How did you get his number?" Kelli asked.

"He gave it to me." She scrolled through her contacts. "Said 'anything you need.'"

Kelli rolled her eyes.

"Hey, Brian? Hi, this is Stephanie London, Kelli's sister-in-law... Doing well... Listen, I hate to bother you again so soon...well, thank you." She mouthed, *He's so nice,* to Kelli and Cyd, then explained the situation. "Really? That easy? You don't have to do that... That would be perfect... Okay...um"—she eyed Cyd— "let's say tomorrow, Cyd and Cedric's house... I'll give you a call on our way back... Okay, thanks so much."

Kelli shook her head. "I can't believe this. You've got Brian coming to the house?"

"He said he'll show us how to use the software to record and how to e-mail it. We can get it back to him on Monday. Problem solved."

"Problem created," Kelli said. "I don't want to see him."

"You don't have to," Stephanie said. "He can show me how to do it and then he's gone. But, Kelli, seriously, is he really that bad? I mean, I've got my share of old boyfriends, and I've definitely held my share of grudges, but don't you think it might be time to let it go?"

Kelli looked away, seeing the past. "It's not that easy."

Cyd put an arm around her. "Whatever it was, it's clear he still cares about you. And he apologized. Counts for something, doesn't it?"

Kelli dismissed the question with a look. "It's easy to apologize and act like you care after the fact. When I needed him to care, he didn't. That's what counts in my book."

They could call it a grudge if they wanted. Kelli just wanted firm boundaries—Brian could keep to his lane, and she would keep to hers.

Chapter Twelve

From the top of the street, Cyd could see the balloons flapping above her mailbox. She kept quiet, peeking at Kelli to see if she'd noticed yet.

As they drove nearer, Kelli exclaimed, "Look! Must be somebody's birthday." Then, "Wait, that's our house! What's going on?"

Cyd pulled into the driveway. Before she even cut the engine, the front door opened and bodies poured out—Cedric, Lindell, Dana and Scott, Phyllis and Hayes, all their children—all holding colorful hand-made signs that said *Congratulations!* and *Future Songwriter of the Year!*

Kelli stared out the passenger side window, eyes wide.

Stephanie tapped her shoulder from behind. "What are you waiting for, girl? Join your party!"

The party joined them, surrounding the car and opening their doors.

"Welcome back!" Dana said as the women got out, stretching from the four-hour drive.

"I can't believe you all did this." Kelli looked from face to face, then turned to Cyd and Stephanie. "You two knew about this?"

They shrugged, unable to hide their smiles. "Perhaps," Cyd said.

Cedric gave Cyd a welcome kiss and hug, then hugged Kelli so tight he lifted her off the ground. "We're so proud of you, sis. I always knew your talent was special."

Lindell hugged her next. "You got it honestly, from your big brother Lindell."

Stephanie howled. "If you had any musical sense whatsoever, we might believe it was true." She kissed him. "Hey, babe."

Cedric and Lindell lifted their bags from the trunk and everyone moved inside, where the travelers got an even more enthusiastic welcome from Reese.

Kelli bent low to respond. "Did you miss me, sweetie?"

Cyd laughed. "Probably slept in your bed just to feel like you were with her." She kept walking toward the kitchen. "Mm, do I smell baked beans?" She looked at Dana and Phyllis. "Who brought those?"

Cedric put his hand to his chest. "Who brought those? I'm hurt. That's my gourmet beans recipe."

"Oops." Cyd made a face. "Sorry, babe, but you've never made baked beans. I didn't know."

"I've got lots of recipes up my sleeve. That's what happens when it takes decades to find the right woman." He pecked her on the lips.

Dana's ten-year-old son, Mark, made a face. "Eww."

"Least it wasn't a *movie* kiss," said Mackenzie, two

years older. "Aunt Cyd, did you really meet Monica Styles? I have, like, *all* her music in my iPod."

Cyd tweaked her chestnut ponytail. "It's true, Miss Mackenzie. And guess what? One day you might have Kelli's song in your iPod, because Monica might record it."

Mackenzie blinked. "You're, like, serious?"

Mark frowned at her. "Why do you think we're having a party? Even I knew that!"

Phyllis's oldest son, Cole, piped in. "Here's what *I* want to know." His eyes swept Kelli, Cedric, and Lindell. "Mom said you all know Alien. I mean, like, *know* him." He paused, his face incredulous. "How come nobody told me before now? I'm his biggest fan."

Cedric laughed. "Nobody told me either. I just know him as Brian, the kid who used to be at the house every time I stopped by. I thought my mother had adopted him."

Kelli rolled her eyes. "Whatever, Ced."

"Cole is crazy about this Alien," Phyllis said. "Last month he begged to go downtown to this outdoor concert thing at the Arch, but Hayes was out of town and I wasn't about to tackle that crowd by myself with three boys and a busy toddler." She looked down at Ella, who was trying to pull Reese's tail. "Cole pouted for days."

"Aw, you could've left Ella here," Cyd said.

Phyllis glanced at Cole to see if he was listening, then turned back to Cyd. "Don't be blowing my cover. There were over fifty thousand people down there. Ella was a good excuse."

"Well, look how it worked out, Cole," Stephanie said. "You didn't have to go downtown to see Alien looking like a speck on the stage. You can see him up close. He's coming over today."

Cole's expression turned grave. "*Alien* is coming *here*? Is this a joke?"

Most of the adults laughed. Kelli seemed to be taking it in stride.

"No joke, buddy," Cyd told him. "He's bringing his laptop so Kelli can record her song."

"I still can't believe it," Dana said. "Just a week ago we were praying about all this in the pancake house. I'm so happy for you, Kelli."

"Me too," Scott said. "They tried to make this celebration a DF thing, but I protested. I wanted us all to celebrate. This is unbelievable."

Kelli leaned her backside against a kitchen counter. "I know Steph's gonna kill me—and I'm definitely thankful you've done all this—but isn't the celebration premature? They haven't said yes yet."

"We're believing they will," Lindell said. "But you know what? The fact that Monica and her manager loved your song is reason enough to celebrate. I think that's great confirmation of the gift God has given you."

"Well said, bro." Cedric picked up the *Future Songwriter* sign from the counter and waved it. "Kel, we're not just celebrating what is. We're celebrating all that God's going to do."

The doorbell sounded, and everyone's face turned.

"I wonder if that's Brian," Stephanie said. "I didn't expect him so soon."

"I'm going to see." Cole took off for the door, and the rest followed, except Cyd, who lagged behind with Kelli.

A swell of conversation filled the foyer the moment the door opened.

"Hey, man! Why didn't you tell me you were some big star now?"

"Brian! Good to see you. Come on in."

"Guess that's my cue." Kelli started for the stairway.

"But this is your party," Cyd said. "Don't let Brian's presence drive you away."

Kelli was halfway up the stairs already. "Hopefully he'll drop off the laptop and leave."

Cyd went to greet Brian as the others headed into the family room, everyone chattering at once. He had a gaggle of kids hanging on him, literally. Even Ella, who'd gotten caught up in the excitement, was pulling on his leg. For Reese, it was a chance to pounce on them all.

Hayes walked beside him trying to exert some crowd control. "Kids, give Brian some space. He just got here."

Brian smiled. "They're fine. I love kids."

"We haven't met yet," Cyd said. "I'm Cedric's wife, Cyd."

Brian tossed a glance to Cedric, then back to Cyd. "So you're the amazing woman who got him to settle down?" He bowed. "I'm honored to meet you."

"Don't start, man," Cedric warned. "You'll get a quick escort to the door."

"Nah, man, really… I'm happy for you. Must be awesome to be with the person you know is made for you."

While the kids got distracted with something else, Hayes spoke up. "I was a huge rap fan as a teen and young adult. When Cole told me about 'Christian rap,'

I thought for sure it'd be corny." He looked pointedly at Brian. "But your songs make me think."

Phyllis couldn't hide her surprise. "I didn't know you were listening to Alien's music."

Cyd waited with interest for Hayes's reply. Phyllis had lamented to the women over the years that she couldn't even listen to Christian music around Hayes because he'd complain that she was trying to preach to him.

Hayes paused, maybe realizing he'd revealed more than he'd intended. "I got tired of battling with Cole about what to listen to in the car. Alien's album snuck up on me. I started letting it play even after I'd dropped Cole off." He looked at Brian again. "I…walked away from church as a kid because my mother had an affair with the pastor, and my dad left us. But I'm starting to see it's not about one pastor or even about 'church.'" He paused, and it was clear he was reflecting. "Your songs penetrate."

Brian and Hayes continued their conversation, and Phyllis turned toward Cyd.

Wait till Cole hears this, she mouthed. And then in a low tone, "He's been praying so long for his dad."

"Excuse us a sec, Phyllis," Cedric said. He pulled Cyd aside. "You plan to talk to Dana and Scott while they're here?"

Cyd glanced over at them and sighed. "I think I have to, but I sure don't want to." She looked into Cedric's eyes. "How did you know I'd decided?"

"I could hear it in your voice when we talked this morning. I knew that's how God was leading you."

From the time Cyd talked to Logan, the conversation had weighed on her. Stephanie and Kelli had been

so focused on the Monica development that they'd forgotten to ask about it, which was fine. She wanted to
pray and talk to her husband about it. "This is one of
the hardest things I've ever had to do."

"Cyd." He tipped her chin. "I remember another hard
thing you had to do. You had to beat me back with a
stick when I was trying to lead you places you didn't
want to go. You will never go wrong when you do what
you know God wants you to do."

"I know." She sighed again. "But she's my best
friend, and I know this will hurt her."

Cyd took the seat across from Dana and Scott at the
dining room table.

"This seems so serious," Dana said. "Why do you
need to talk to us right now? Did something happen?"

Cyd nodded slowly. "At the conference." She looked
into both their faces. "Heather was there."

"Heather? That's what this is about?" Dana's face
tensed. "Come on, Cyd. She's the last person I want
to talk about."

Cyd put her hand up. "I totally understand. This
whole thing took me by surprise."

Scott reached for Dana's hand on the table. "What's
going on, Cyd?"

"I don't know the whole story, but somehow Heather
ended up without a place to stay, and Logan put her
up in his room."

"She's got her sights on Logan now?" Dana's voice
rose an octave at least. "He can't be that stupid. She'll
be the downfall of his ministry."

"He wasn't in the same room. He stayed with a
buddy." Cyd chose her words carefully. "From what

he said, though, whatever happened caused Heather to really examine her life. Logan prayed with her." Cyd paused. "She committed her life to Jesus."

"Praise God," Scott whispered under his breath.

Dana cut her eyes at him. "Praise God? You're falling for this? It would be nothing for her to fake a spiritual experience just to get next to Logan."

Scott didn't respond but looked at Cyd. "Where do you come in with all this?"

Cyd took a deep breath. "Logan said Heather needs someone to disciple her, that she doesn't know much about the Bible and has a lot of questions. He asked if…if I'd be willing to do it."

Dana let go of Scott's hand and sat up. "You told him no, right?"

"I told him I'd pray about it."

"Cyd, how could you?"

"How could I pray about it?"

"How could you even consider helping her after what she did to me? She was in my *bed* sleeping with my *husband*. She's despicable!"

Scott lowered his eyes.

"Dana, I was there." She gazed into the eyes of her friend. "I'm the one who wanted to slap the girl. This is not easy for me. But God reminded me that I started praying for her a little while after that, for her to be changed. What am I supposed to do now that He's answered?"

Scott put his hand over Dana's. "The last thing I want to do is relive everything we went through last fall, but I was as much to blame for what happened as Heather. And I was shown mercy and given another chance." He paused. "What if Heather really has committed her life to Jesus? What if she truly wants to learn and grow? Shouldn't she be given a chance too?"

"You know what, Scott?" Dana said. "I really don't feel like hearing you defend her. But fine. Let's agree she should have every chance in the world to learn and grow. But it should be with someone else's best friend." Dana lifted her hands in frustration. "I can't believe we're even having this discussion. Doesn't Logan know we're best friends? Why would he ask you to do this, Cyd? It's not fair."

Cyd was on the verge of tears. It really *didn't* seem fair. "I think," she said slowly, "Logan asked because I was there when the need arose. But I also think"— *Help me, Lord*—"that somehow, even that might've been part of God's plan. I wanted to reject Logan's request instantly, but I couldn't. And I kept praying for God to give me a peace about telling him no. Instead, He gave me a peace about doing it."

Dana stared at her for long seconds. "So that's it? You're going to disciple the girl who almost tore my family apart?" She pushed back from the table. "I need to go for a walk."

"I'm going with you," Scott said.

Dana turned. "I need to think this through by myself right now." She cast a glance at Cyd and went out the door.

Cyd's heart was breaking. She couldn't remember the last time she and Dana had had a disagreement, but she was sure this one beat every one they'd had since junior high.

Scott stared at the door. "I understand how Dana's feeling, and I know this will rehash a lot of stuff

I'd rather leave alone. But how can I not be glad for Heather? And she couldn't ask for a better mentor."

"Well…pray," Cyd said. "I still don't *like* her. But I really want to see her as God sees her."

"I'll be praying. For Dana too."

"Brian? Did you hear me?"

Brian snapped his attention back to Stephanie and the laptop in front of them. They were in the office just off the family room.

"Uh…can you repeat that?"

"Show me one more time what to do once we're done recording. How do we convert it to, whatever you call it, so we can e-mail it?"

"The mp3 file? Yeah, that's easy." Brian walked her through it.

"This is great. I don't know how to thank you."

"No problem at all." His thoughts drifted again. He'd hoped to get a glimpse of Kelli, but she was obviously determined to steer clear of him, to the extent of missing her own party. He'd stayed longer than expected, but with the tutorial done, it was time to go. His phone rang, and he glanced at it. "Excuse me, I need to get this."

Stephanie stood. "And I need to see what's taking these guys so long to get this food off the grill."

He answered as Stephanie left.

"You won't believe it," Harold said. "Got some good news."

"What's up?"

"My old connections paid off. I sent your stuff to G-Freddie, and he digs your style. Said he'd be willing to guest on your album. That's huge, man! Crazy airplay on the radio. He could put you in the stratosphere. And check this out. He thinks you'd be helping him too. A feature on your album might clean up his image…he had a little problem with that jail stint recently." Harold laughed. "What do you think?"

Brian had to temper what he wanted to say. "I think we need a face-to-face. Let's set a date. Will you be in St. Louis anytime soon?"

"What about? Just tell me now."

"Okay." Brian nodded, resolved. "This isn't working, Harold. We're not seeing eye-to-eye, and I don't even think you're listening to me anymore."

"Oh, you just gonna dump me now? After I got you where you are?"

Calm coated Brian's insides. "You helped me get a deal, and I'll always be appreciative. But God got me where I am. If I had followed your advice along the way, I wouldn't have the ministry or the following I have now."

"True," Harold said. "You'd have a bigger following—but it's all good. I feel like God's been telling me to go back to secular anyway. Maybe He wants me to minister to those artists."

"I appreciate your understanding, and I wish you well. I'll hit you up later this week so we can talk more about what we need to do."

Brian got up, exhaling, feeling one weight lifted… but he still had a ton on his mind. He found Cyd and Phyllis in the kitchen setting out plates, glasses, and soft drinks.

"You're staying to eat, aren't you?" Cyd asked.

He put his hands in his pockets. "Thanks, but I need to head home."

"You got a home-cooked meal waiting for you?"

He smiled slightly. "Grandma usually cooks, but she made Sunday her day off. There's always leftovers, though."

Cyd stepped closer. "Let me put it this way. Are you hungry?"

"Well…"

She passed him a plate. "Brian, get some food."

"But I saw the balloons and signs and everything. This is Kelli's celebration, and I know she's upstairs because of me. I need to go."

The women looked at one another.

Cyd took the stoneware plate from him and exchanged it for two paper plates. "Pile the food high, and I'll wrap it up for you."

"That'll work," he said.

Phyllis passed him the baked beans and potato salad on her end of the counter. "Are you working on your next album?" she asked.

"Good question." He gave an empty chuckle. "I should be, but nothing's really coming to me."

"How can we pray for you?" Cyd was taking some macaroni and cheese out of the oven. "You've got to get some of this. It's Phyllis's specialty."

"Oh, that's awesome—the prayers, I mean," Brian said, then added, "but the mac 'n' cheese looks awesome too." He turned from the food. "Please pray for direction. A couple of months ago I thought God was moving me away from my graduate studies and telling me to focus on music. But now I don't know… He might be saying the exact opposite."

"Oh, Lord, please keep him in music," Phyllis said.

"Anybody who can reach my husband needs to keep doing what he's doing."

Brian gave her an appreciative smile.

"Brian, I think we should all pray for you while you're here," Cyd said. At his nod of agreement, she walked to the back door and called everyone in.

They trooped into the kitchen moments later, though he noticed one of the families had left. The dog trotted in with them, panting from an obvious workout outdoors, and went straight to her water bowl.

"Time to eat?" one of the little guys asked.

"Yep," Cyd said, "but first we're going to pray for Brian."

They formed a circle, and after Brian shared his heart with the entire group, Cedric began to pray. Brian was suddenly teary-eyed. Maybe because it was remarkable to see how far God had brought them both. Maybe because he had been needing a close circle like this more than he knew.

But maybe the tears stemmed from something else. Maybe because the one person he wished was in the circle, holding his hand and praying with him, was upstairs avoiding him.

Chapter Thirteen

Kelli bounded down the stairs Friday, ready for a fun night out with her brothers and sisters-in-law. After dinner they'd catch a movie, and if they still had energy she'd pitch a stop at Ted Drewes for frozen custard, a St. Louis favorite she hadn't had in a long while. Being able to spend time with family like this was a new treat, but she looked forward to it for another reason as well—to get her mind off the mental roller coaster it had been riding all week.

She looked down at her constant companion. Reese had already fashioned new headquarters in her room, complete with a blanket the dog had dragged upstairs and lodged in a corner, along with a collection of toys. And now she'd started letting Kelli know when she wanted a walk. She'd just dropped her leash at Kelli's feet.

"Didn't Cedric walk you when he got home? And I know I walked you this morning." Kelli rubbed her behind the ears. "I think I'm spoiling you."

Cyd and Cedric were upstairs getting ready. They

had thirty minutes before they needed to meet Stephanie and Lindell at the restaurant. Plus those eyes looked
so pitiful.

"Okay, girl, come on. I'll give you a quick trip
around the block."

Kelli attached her leash and led Reese out the back
door and down the driveway. A downpour earlier in the
afternoon had ushered in a nice cool summer breeze.
Kelli breathed it in as they trekked down the sidewalk
and tried to breathe out everything on her mind.

The week had started on a high. She loved the experience of recording the song, even learning how to
use the computer keyboard and other instruments in
GarageBand on the Mac. Laying down her own music
and lyrics and hearing them back gave her a thrill she
hadn't expected, permission to bask for a moment, to
accept that God might very well be about to bless her
with a deep desire of her heart.

The excitement increased after they'd sent the mp3
late Sunday to Monica's assistant. Monica replied
herself the next morning, excited to receive it, saying
she'd already forwarded it to the production team. She
added—with a yellow smiley face—that she'd be calling her team within the hour to get feedback and told
Kelli to expect an update soon.

The rest of Monday and all day Tuesday, Kelli's
imagination soared. Maybe she'd get to go to the studio to watch Monica record the song. And maybe, just
maybe, she'd get to sing some background vocals.
She'd never dreamed of being a singer—so many did
it better—but Monica's comment about her voice had
encouraged her. She caught herself singing the background melody to the song as she went about her day.

When no word came by Wednesday evening, Kelli began to back away. It didn't take three full days to listen to a four-minute recording. They didn't like it. They'd moved on...and neglected to let her know.

On Thursday she focused her energy where it should've been the last two weeks—on finding a job. She reviewed her folder of information on public relations firms and corporate marketing departments in the St. Louis area and perused their websites. She would target those who were hiring first, hopeful that Cedric could get her in the door with a few of them.

Miles had helped focus her too, e-mailing a *Dallas Morning News* article that profiled a local PR firm and its successful launches of different brands. Felt good to get her head back in the game, remember why she'd gone to graduate school. She didn't need to be up in the clouds thinking about music again. She needed to find a position and start working.

But Stephanie had called to give her a pep talk that morning. "We haven't heard anything, and I know you're thinking the worst, but there could be a million reasons for the delay, none having to do with you or the song. Don't forget—Monica loves it!"

Kelli smiled at a dog walker coming her way and moved Reese to her other side, fearing the Great Dane might come at her. But little Reese was the one who caused the beef, growling and straining to get at the other dog.

"Reese, no," Kelli said, using both hands to pull her back.

The man smiled, tightened the leash, and moved his dog onward.

Kelli rounded the bend back to their street. All day she'd teetered between the clouds and the ground, not sure which to cling to, praying for an answer. But tonight she just wanted off. She didn't even want to talk about it. She just wanted to enjoy the company of her fam—

Was that Stephanie and Lindell's car?

Kelli watched as the car pulled up in front of the house and Stephanie and Lindell got out.

"Hey, guys!" Kelli called. "Decided to meet here instead of the restaurant?"

They glanced at her, then at one another.

Kelli frowned a little as she came closer. "Y'all look funny. What's up?"

"Why don't we go inside," Lindell said.

Kelli walked in and unhooked the leash as Cyd and Cedric came down the stairs. She noticed the four of them eyeing one another.

"Okay, what's going on?" Kelli said. "You two knew Steph and Lindell were coming here?"

A big smile eased onto Cedric's face. "I guess we can go ahead—"

"Wait," Stephanie cut in. "Cyd and Cedric don't know this either. I sent Monica an e-mail today, asking for an update. I got a reply from her assistant only a few minutes ago." She pulled out her phone, pulled up the message, and passed it to Kelli.

Kelli's hand shook as she took it. The message was two lines.

Our team liked the song but decided to go another direction. We apologize for not getting word to you sooner. Best, Laura

Decided to go another direction...decided to go an-other direction... Kelli forced her eyes away from the words and passed the phone back.

"Let me see that," Cyd said. She and Cedric read it together.

Kelli picked up her purse from the chair by the door and slung it over her shoulder. "Ready?"

Cedric eyed the others before responding. "Kelli," he said, "we've got something for you. That's why we'd already planned for Lindell and Stephanie to come here first."

Kelli stared at them. *Please don't let it be music re-lated.* She simply wanted to pretend that none of this had happened and get back to life as usual. Maybe they got her a MacBook, and she could use it for her job. "What is it?" she asked.

Cedric and Lindell slipped back out the front door, Cyd and Stephanie following. She heard a trunk slam. The women returned first, with Cyd holding the door for the guys. Lindell walked in with a big black stand and set it in front of her, then Cedric brought in a key-board and placed it on the stand.

Kelli walked away from it. "We have to take it back."

"I told them you'd say that," Lindell said, "but so what if Monica's camp turned down the song? They af-firmed you as a songwriter by giving it consideration."

"This is our way of tangibly saying we support you," Cedric said. "We want you to have what you need to create fantastic music. You might have several more rejections before you hit—but you've got to keep plug-ging. Don't give up."

Cyd nodded. "Monica's just one recording artist.

I know God will open a door for you. I just know He will."

"No, He won't, and it's okay." Kelli inhaled, trying to keep it together. "God's just making clear what I already knew. I shouldn't have gotten my hopes up. I'm done with music."

Cedric touched her shoulder. "Kel, it's one rejection. Don't let that stop you from—"

"That's not what's stopping me."

They'd never understand—or leave her alone—unless she made it plain. She took a big breath, making eye contact with each of them.

"It's me. All me. Okay? I'm the one who messed up God's call on my life. Everything changed when I..." Her voice gave out on her. She looked down, mustered strength. "When I had the abortion."

The tears came halfway up the stairs, and they came like a flood. She hadn't realized how much she'd been clinging to the clouds, to the only dream, the only heartfelt passion she'd ever known, clinging to the faint hope that maybe God did have plans for her music, maybe He would give her a second chance.

It was a long fall from those clouds.

She collapsed on her bed, watching as Reese eased slowly into the room, as if aware something was wrong. She jumped onto the bed, nuzzling Kelli's chin. Kelli wrapped her arms around the dog and cried into her fur.

The stairs creaked under several sets of footsteps. All these years she'd kept her secret. What would her brothers say? What would Cyd and Stephanie think of her? She felt the bed sink as bodies joined her and Reese. Cedric sat closest, took her hand. For the longest time, the only sounds were Kelli's sniffles.

Cedric cleared his throat. "Kel, I'm so sorry. I had no idea you were dealing with this." He kept silent for several seconds. "You said everything changed. Was this in college? Grad school?"

"End of high school."

Lindell said it. *"Brian?"*

Kelli nodded into the fur.

"Dear God…" Lindell muttered. "You were so young. Was Mom there for you?"

"I never told her," Kelli mumbled.

"What about Brian?" Cedric asked.

"He wasn't there either," she said amid more tears. "He wasn't with me at the clinic, and he wasn't there for me afterward."

"He left you to deal with it alone?" There was anger in Cedric's voice.

"That's why I have nothing to say to him."

Cedric stood, letting out a heavy sigh, and walked a few feet away.

"Sweetie," Cyd said, "is that why he wanted to talk with you at the conference?"

Kelli nodded again. "He asked me to forgive him."

Cedric sat back down, shaking his head. "I was ready to pick up the phone and go off on him and then…" He paused, emotion building in his voice. "Then God pulled me up. Reminded me that I did the same thing to somebody else's sister."

Kelli lifted a little, looked into his eyes.

"Cyd knows I've repented of a lot of things, and that was one of them," he continued. "I was in my early twenties. And unlike Brian, I've never gone back and asked forgiveness. I've got big respect for that."

"Kelli," Stephanie said, "I'm finally understanding the rift between you and Brian, but I'm not getting the music part. Why did everything change with the music?"

Kelli wasn't sure how to explain it. "I used to write all the time. Melodies and lyrics would come to me in school, at the dentist's office, wherever, and I'd keep my pad with me to get it down."

That time was hard to imagine now. It had been so long since she and God flowed like that.

"After I got pregnant, one night I was freaking out, crying half the night, wondering what I would do. And a song came to me. It was so clear I got up, turned the light on, and wrote down the words. I knew God was speaking to me, letting me know I didn't have to be afraid. He would be there. He would help me. He would love me and the baby through it."

Stephanie gasped. "The wedding song? 'I Will Love You'?"

Kelli nodded. "I made up my mind. I had to keep the baby. And I couldn't wait to share it all with Brian the next day. But he'd made up his mind the night before too. Before I could say anything, he told me I could do what I wanted, but he was still leaving for college. He said not to expect him to be there. We argued. We broke up. And the peace I'd gotten the night before was gone."

Kelli started shaking with the remembrance. How could she have allowed fear to override her clear sense of what was right? It took her a few moments to gather herself, her mind lodged in that one space in time.

"I remember the song playing in my head the morning I woke up after...afterward." She always found it hard to say. "It was haunting me, accusing me. God had spoken to me through a song to keep my baby, and I didn't listen. He hasn't given me another song since. And obviously He's not going to use anything I've already written."

"Kelli, back up a minute," Cyd said. "You heard the song playing in your head the morning after the abortion? You thought it was haunting you, but it strikes me totally differently. Sounds like God was saying 'I will love you' even through *this*."

A chill danced up Kelli's arms. She'd never thought of it that way.

"The story about that song is deep," Cedric said. "I heard you playing it when I stopped by the house, but of course I didn't know what was behind it. I just knew it was beautiful."

"That was me drowning my sorrows at the piano the night we broke up. If I'd known you'd come in, I would've clammed up."

"If you ask me, I was meant to hear it," Cedric said. "Otherwise, I wouldn't have known to ask you to sing it at our wedding."

"Yeah, thanks a lot. That's what jump-started this whole music thing again, and look where it got me."

Stephanie looked miserable. "I'm the one who pushed you on the music, and I'm so sorry. I thought you just didn't believe in yourself. I should've left it alone."

"I can go you one better," Kelli said. "I should've stayed in Austin, where I wasn't thinking about music, didn't have to deal with the past, and definitely didn't have to deal with Brian."

"I don't know about all this woulda-coulda-shoulda stuff," Cyd said. "I think you're right where you need to be, and all this happened for a reason. Maybe it's time to deal with these things. Might bring healing."

"More like pain," Kelli said.

Cyd smiled sympathetically. "Pain is part of healing. Let God bring you through. You never know what's on the other side."

Kelli's brow wrinkled. Did she need *healing*? She'd always felt she'd moved on as best she could, functioned well, gotten her degrees. But then, until these last couple of weeks, she hadn't realized that the pain was still there, still intense, until it was resurrected. Was it even possible to get to the other side of it? Was it possible to fully heal?

Chapter Fourteen

Heather felt a rush of nerves Saturday as she got in her car to head to Cyd's. All day at work it was there, turning over in her mind—the three o'clock meeting in Cyd's home. What would it be like? How would Cyd receive her? She'd been nice enough on the phone when they set the date and time, but things were bound to be awkward. Heather had second-guessed the decision a million times.

She pulled out of the almost-empty parking garage on Francis Place in Clayton. The dental office where Heather worked was one of only a few in the area that took Saturday appointments—and it was mere minutes from Cyd. Heather dealt daily with clients who lived in the area, but she'd never actually visited anyone's home there. It only added to her angst. Cyd was above her, in another class. A college professor, for goodness' sake.

Heather had only gone to community college and barely finished that. In the space of six years she'd worked at two retail stores, a restaurant, a veterinarian's office, and, for the past eight months, a dental office. She liked it well enough thus far—much as she could like anything apart from singing—but didn't feel she was accomplishing much. And now that she'd set aside her singing dream, she wasn't certain she'd ever accomplish anything. Being with Cyd in her home was bound to make her feel extremely small.

Her cell phone rang at a red light. Her insides smiled when she saw the name. "Are you checking up on me?"

"Yes. Headed to your appointment?" Logan asked.

"Unless I change my mind within the next two miles, which I might."

"You won't. It'll be great."

"What makes you so sure?"

"Because I know Cyd, and I know you."

"Well. You don't know me *that* well. *I* don't know me that well." Heather made a right turn, smiling.

Logan laughed. "Okay, good one."

Ever since the "old Heather" comment, her running joke had been trying to figure out what the "new Heather" was like.

"I wonder if I like zucchini now," she'd said two days ago.

Logan assured her she would, told her to do a stir-fry of all the veggies she once hated and behold her changed taste buds.

"I'll tell you what I know about the new Heather," he said now. "She's hungry to know God. She's hungry to know the Bible. And she's hungry to know her new self."

Heather's eyes misted. Such words had never been used to characterize her. She saw the turn and flicked the left signal. "Almost here. Say a prayer for me?"

"Already done. Let me know how it goes."

Heather clicked off and pulled in front of Cyd's house, taking in her surroundings. Gorgeous homes and stately trees lined the street. She could hear lawn mowers, and a couple of kids whizzed by on their bikes on this lazy Saturday afternoon. Seemed so peaceful. Her apartment building was situated on a busy road.

Heather grabbed her purse, Bible, and notebook and walked to the door. She rang the doorbell, then waited.

The door opened, but it wasn't Cyd.

"Hi, Heather, I'm Kelli. Come on in."

"Thanks." Heather stepped inside, feeling self-conscious, wondering what Kelli knew about her. Probably the worst. Heather heard a bark and jumped as a little wavy-haired dog came gunning for her from around the corner.

"Reese, no. Come!" Kelli said. But the dog had already pounced, throwing her full weight at Heather, knocking her back a couple of feet.

"Whoa!" Heather said, laughing. "You're more solid than you look."

"I'm sorry. We usually gate her when company comes, and I forgot."

"It's fine." Heather rubbed the top of the dog's head. "Guess she's a nice ice breaker."

"Cyd thought she'd beat you here," Kelli said. "She had to run a quick errand. Can I get you something to drink?"

"Um, sure," Heather said. She followed Kelli to the kitchen. "Cedric's your brother, right?"

Kelli turned as she walked. "How did you know?"

"From Stephanie and Lindell's wedding." The second she said it, she wished she'd left it alone. That wedding was the day after she and Scott were caught, and she only went to the wedding out of desperation because he wouldn't take her calls.

Kelli got a glass from one of the cabinets. "I didn't realize you were there."

Heather heard something in the comment. Kelli definitely knew who she was.

Kelli opened the refrigerator. "Water? Cranberry juice? Coke?" She smiled. "We've got a few choices."

"Cranberry juice sounds really good, actually," Heather said. Her eyes traveled around the kitchen, which so looked like Cyd—understated and classy.

Kelli handed her the glass, and Heather sipped lightly, both of them standing in silence.

Maybe the new Heather could just speak from the heart.

"Kelli, I—"

"Heather, I—"

They laughed faintly together.

"You go first," Kelli said, "and we might as well sit while you're waiting."

Heather pulled out a chair at the kitchen table and sat. "Please, you go ahead. What were you about to say?"

Kelli joined her at the table. She clasped her hands in front of her and stared at them a moment. Finally she looked at Heather. "We don't know each other, but in a strange way I feel like we have something in common."

Heather's brow creased. "How so?"

Kelli paused again. "I know what happened with you and Scott and how you left the church and everything."

Heather stared into her glass.

"And though you want to put it behind you and move

on, I bet it's hard. Sometimes, I bet you think you're the worst sinner in the world."

Heather looked directly at Kelli. "I feel like I'll always carry a big scarlet A for adultery on my chest. But what would you know about that?"

"Because I feel like I'm the biggest sinner in the world." Her head bowed slightly. "Ugh… I did *not* want to cry again today."

Heather saw a box of tissues on the counter and brought it over. She pulled out a couple and gave them to Kelli.

"My big A is for abortion, and even though it was seven years ago, it's still hard…and especially fresh right now because I just told my family last night. And I know you're wondering why I'm bringing all of this up." Kelli dabbed her eyes. "I figured it couldn't be easy for you to come here, and I wanted you to know that you're not alone. You're not the only one who's done something you regret."

Now the tears started in Heather's eyes. She'd never felt such an instant connection with someone. "And it sounds like I'm not the only one who has to learn how to accept God's forgiveness."

"No. That's me too."

The back door opened and closed, and Cyd came quickly into the kitchen. "I'm so sorry I'm—" She walked further in. "What happened?"

Kelli looked at her. "God. I think."

Heather stood. "Hi, Cyd."

Cyd came near to her. "Hi, Heather. Welcome to our home." She hugged her. "I'm really glad you're here."

"Really? I guess…" She flicked a tear away. "I know it wasn't an easy decision."

"It wasn't as hard as you might think," Cyd said. "And once I got going with it, God gave me all kinds of ideas. That's why I'm late." She surveyed the two of them. "And by the looks of things, God was doing His thing, so I shouldn't have worried."

"What do you mean?" Kelli asked.

"I came in the door with a question to ask you two." She looked at Heather first. "You and I are supposed to be meeting. It came to me a little while ago that it might be beneficial to include Kelli too. But I won't do it if it makes you feel uncomfortable, Heather," she added quickly. "And, Kelli, I totally understand if you say thanks but no thanks. It's just an idea."

Heather and Kelli looked at one another.

"I'd really like that," Heather said. "Will you do it, Kelli?"

"I think I *need* to do it. Count me in."

Cyd clapped her hands. "Fantastic! Be right back." She dashed down the stairs to the back door and returned holding two flowery gift bags. "One for you"— she handed it to Heather—"and one for you."

"Should we look inside?" Heather asked.

"Absolutely."

Heather and Kelli tore into the bags like it was Christmas, tossing tissue paper onto the table.

"Oh, thank you, I've never had one of these," Heather said, lifting it out. "Is this a journal?"

"It is," Cyd said. "Given with no pressure. I've started a million of them and can never stick with it. Some people write daily. If you think you might want to write down your prayers or thoughts about what you're learning, you've got some pages to do it in."

"Pretty pages too," Kelli said. "Love this. Thank you!"

Heather showed hers to Kelli. "Did you see the pen tucked inside the spiral binding? Nice."

"Keep going," Cyd said. "There's one more thing in the bag."

The sound of swishing ensued again, and Heather and Kelli each pulled out a laminated bookmark.

"I was more excited about the bookmark than the journal," Cyd said. "When I saw it, I knew it was made for you two."

Heather held it between her fingers and read the words out loud:

- Done.
- Gone.
- Covered.
- Cleansed.
- Wiped.
- Washed.
- Renewed.
- Restored.
- FORGIVEN.

She turned to the back, which read,

As far as the east is from the west, so far has He removed our transgressions from us. ~Psalm 103:12

Heather stared at it, reading the verse again and again, then looked over at Kelli, who was apparently doing the same.

"I never thought about forgiveness this way," Heather said. "I knew God was forgiving, but I felt like He'd always be mindful of what I did, like I'd never really get away from it. This makes it seem like He forgets about it. How can God forget something?"

Cyd smiled. "It's amazing, isn't it? He chooses to forget it. He chooses to blot it away. That's how much He loves us."

Kelli was still focused on the words. "It's hard to believe God would cover what I did. Just wipe it away. It's not like I deserve that."

"That's why I was excited about the bookmarks—because it's exactly what I had already prepared for our first session. I want us to take a good look at God's love for us and what the Gospel really means for each of us. We don't have to pay the price for our sins. That's why Jesus died." Cyd gave them both a big hug. "I'm thrilled about what God is going to do in each of your hearts. Let's go into the family room and get comfortable. Don't forget to grab your Bibles."

Heather kept the bookmark in her hand as she walked, staring down at it.

The new Heather is completely forgiven.

Cyd cruised the parking area of the St. Louis Galleria, trying to catch someone pulling out. "This is hopeless. If you two didn't *really* want to go to the Cheesecake Factory, I would *so* be headed someplace else. Everybody and their momma is out here this evening."

After more than two hours of studying, talking, and praying, the three realized how famished they were. With Cedric at a client dinner, Cyd offered to treat the young women to the restaurant of their choosing.

"Back-to-school shopping probably," Heather said.

"Everybody was talking about it at the dentist's office today. Tax-free weekend."

"And look, that new Five Guys is open now," Kelli said.

Cyd sighed. "We'll never find a spot."

"Over there," Kelli said, aiming a finger. "Quick. That lady's coming out on the other side."

Cyd sped up and whipped around the corner, flicking her turn signal. "Parking spot conquered," she said, moving into the space. "Now for the famous two-hour wait."

"Oh, it won't be so bad." Kelli hopped out. "We called ahead."

Cyd smiled as she walked with them. She couldn't have asked for a better first meeting. Kelli and Heather had hit it off, and the three of them enjoyed rich, open discussion. Most surprising, Cyd found herself genuinely liking Heather. Unlike the woman who'd been caught in bed with Scott—gum-popping, unapologetic—this one had clearly been broken. She had a real humility now and an eagerness to grow in Christ.

They approached the hostess stand and gave their name, and the woman passed them a handheld buzzer. "About an hour," she said.

Cyd regarded her companions. "An hour, *with* call-ahead seating."

Heather smiled big. "Better than two hours."

They left the restaurant and entered the mall, idling by the seating area with others.

"Hey, Heather," Kelli said suddenly, "we should go to f.y.e."

"Totally."

"The music store?" Cyd asked.

Kelli nodded. "We found out we have that in common too—a love for music."

Cyd took the stroll with them, but after a few yards she spied a train wreck coming around the corner, headed straight for them—Dana, Scott, and the kids, armed with shopping bags.

Scott did his best to avoid looking at Heather, distracting himself with the kids, but Dana mowed her down with a stare.

Cyd's stomach cramped. "You guys must be taking advantage of the tax break." She could hear how phony she sounded. Like she was talking to neighbors she barely knew.

"Aunt Cyd, you should see what I got from Justice," Mackenzie said, reaching into her bag. "Look at this silver sparkly fashion scarf—" She seemed to just notice the others then. "Oh, sorry… Hi, Kelli…and…"

"And nobody," Dana said. "Scott, we have to go."

"Wait a minute, Dana," Cyd said.

Kelli whispered to Heather, and they continued on.

"Kids, let's check out the new stuff in the Apple store," Scott said. "Dana, meet us over there."

Dana didn't comment. The pointed stare was now directed at Cyd.

"I can't believe you said that, Dana, and in front of Mackenzie. That was uncalled for."

"Great. Now you *and* Scott can take up for poor Heather. Fun night out for the girls?"

Cyd sighed, trying to find the right words. "I really don't want this to be a source of tension between us. You're my best friend, and I love you. But does that mean I have to hate Heather?"

"You're hanging with her in the mall."

"We just came to get something to eat after our Bible study."

"Don't you think that's going beyond the call of duty? I can't even tell you how this makes me feel."

"Dana, I know how you feel. I do. But she's not the person she once was." Their earlier lesson came to mind. "There comes a time when you just have to... you just have to forgive."

Dana's face said the suggestion was ludicrous. "I've got to go, Cyd. I'll talk to you later."

Cyd let out a breath as she went to catch up with Kelli and Heather. Why did God put her in the middle? Why did they have to run into Dana and Scott? Would she lose a friendship of almost thirty years because of this?

Lord, please, somehow...touch Dana's heart. Give her eyes to see Heather as You see her. As hard as it might be, help her to forgive Heather, for her own peace of mind.

Kelli came to Cyd the moment she entered the music store. "Heather has barely said two words. I know she brought all this on herself, but I can't help but feel bad for her." She looked over at Heather, who was standing by a selection of oldies, her head down. "Don't you think Dana was kind of mean?"

"Kelli, I will never forget the pain and devastation Dana felt when she discovered Heather in her bed. If I were in Dana's shoes, I probably would've done the same—or worse—if I ran into Heather." Cyd glanced over at her again. "The funny thing about forgiveness is that God is much freer with it than humans are."

She looked at Kelli. "Think about it. You feel bad

for Heather, and you think Dana should've treated her differently. But how have you treated Brian? Have you forgiven him?"

Chapter Fifteen

Kelli thought about Cyd's question all through dinner and on the way back to the house. Not that she didn't know the answer—but for the first time, the answer was starting to bother her…especially after an afternoon with Heather marveling at how freely God had forgiven *them*. It was basic, but it hit her between the eyes nonetheless—Brian deserved forgiveness too.

They parked and waved good-bye to Heather as she got in her car and took off. On the way inside, Kelli's phone rang. A wireless number she didn't recognize.

"Hello?" she said.

"Hi, Kel."

Her breath caught. Why, after all these years, did he still have an effect on her? "How did you get my number?"

"I'm not supposed to tell."

"Stephanie."

"When she returned my laptop Monday, she asked if there was any way she could repay me. Don't be too mad at her."

"I'm not mad at her. But I'm wondering why you decided to call, since I told you not to speak if you see me."

"You gonna hang up on me?"

Kelli watched the branches sway in the gentle evening breeze. She hated how well Brian knew her. If she was planning to hang up, she would've done it already. She sighed into the phone. "Just tell me why you called, Brian."

"I'm sorry things didn't work out with Monica."

"Stephanie told you?"

"No." Brian paused. "Monica and I are good friends. She told me."

"Well. Thank you anyway for letting me use the laptop." Her tone didn't exactly sound thankful.

"I was glad to do it."

"So that's why you called?"

"Actually, no. I need to talk to you about something. Would you be willing to come to the studio? I can pick you up."

"Brian, seriously...first a phone call, and now you think I would go somewhere with you? Why are you acting like we're cool?"

"I know we're not cool, Kelli. I know you hate me. I wouldn't ask if it weren't important. It has to do with my album."

I know you hate me.

Kelli remembered her thoughts just before her phone rang. The forgiveness thing. Only, she didn't feel like forgiving him. Having an attitude with Brian had become second nature.

Darkness was settling in. She looked at her watch. Almost eight thirty. "Where's the studio?"

"In my house."

"Your house?"

"I set it up in the basement. I promise I won't keep you long."

"Why can't you just tell me what it's about?"

"I need to tell you in person. It's something that's been on my heart for the last four days, and I can't shake it."

Kelli was frustrated with herself for even considering it. *His album isn't your concern. Tell him no and be done with it.*

If he had called any other day, that would've been easy. But after that Bible study...plus, she had to admit she was curious. Whatever the reason, something in her wouldn't let her dismiss this. "I can't stay long," she said finally, "and I can drive myself."

"That's fine, but I'm right around the corner at Home Depot picking up mulch and other yard stuff for Grandma. I could scoop you up and bring you back, no problem."

Ugh. "Fine, Brian."

"Thanks, Kel. Be there in fifteen."

A million memories flooded Kelli's mind as she opened Brian's car door and got in. How many times had he rolled by her house to pick her up? She remembered the day his great-uncle gave him a car, a hand-me-down with more than 150,000 miles and a good amount of rust, but Brian was thrilled. He drove straight to Kelli's, and they celebrated with a trip to the Science Center, chatting nonstop as always.

Now he drove an SUV, and instead of easy conversation, she wasn't sure what her first words would be.

He backed out of the driveway, glancing at her. "Hey."

"Hey." Her eyes dusted him, then moved out the window.

He drove slowly down the street, peering at the houses. "Remember we used to wonder who actually lived over here?"

Kelli took a good look around herself, remembering what it was like to ride the school bus through the neighborhood. "We thought they must be millionaires."

"With no problems."

"Yeah," Kelli said. "I'll have to ask Cedric and Cyd if that's true."

Brian turned onto Clayton Road. "So how do you like being back in the Lou?"

Kelli shrugged, her honest answer. "I'm sure it'll start looking up when I find a job."

"Doing what? What's your field?"

Weird. They didn't know even basic information about each other anymore.

"Public relations and communications. Best-case scenario, I'll be able to work on behalf of organizations whose mission and message I can get excited about promoting."

"Sounds perfect. You'll be really good at that."

She nursed her own question, not wanting to show interest in his life, but she couldn't resist. "Never would've guessed you'd be rapping. How did it happen?"

"Long story." Brian's expression changed as he reflected. "What I did to you...to us...to the baby"—he blew out a sigh—"it haunted me for weeks when I went away to college. I had nightmares where I would call you and say, 'Kelli, stop, I changed my mind. Don't do it!' Then I would see this empty cot in a clinic and no one in sight. Shook me so bad one night I got out of bed and on my knees. I said, 'God, I can't live with this. And yet I can't make it right. I can't bring that little life back.'"

His emotions filled even now, and Kelli watched as he took a few moments, staring at the highway.

"'But I can give You *my* life.' That's what I said. Just told God to take my life and do whatever He wanted with it." He gestured with his free hand. "Fast-forward to sophomore year. I was going to this campus Bible study, and a couple of the guys who led it were big into Christian rap, even had a ministry at the local jail where they would share the Gospel in rap form." He glanced at Kelli. "You might know them. They're pretty big now—TruLife and AFG."

Kelli gave a blank stare. "AFG?"

"All for God."

"Never heard of them."

"Really? Those are my boys." He took the familiar exit that led to his house. "They took me under their wings and mentored me. Meanwhile, God started giving me rhymes, out of the blue it seemed. When I shared them, the guys encouraged me. The next year, they gave me a feature on their albums and let me tour with them a little over the summer. One thing led to another, and I got my own deal."

"That's incredible, Brian. Looks like you're pretty big yourself." She might as well admit it. "I looked you up on Facebook, and you've got almost forty thousand fans."

"It's crazy, isn't it?" He paused. "I thought I'd spend

my life working alone in a lab...which still might be the case. I'm confused about what God wants me to do. Haven't made any headway on this new album."

"I heard they prayed for you on Sunday."

He nodded. "Your family's awesome. God might be finally answering. That's why I needed to talk to you."

How could she possibly help? Did he want her to come up with some rhymes?

When he drove down his street—always busy with folk sitting in front of their homes or on the corner, though *usually* peaceful—it struck Kelli that she'd never had a chance to talk to him about his mother.

"Brian, I didn't come back when your mother died this spring. My mother told me, but to be honest, I let all the stuff between us get in the way of paying my respects to her. I'm sorry."

He pulled up in front of his house. "I didn't expect you to come, Kel."

"What happened to the drunk driver?"

"He was her boyfriend. They arrested him, but who knows if he'll actually do time." He gazed downward. "At least she died instantly."

"That had to be hard." She'd thought that a lot when they were younger, that Brian's life was hard, with his mother on and off drugs, in and out of work. Kelli's home had always been stable. Even after her father died from prostate cancer when she was young, her mother worked to maintain a strong sense of family, which Brian glommed on to. He was always welcome in their home and often said if it wasn't for his grandmother and Kelli's family, he didn't know what he would do.

He looked briefly at Kelli, then back to the steering

wheel. "You know how much I went through with her. But she was still my mom, you know?"

Kelli's head filled with memories as she walked into Brian's childhood home. The sofa and chairs in the living room, the paintings on the wall. The green magic marker stain on the carpet that Brian affixed on purpose. She warned him it wouldn't come out with his homemade mix of chemicals, but he did it anyway and got into big trouble.

Her eyes drifted to the stairs. She could picture the two of them walking up to his bedroom while his grandmother was at work, carried away by the moment…

"Lord, have mercy… I know that's not Kelli London."

Kelli looked toward the kitchen where Brian's grandmother was standing in the doorway, a hand to her hip, looking spry in jogging pants. A huge heart smile came onto Kelli's face.

"Grandma Howard, it's so good to see you!" She went to hug her.

Grandma Howard stepped back, hands to Kelli's shoulders, and looked upward. "Thank You, Jesus."

Kelli looked over at Brian, then back to Grandma Howard with curious eyes.

"Ever since this boy graduated college and came back home, I been wondering about him. He so busy it's hard to see, but I know my Brian. He ain't the same as when the two of you were running around here."

Brian gave her a look. "Grandma, what are you talking about? I'm not supposed to be the same. I was a teenager back then."

She addressed Kelli rather than Brian. "I'm tellin' you, something's missing. The boy is lonely."

"Grandma!"

She ignored him. "When he told me you moved back, I said, 'Lord, that's exactly right. Please get these two young people together. I know they was meant for each other.' And here you are."

Brian shook his head. "Grandma, we're not back together. Kelli's here for *one* visit because I need to talk to her about an idea for the album."

Grandma Howard addressed him directly now. "I thought you would've seen by now that school is where your focus needs to be. There's a reason nothing's been coming to you for this album."

Brian sighed, and Kelli could hear in it a thousand conversations he and his grandmother had had.

"You might be right," Brian said. "But you always said keep seeking Him until you know for sure."

Grandma Howard eyed him. "Can't argue with that." She moved toward the stairs. "Kelli, go on in there and get you some of that chicken. Don't act like you ain't at home. This is still your home."

Kelli smiled. "I already ate, Grandma Howard, but thank you."

Brian opened the door to the lower level, and they descended the stairs.

Kelli shivered, rubbing her arms. "It was always cold down here."

"Why did I know you'd say that?" He turned to look at her. "I'll turn on the space heater down here—in the middle of summer—just for you."

She made a face. "Thanks."

When she got near the bottom step, she could see

the transformation. The living space, once filled with an old sofa and floor television with a pool table off to the side, now had a long wooden desk against a wall, with two big computer monitors on top and racks underneath with tons of equipment. "This looks serious. You can actually make music down here?"

Brian nodded. "I've got everything I need." He plopped down in a swivel seat in front of the equipment.

Kelli was still looking around. "What's that behind the mic stand?"

"Reflection filter. Helps with the sound."

She was intrigued, wanting to ask about everything she saw, like the diamond-shaped foam on the walls, but she caught herself. She came for a limited purpose.

"So tell me why I'm here." She took the other chair at the desk.

Brian swiveled toward her, his forearms on his thighs. "I heard the song you recorded on my laptop."

Kelli felt sick. How could she have been so absent-minded? She'd meant to delete it from his hard drive once she'd sent it to Monica and burned it onto a disk for herself.

"Something about it grabbed me and wouldn't let go. I played it over and over and over. Kelli, it's beautiful."

She whispered, "Thanks," her arms trembling slightly.

"The next day the chorus was still going in my head," he said, "but with a slightly different arrangement, over another beat."

Kelli frowned slightly, wondering what that would sound like. "Okay…"

"I had to test it. I sent the song to one of my favorite producers, told him what I was thinking, and asked him to remake it. Got it back, and it blew me away."

"I'm not getting where you're going with this."

Brian scooted a little closer. "For the first time, I'm truly feeling a song for this album. I don't know why, but I'm connected to it. The love theme is powerful. When I found out Monica wasn't using it, I felt bad for you, but I also wondered if it might be a God thing."

"You want to use *my* song for your album?"

"A remake of it, yeah. I'd come up with my own verses, maybe ask Monica to sing the chorus."

"No." She got up, her heart beating fast. "You can't use it."

His face fell. "Why not?"

She walked across the room. "I don't have to give you a reason, Brian. I just don't want you to."

"But you were going to let Monica use it, weren't you?" He sighed. "I get it. I'm not Monica. I was so drawn to the song—not to mention the fact I was finally inspired—that it didn't occur to me, 'Hey, you're the guy who broke her heart. Why should she do anything for you?'"

"It's not that. At least, not the main part." Kelli felt an inner urge to tell him the real reason, but how could she?

"You won't tell me what the main part is?"

She closed her eyes tight, to keep the dam plugged. "I just can't."

"Is it because it's something personal?"

She found that funny, in a desperate sort of way. "Oh, it's personal all right."

Why couldn't she stop trembling?

She blew out a breath. Fine, why not tell him? She'd

tried all those years ago, and he wouldn't listen. Would probably hurt him to hear it now...and in a way, it would serve him right. "That's the song..." Tears spilled onto her cheeks.

Brian got up, came to her side. "What is it?"

She couldn't look at him. "The last song I wrote, the night before...before you broke up with me. God gave me that song for our baby."

Brian stood stock-still, afraid to grasp the meaning of what Kelli had just said. "God gave you a song... for our baby?" He barely made sense of the words, yet they were piercing his soul. "Why didn't you tell me?"

"I *tried*. That's why I came to see you."

Kelli was shaking, and Brian wanted to hold her but he knew she wouldn't let him. He brushed her tears instead.

"You didn't want to hear it," she said. "Remember? 'I know you're here to try to talk me into keeping this baby'"—her tone mocked him—"'but I've made up my mind. You can do what you want, but you'll be doing it alone.'"

He remembered all right. Upstairs in the foyer. Wouldn't even let her further into the house. Just wanted to say it and get it over with.

"Oh, my God," he whispered to himself. He walked to the computer and pushed a couple of buttons. The original song Kelli recorded played through the speakers. He wanted to hear it anew, hear it in light of this revelation...and the weight of it crushed him.

I will love you...

And I will love you...

He fell to his knees beside a speaker and wept. Hearing Kelli's voice on the song, seeing her face when she came to talk to him that day, with his baby...

I will love you...

His face buried, he bawled as he replayed the day in his head. Would the song have made a difference, if he had known? He didn't know that boy in the foyer anymore, couldn't understand his mind-set. Maybe he still would have walked away. But this song let him know as never before that God was in the midst of their situation, and Brian hadn't cared to look to Him.

He flinched when he felt a hand on his shoulder, then grabbed it and held tight. Kelli came to her knees beside him, and they stayed that way, hands locked, silently weeping.

God, I feel like I'm being punished. I thought You had forgiven me. I thought You had helped me move on. Why are You dropping this on me right now?

The original song faded, and in the quiet he heard the remake in his head. And he knew. Just like that, he knew.

"Kelli." He felt a surge of adrenaline as he sat down on the carpet, wiping tears with the palm of his hand. "I know why I felt so connected to the song. It's about more than the album. This will be a dedication to our baby, a love letter."

Kelli stared at him, her eyes glistening with surprise, then she looked downward as she sat beside him. "Cyd said I still needed to heal, and I did an online search on post-abortion recovery. It said for some people it helps to release their child into God's care, to acknowledge that the baby is with Him. They might say a prayer or hold a memorial service, name the child, maybe write a poem." She looked at Brian. "Dedicating a song? A love letter?" Her voice broke. "That's…that's beautiful."

He nodded. "There's something else, Kel. You have to sing the chorus. You and me on the same song, for our child."

She shook her head. "I don't think I could do it. It'd be too emotional."

"And I think we should do it tonight."

Her eyes got wide. "What?"

"It would be powerful to do it while we're in this very moment."

"But you haven't even written the verses."

"I can't explain it, Kel. I just feel it. I know the lyrics will come."

"Well, that's good for you, but what about me? I'd have to tweak the chorus and arrange background vocals. How could I do that so quickly?"

He paused, not wanting to overstep. "Would you mind if we…if we prayed together about all this?"

Chapter Sixteen

Kelli fought to stay awake. Pastor Lyles's sermon had her interest, but she hadn't hit the bed until three in the morning, and even then she couldn't sleep. She'd planned to attend the eleven thirty service, but once again Reese had been her alarm, barking frantically at eight o'clock in a doggie duel with the Border collie that lived behind them. Once awake, there was no going back. The song took over, looping in her mind, filling her with a rush of wonder. Had she and Brian really made a recording for their baby? It didn't seem real, even though she had a CD to prove it.

Sleep deprivation hit a third of the way into the sermon, without much to counteract it...except passing notes. Kelli peeked down at the phone inside her purse, stomach buckling to hide her laughter. She'd just texted that to Heather—and Heather texted back.

if teacher comes for note, delete my name. heather = double detention.

It was funny and sad at the same time. Kelli looked up, trying to track with the sermon, but when Pastor Lyles mentioned that nothing could separate us from God's love, not even our sins, it made her think of Heather again. She poised her fingers inside her purse.

good stuff about god's love in sermon. wish you were here.

Stephanie bumped her with a shoulder, her eye on Kelli's handbag.

Kelli bumped back. "What?"

She glanced down the pew at Dana and Scott. What would they think if they knew she was texting Heather right now? She almost felt bad for being happy about their friendship, but she couldn't help it. Heather was one of the first people she wanted to tell about last night. She knew Heather would totally get how difficult it was emotionally—the song, as well as working with Brian—yet amazing in its totality.

A new text flashed across her screen. :-(would love to hear. need to find a church. pray for me.

Kelli made a sad face as well as she stared at the message, and Stephanie bumped her again to show her that people were getting to their feet. How did she miss the wrap-up of the sermon? She'd have to make sure she got the CD—*Duh!* She could get Heather one too.

They sang along with the praise and worship team, Logan leading. Heather hadn't said a word about him, but Kelli knew he'd somehow been there for Heather in Indianapolis. She gave God a curious glance upward, thinking it kind of funny. She and Cyd weren't the only unlikely ones to befriend Heather. The most sought-after bachelor in the church had done so as well.

The closing prayer barely uttered, Stephanie started chattering. "Okay, so what's the deal? We're heading to Cyd and Cedric's to hear the song?"

Kelli was moving out of the pew. "Yes. I want to tell you all about it at the same time and then let you listen."

Stephanie gave a half glance behind her. "Are you inviting all of Daughters' Fellowship? Dana and Phyllis have been praying about your music too."

"I know," Kelli said, moving into the aisle. "I thought about that. But to be honest, I'm just not ready to tell anyone outside the family yet about…about my past." She leaned in further. "I did invite Heather to listen. She's the only one other than you all who knows."

Stephanie's eyebrows rose. "Definitely can't have Dana and Heather at the same gathering, now can we? Woo-boy… Shoot, Dana and *Cyd* together is starting to be a trip. Never thought I'd see the day."

"Yeah, I noticed they sat on opposite ends of the pew. They normally sit near one another, don't they?"

"Girl, side by side most times, since junior high."

"What are y'all whispering about?" Lindell asked.

Stephanie smiled at him. "Nothing."

Cyd and Cedric had been talking with another couple, but they walked over just as Dana, Scott, and Phyllis joined the circle. The guys branched off to the side, leaving the women to gab.

"Are we sneaking off to the pancake house again?" Phyllis asked. "I've got a taste for some."

Kelli's stomach tightened.

"I can't," Dana said. "Scott and I said we'd help out

in children's ministry after first service. With summer and families going on vacation, they've got a shortage."

"I might as well see how I can help out too," Phyllis said. "I guess my stomach can hold off till I get home."

"Let's plan a DF dinner for one night this week," Cyd said. "I can call everyone and arrange it."

"Sounds fabulous," Phyllis said.

Stephanie nodded. "Works for me."

Kelli smiled. "You know it works for me. What else do I have to do?"

"It's a busy week for us," Dana said. "Different things going on with the kids. I'll have to see."

Cyd looked at her. "I'll call you, Dana. We'll work around your schedule."

Dana half-nodded, then nudged Phyllis. "We'd better get out of here."

Kelli stared after them, and it struck her that she would've been one of them, a mommy in the fellowship. She would be heading over to children's ministry to help—probably with the first graders, which was what her child would be right now.

Cedric put his arm around Cyd. "Everybody ready? I can't wait to hear this song."

"Isn't that Brian over there, headed out to the lobby?" Stephanie asked.

Kelli looked across the sanctuary. "It is. Surprised he made it to first service."

Stephanie upbraided Kelli with a look. "Well, why is he all by his lonesome? You need to invite him to come sit with us."

"Why? We recorded a song. We're not best buds."

"You should at least invite him to our listening party," Cedric said. "Wasn't the song his idea?"

Kelli walked a little slower as she considered it. It wasn't that she was opposed to Brian taking part. It *was* his idea. And she did forgive him, though she hadn't exactly told him. As she thought about it, she realized it might even help to have him there when her family heard the song, since it made her so emotional. And he could better explain his plans for the album.

But she'd have to make sure they kept their distance. She didn't want him thinking they were inching back into one another's lives, not even as friends. She could never turn back down that road. She couldn't do that to her heart.

Brian sat in the overstuffed chair in Cyd and Cedric's living room, overwhelmed by the response to the song he and Kelli had recorded. The women were wiping tears, and Cedric and Lindell were at the least misty-eyed. Brian had played it so much that he could half manage his emotions while listening, but he doubted he'd ever hear it without a deep tugging at his heart.

Cyd clutched a tissue. "God certainly brought beauty from ashes. That song is incredible."

"As much as I loved your version, Kelli," Stephanie said, "this is a whole 'nother level. The two of you on the song together, for your baby… I don't even know what to say." She shook her head. "Well, actually, I do. Thank you, Monica and team, for passing on the song."

"And, Kelli, your voice." Heather sat cross-legged on the floor beside Kelli, Reese resting between them. "Why do you minimize your vocal talent? Girl, you're the bomb."

Kelli gave a faint smile. "Thanks, Heather."

Brian nodded. "I've told her that a thousand times."

Cedric looked at Brian. "Gotta be honest, man. I was ready to go off on you when I heard what happened with Kelli. But the apology and now the song?" His eyes were filled with emotion. "Will this be on your upcoming album?"

"Oh, definitely," Brian said. "It's the first love letter."

Kelli looked at him. "The *first* love letter?"

Brian had planned to talk to Kelli about it in private, but maybe it was just as well discussing it here in the open. He might need her family's help.

"It came to me this morning," he said. "I went back down to the studio and listened to the song ten times at least, and finally I could see it—a vision for the entire album." He paused. "God is finally answering prayers in a big way."

"Well? What's the vision?" Kelli asked.

Brian smiled at her, and Kelli lowered her eyes. He knew she was still on guard. He cleared his throat. "Love letters, that's the concept. I haven't thought out each one, but there's the love letter to the baby, and there will be a love letter to the world—you know, like 'God sent His son to die for you because of His love for you.' And I'm thinking several love letters to the body of Christ. Could be a love letter to the persecuted, love letter to new believers—"

"You could do a love letter to fellow aliens."

Brian looked to see if Kelli was joking.

"No, really," Kelli said. "The song would tell them it's okay to be different, set apart."

Brian was smiling again. "You're hired."

"As what?"

"My co-collaborator."

"Uh…no."

"I'm serious, Kelli," Brian said. "I was already planning to ask you. I'd like you to collaborate with me on the writing of these love letters. And I'd like you to sing the choruses as well."

"This is just too much." Stephanie got up and paced the floor. "I knew it, I knew it, I knew it. I *knew* God was going to use your music, Kelli." She stopped to look at Kelli. "I kept saying all things were possible, but I did kinda stop believing after Monica's rejection. This is so awesome."

Kelli raised her hand partway. "Before you get too excited… I'm not working on any more songs for the album. Not interested in any co-collaboration."

Brian's countenance fell.

Stephanie put a hand to her hip, staring at her. "Excuse me, Miss Thing, but did you acknowledge God while I wasn't looking? Or are you leaning again?"

Kelli pursed her lips.

"Good point, Steph," Cedric said. "We shouldn't assume either way. Pray about it, Kel." He turned to Brian. "How soon do you need to start working on the other songs?"

"Like, last month," Brian said, "and I wish I were joking. For months, I couldn't come up with anything that was worth anything. I couldn't understand why God wasn't giving me what I needed."

Heather spoke quietly. "He was waiting for Kelli to come back."

Everyone in the room seemed to ponder that.

"That's what I'm starting to see," Brian said. "Anyway, I got a couple of extensions. So now I'm supposed to turn in the album three weeks from now, at the end

of August. Release date is end of October." He cringed
at the tight time frame.

"Come on, circle up." Stephanie waved everyone
forward like little chicks. "We have to put some more
prayer on this album"—she eyed Kelli as she extended
her arms—"now that we know what God is up to."

Kelli linked hands with Stephanie. "*Think* you
know."

"Hmph."

Brian wanted to take Kelli's free hand, but he positioned himself between Cedric and Lindell instead,
lowering his head.

"Father God," Lindell started, "we thank and praise
You for what You've done since last Sunday, when we
prayed that You would give Brian direction. We're
praying now, Lord, that You bless the continued work
on the album, and specifically, that it would be clear
who is to work on it."

Reese wove between legs, trying to find a suitable
spot in the circle.

"And, Lord, just to break it down further," Stephanie said, "if You want Kelli to collaborate on the writing and also sing on this album, I pray You would give
her neither rest nor peace until she agrees."

Brian peeked to see Kelli's response. Her head was
up, eyes narrowed on her sister-in-law.

Cyd cleared her throat. "Lord, we thank You for
Brian's heart. He didn't want to throw any ol' thing together on the album and call it a day. He wanted to hear
from You. And we pray believing that this album will
be inspired by You and that it will glorify You. We pray
it goes far and wide and blesses everyone who listens."

"Father, I've known this young man since he was

a boy," Cedric said, "and I'm in awe of what You've done in his life. Keep him humble and connected to You. And I'm praying for my sister—"

Kelli's head popped up again.

"—that You would help her to put the former things behind her and look for the new thing You might be doing."

Brian stared at the floor, eyes wide.

"Jesus, thank You that Kelli's willing to be my friend," Heather said. "And thank You for her talent. Could You love on her and do big things through her?"

Brian watched Kelli slip an arm around Heather and hug her. The room grew silent. Should he pray? Certainly, music wasn't the only big thing looming in his world. When the quiet continued, he decided to throw in another request.

"Lord," he said, "even if the album comes together like I'm seeing it, I've still got a huge issue. What do I do about school? Fall semester starts before I know it, and I need to give them an answer. Please show me Your plan. Show me what to do."

Murmurs of agreement rose from the circle, then it grew quiet again. After several seconds, Brian wondered who would wrap it up.

Suddenly he heard sniffles and looked in Kelli's direction. Her head sagged, and she seemed to be crying. His brow knit. Wasn't she fine a minute ago?

Everyone looked at everyone else and waited.

Kelli let go the hands she'd been holding and covered her face, then walked across the room and got a handful of tissues. She blew her nose, turning toward them.

"When the circle got quiet," she said, "I heard a melody and lyrics." She paused, wiping a tear from her face. "That hasn't happened in seven years. I thought God would never give me another song, but it was so clear, like it used to be." She paused again. "And the words were for a love letter to the suffering."

Brian looked at her, hope moving to the edge of his heart.

"I've got all kinds of hesitations, Brian," she said, looking back at him. "I need to find a job, and I've got to be honest—I don't really want to work with you. But I guess I can't ignore what God just gave me." She looked downward, thinking to herself, and let loose a sigh. "I'll do it. I'll collaborate with you. But if at any point it's not working out, I'm sorry, but I'll have to stop."

Brian took a couple steps toward her. "I understand, Kel. It can't be easy to… Well, just, thank you."

Kelli nodded, and it struck Brian that he didn't know what to feel. He should be happy she agreed, happy he could pursue the direction he was finally getting. But Kelli had said in front of everybody she didn't want to work with him. What if she bailed after the first session? What if they found they simply couldn't get along?

He pushed back on the hope skirting his heart. For now, it was nothing but tentative.

Chapter Seventeen

Heather embraced Kelli, congratulating her on the breakthrough. Kelli didn't exactly seem thrilled, but how awesome it was that Kelli was hearing new music in her head after seven years. Given Kelli's long wait, Heather realized it might be a long time before she knew what God would do with her own singing career, if anything. But she was okay with that. At least, she wanted to be. She was praying to be. Right now, crazy as it sounded even to herself, she just wanted Jesus to be enough.

As others surrounded Kelli, Heather heard her ringtone and stepped away to grab her purse from the floor. Missed call from Logan. Her brow creased. She hadn't expected to hear from him today. She'd assumed now that he'd sort of handed her off to Cyd, his Christian duty done. She dialed him back, leaving the family room so she could hear.

"Heather, are you home?" he asked.

"No, I'm at Cyd's house."

"Two days in a row, huh?"

"They've been really good to me, but what's up?"

"Guy on the worship team can't make the Cards game. He gave me his tickets, but it starts in less than an hour. Wondered if you'd like to go."

"Is that baseball?"

There was a pause.

"Seriously?"

"What? There's a Cardinals football team in St. Louis too."

"... that left in 1987. Didn't you grow up here?"

Heather laughed. "I never paid much attention to sports."

"You think?"

"Okay, smarty...you can see I wouldn't exactly be the best sports companion. You might want to ask some others and use me as a last resort."

"Already did. You kinda *are* the last resort."

"Gee, thanks."

"Just sayin'."

Heather thought a moment. "Well. This wouldn't be a date, would it?"

Logan paused. "Can't say I'd thought of it that way, so no. Been awhile since I considered myself on a 'date.'"

Same was true for Heather. Guys were interested in hooking up with her, not dating. "Okay, then. Long as you don't mind telling me what's going on. I should have it down by the ninth quarter."

"Ha-ha. Makes more sense to pick you up from Cyd's and shoot downtown, if you don't mind leaving your car."

"Sounds great. See you."

* * *

Twenty minutes later, the doorbell rang as Brian was saying good-byes in the foyer.

"Wonder who that is," Cyd said.

"Probably Logan," Heather said. "We're going to a baseball game."

"You're headed to Busch Stadium?" Lindell asked. "They're playing the Reds today. Sweet!"

Brian was closest to the door, so he opened it. "Hey, man," he said. "Saw you at the conference. Love the praise and worship at church, but we haven't formally met. I'm Brian."

Logan stepped inside, shaking his hand. "I'm a fan. Love what you do. We should get together soon."

"Thanks. Definitely."

While Logan exchanged greetings with Cedric and Lindell, Heather said her good-byes to the women.

"Hope you don't mind if I leave my car outside your house a few hours," she told Cyd.

"'Course not," Cyd said. "Have a good time."

Stephanie glanced between Heather and Logan. "Hmm."

Cyd pushed her. "Mind your business."

Heather smiled. "I know what you're thinking—but it's not like that. For some reason, God's just giving me real friends. I've never had that."

Stephanie came closer. "If God's giving you real friends like him, girl, you know you're blessed." She peered over at him. "Our family has known Logan for years. He's a really good guy."

"I'm so glad you came over," Kelli said, hugging Heather.

"I would've been mad if I missed it. Now I can say

I was one of the first to hear the hit song 'I Will Love You.'"

"Whatever."

"Seriously. And I'm expecting big things from the rest of the songs you two will write."

"Yeah, well, I'm not sure yet about any of it," Kelli said. "But if it does work out, would you consider doing background vocals? Cyd said you've sung some beautiful solos at church."

The question took Heather off guard. "That would be a dream come true. But much as I'd love to say yes, I'm still feeling like music is a no-go for me right now."

"Heather, we'd better leave," Logan said, turning from his conversation with the guys.

They said good-byes and scurried out. Logan opened the passenger door, and Heather got in, then watched him walk to the driver's side. When they were on their way, she said, "Hey, I just learned something else about the new Heather."

He glanced at her. "What's that?"

"I used to get this skitter thing whenever I saw you. You know, because you're so cute."

He tossed his eyes in embarrassment. "Wait. *Used to?*"

"Yep. Skitter's gone. Just noticed it. Guess I really am starting to see you as a big brother."

"Cool. Never had a little sister. Maybe God thinks I need one." He paused, rubbing his chin. "That was off the cuff, but there's probably truth in it. I don't have any women in my life who I really talk to. Maybe because women tend to make it known that they're interested in me romantically. I only share that to say I think I've put a wall up—or maybe God put it up. Until I'm ready for a serious relationship, I don't see the point in letting anyone get close."

Heather stared at him, appreciating his honesty.

"So, seems like God is up to something here," Logan said. "Who knows? Maybe He wants to show you it's possible to have a man in your life who doesn't have an agenda. And maybe He's taking my wall down a bit. I spend a lot of my time ministering to people, but funny thing is, I don't have to share a whole lot of myself. Maybe I've gotten too comfortable with that."

"I noticed that in the choir," Heather said. "You were always there, always available, but it was also clear you kept your distance."

Logan grinned and waggled his eyebrows. "Yeah, betcha didn't know that beneath the praise-and-worship leader exterior was a big kid who could spend hours at the go-kart track or Six Flags."

"*Now* we're talking," Heather said. "No offense to the love-of-sports thing, but I'd do go-kart racing in a minute and I could ride the Screaming Eagle all day."

"Is that your favorite too?" He looked at her. "Every year they've got some newer, fancier roller coaster, but give me the Screaming Eagle over all of them."

"Well." She looked at her watch. "Don't know if you realize it but it's August. Park's only open a little while longer. And I don't know about you, but I haven't been this year."

"I haven't been in *two* years. So pack a lunch because when we go, we're staying all day."

Heather laughed. "Any chance we can ditch the ballpark right now for the amusement park?"

"Not on your life."

* * *

"Woo-hoo!"

Heather high-fived Logan, and they came to their feet with the rest of the crowd, pumping fists and cheering wildly as the ball sailed clean over the wall.

"Grand slam, baby!" the guy behind them yelled. "How ya like *them* apples?"

Heather peeked at the guy to her left. A Reds fan, he'd been battling the guy behind them throughout the game. Until this moment Cardinals fans had been dejected, thinking the game lost, and Mr. Reds had been talking trash. Now he was the only one around them still sitting.

"I *knew* Pujols would knock it out," Logan said, beaming. "He is such a clutch player. What a way to end it."

Pujols did his victory lap around the bases as the music blared.

"Look at Fred Bird gettin' down," Heather said. The team mascot had been major entertainment. "He's hilarious."

They lingered in the celebration a few minutes more, then filed out and up the stairs with the rest.

"So what'd you think of your first major league baseball game?"

"Way more fun than I thought it'd be." She took a sip of the Mountain Dew left in her cup. "There's so much energy in the stadium, it's hard not to get into it."

"Didn't hurt that we had primo seats either. I didn't realize we'd be so close."

Logan guided her through the throng, past the concession stands and wastebaskets overflowing with empty popcorn tubs and hot dog wrappers, until they found the exit doors closest to where they'd parked.

"And thanks again for the shirt," she said as Logan held the door. She'd changed in the bathroom and stuffed the one she'd had on into her purse.

"You're welcome. Had to get you in the spirit."

They strolled down Broadway, the late afternoon sun following overhead.

Logan gazed over at her. "So…just curious…why'd you want to make sure this wasn't styled as a date?"

"Remember in Indy we prayed about God's plan for me? And you said pay attention to the ways God might respond, how He might lead me?"

"I remember."

"Well, I started reading John, like you suggested, and…it may sound weird, but I feel like I'm actually spending time with Jesus. And the more I know about Him, the more I want to know." She shrugged. "So I'm thinking that's the plan right now. Not music or romantic involvement with a man. Just hanging with Jesus."

A smile lit his face. "I am so excited for you," he said.

"Why?"

"I can see that fresh wonder in your eyes. There's nothing like being rocked by Jesus. And you never know what He'll do or where He'll take you. So get ready for the ride."

She turned that over in her mind. She'd been thinking she might need to get used to the idea of staying at the dentist's office the rest of her life…which wasn't so bad. But what if something totally new and unexpected unfolded? "Whatever's in store," she said, "I just want Jesus with me."

"That's a given," Logan said. He poked out his lip. "But what about your bro?"

Heather chuckled, her heart lighter than she could ever remember. "I hope Jesus brings you along too."

Chapter Eighteen

They sat tight in the booth Tuesday night, Dana, Phyllis, and Cyd on one side, Stephanie and Kelli on the other. Cyd didn't know how the arrangement worked itself that way, but she was sure it had the effect Dana wanted. She could practically ignore Cyd from her position.

So far there'd been light banter about the Maggiano's menu, but with orders placed and the server gone, they were set to focus on one another and the news Kelli waited to share.

"Quick housekeeping question," Phyllis said. "Last couple of DF gatherings have been over a meal, which is great, but when's our next real meeting? I miss the Bible study."

"You're right," Cyd said. "We've gotten off track. I miss it too."

Dana lifted her water glass. "I figured you didn't have time for two Bible studies, so DF was on hold."

Cyd glanced over at her. "I always have time for DF. We should plan the next meeting before we leave."

"Great," Phyllis said. "Okay, I cannot wait another second. What's the news?"

Kelli sat up, looking into their faces. "I told Brian I'd work with him on his new album, helping to write as well as singing."

Phyllis stared. "You just said that so calmly, like it's no big deal. You're going to be on the next Alien album?" Phyllis practically screamed it, albeit with an inside voice. "Cole will absolutely flip."

"Kelli, this is way bigger than the Monica opportunity," Dana said. "Talk about answered prayer. And I'm so excited you'll be singing. I love your voice."

"Thank you, but like I told Brian, I've got a lot of reservations. If it looks like we can't work together, I'm bowing out."

"Wait..." Phyllis frowned as she broke off a piece of bread. "A little over a week ago you couldn't stand to look at Brian. How did things change?"

"Well..." Kelli was obviously measuring her response. "I was upset with him about something in the past, but a series of circumstances made me see he deserved forgiveness like everybody else."

Cyd wanted badly to look over at Dana to see if she might have made a hint of a connection, but she kept her eyes on Kelli, who continued.

"Around that same time, Brian heard 'I Will Love You' and wanted to do a remake. He asked me about it, and we recorded it that same night."

Phyllis's mouth dropped. "You already recorded a song? I *know* it's fabulous."

"It's still weird for me," Kelli said, "hearing my recorded voice. But I guess it turned out okay."

Stephanie gave Kelli her familiar look. "I don't know

what she's talking about—'I *guess* it turned out okay.'
The song is blazin'."

"You've heard it?" Dana asked.

Stephanie glanced at Cyd and Kelli. "Was I not supposed to say anything?"

"It's fine," Kelli said. She looked at Dana and Phyllis. "Brian and I played it for them on Sunday. We're
not sure when we'll let others hear it. There's a lot of
story behind it that we haven't shared openly yet."

Dana nodded. "I understand. Makes perfect sense
to let family hear it first."

Cyd concerned herself with her water glass.

"Did Heather hear it too?" Dana asked.

Eyes went wide around the table.

"Now, why would you ask that, Dana?" Phyllis
asked. "I was hoping we could stay off the subject of
Heather tonight."

"I'm asking because we drove by Cyd's house after
church so Scott could drop off some stuff he needed
to give Cedric. When he didn't stop, I asked why, and
he said that was Heather's car out front. I figured Cyd
must've asked her to spend the night after they went to
dinner. Maybe she's part of the family now."

"Okay, ladies, we've got your yummy entrées."

Cyd stared at hers when the server set it down. She
always got the same thing—baked ziti with sausage—
and it looked delicious. But she thought she'd be sick.

"Enjoy, ladies!" Their server left them in their silence.

"Shall we pray?" Phyllis asked. When no one replied, she began, "Heavenly Father, we thank You for
this food and pray it nourishes our bodies. And we
thank You for Daughters' Fellowship. You've been so

faithful to us, and we're looking to Your faithfulness again. Protect us, Lord, from the enemy's attempts to divide. Bring peace where he seeks to bring strife. May Your joy be our strength. In Jesus' name."

"Amen," Cyd whispered.

Forks clanged as the women tried to busy themselves with their meal—every woman but one.

Cyd could feel Dana's eyes on her.

"Wow," Dana said. "No one answered, which means Heather really did hear the song." She shook her head. "So, Daughters' Fellowship prayed for God to open doors for Kelli's music, and when He opens the door, *she* gets to hear it before we do. I find that interesting."

Cyd looked to the other end of the booth. "Dana, you don't know the whole story. Trust me." She wished she could explain the bond between Kelli and Heather, but that wasn't for her to reveal.

"I guess I don't. But let's see what I do know. You met with the girl on Saturday, took her to dinner afterward"—she ticked the events off on her fingers—"and hung out with her at your house on Sunday. Maybe I should just leave, and y'all can start a new Daughters' group with Heather." A tear fell from her eye. Dana dug in her purse and tossed a twenty-dollar bill on the table.

"You're not really leaving, are you?" Cyd asked.

Dana got up and walked away.

"Excuse me, Phyl."

Phyllis slid out of the booth so Cyd could get out. She caught up to Dana by the bar. "We need to talk outside."

They left the restaurant and walked down the sidewalk, away from the people dining outdoors, Cyd praying every step.

Lord, I don't even know what to say. Please help me.

When they had some privacy, Cyd stopped and turned. "Dana," she said, "please don't blow this out of proportion. You're making way too much of this."

"Really? She nearly took my husband from me, and now she's getting between me and my best friend."

"Dana, that's nonsense... I'll always be your best friend. You've been stuck with me for nearly thirty years and you've got at least another thirty to go. I understand you're hurt, but—"

"No, you don't understand, Cyd." Dana ran her fingers through her hair in frustration. "From the moment her name came up, it was like the scab was ripped off and I started bleeding again. The images of her and Scott are even starting to come back. I need her to move to another universe. I don't want to see her. I don't want to hear about her." She gave a flippant laugh. "But instead, she's hanging out at your house!"

"It's not like that, Dana."

"Actually, it is. The reality is that Heather's world and my world have bumped up against one another— *again*—and my sanity can't take it."

Cyd waited a few beats. "I know I mentioned this before, but...have you ever considered...forgiving Heather?"

"Can't say I have, no. Why? Thinking about a Kumbaya party at your house for her and me?"

"It's not about you and her," Cyd said. "It's about *you*. Forgiveness would go a long way toward your own peace."

"I *had* peace, Cyd, when she was out of the picture."

"I'm not talking about that kind of peace. I'm talking about a real inner peace."

"Well, pray for me, because I'm not feeling it right now." She turned to leave. "I just need some time. And space."

Cyd entered her bedroom and collapsed flat on the bed.

"How'd it go, babe?" Cedric lay next to her, watching ESPN highlights.

"Terrible."

He lifted his head and looked at her. "What happened?"

"Dana and Scott rode past here on Sunday to give you something and saw Heather's car parked out front. In her mind, Heather's become part of the family."

"Ah, makes sense now." Cedric clicked off the TV and turned on his side toward her. "Scott called today about getting me a draft of the promotional materials. We talked about the choices theme, and he said we need to make sure guys understand that bad choices can reap bad consequences for a long time. When you think it's over, it comes roaring back at you. I bet he's dealing with a lot at home right now."

"All because of me. I hate this. I wish I hadn't gone to that songwriters' conference, then I wouldn't be in the middle of this."

"Maybe. No point in second-guessing. I thought you said your time with Heather and Kelli was incredible."

"That's just it. When I focus on Heather, my heart is so sure that I'm supposed to be in her life. But when I focus on Dana, my heart breaks, knowing how it makes her feel."

"Babe." He caressed her face. "Keep focusing on

God. You felt He was leading you to do this, so you've got to trust He'll work it out. Right?"

"I know." She stared off to the side. "But things are only going to get worse." She couldn't hold back tears. "Why now?"

Cedric took her into his arms. "Did you get a chance to tell them?"

"No. Dana left before we'd even eaten. I didn't feel like sharing the news without her." She sniffed into his chest. "Such a huge moment in my life. I'm going to have a baby, and Dana doesn't know about it?"

"Sweetheart, we only found out yesterday."

"Still."

He rubbed her back. "I still can't believe it."

"Me either." Thoughts of the baby lifted her mood. She looked up at him and kissed him. "You and I, having a baby. It's the most exhilarating feeling."

"Uh," he said. "Second most for me."

She frowned at him. "What's the first?"

"Marrying you. I'm still amazed that God actually gave me you as a wife."

"You're making me cry again. And I'm not even a big crier." She sat up suddenly. "I wonder if it's a hormone thing. Oh, joy. I'll be a big fat crybaby now." She sank down again.

"Least you'll be a beautiful big fat crybaby."

She cut her eyes up at him, then snuggled close. "Feeling's mutual, by the way. I'm still amazed God gave me you. *And* I'm amazed you're still giving me roses." She gazed beyond him to the nightstand, at the dozen fresh golden roses he'd brought home after work.

"You didn't think it would stop, did you?"

Cedric had given her roses from the first weekend

they met through to their wedding day—each time a different color with a special meaning. She thought a moment. "I guess I just didn't expect it."

"Good. I like surprising you. But I'm running out of colors. Might have to recycle some old ones."

Cyd smiled. "You'll come up with something, and it'll be perfect. I never even knew there was such a thing as gold roses, let alone that they symbolized a joyous occasion."

"I had to mark this occasion somehow. The two of us becoming first-time parents in our forties? It's wild and wonderful and—"

"Scary."

Cedric sat up on an elbow. "What do you mean?"

"All the stories you hear about high-risk pregnancies. What if there are complications with my health? Or the baby's?"

"Sweetheart, it's not like you to worry."

"But what if something goes wrong with the pregnancy? I'm almost forty-one. I might not get another chance. What if—"

He planted a kiss. "What if we just trust God—with the baby and the pregnancy, with Dana, with everything?"

Sounded like advice she'd given someone else. But with life pressing in as it was, in ways she'd never before experienced, the dial seemed stuck on worry. "So you're saying it's not a good thing to drive myself crazy imagining the worst?"

"Not for you or the baby."

She sighed. "Guess there's nothing I can do to control any of it anyway."

He smiled at her. "There's one part you can control."

She tossed her eyes. "I know. I can trust." She ran her hand slowly across her belly. If only it were as easy as flipping that dial.

Chapter Nineteen

Thursday dawned with a promising opportunity—
and Kelli just knew it was God at work. Earlier in the
week, she had hit the pavement and dropped off cover
letters and résumés at local firms with communications
or marketing personnel. At one place she'd done a little more, after reading a feature in the morning paper
about Tina Schoenfeld. She was being honored as one
of St. Louis's Most Influential Businesswomen—and
she was president of a public relations agency. Kelli included a special letter with a congratulatory note for
her.

She couldn't believe it when she got a call first thing
this morning from Schoenfeld's assistant, who asked
whether Kelli was related to Cedric London. Turned
out, Cedric had worked with Tina in the past, was even
instrumental in helping her secure a prior post. The assistant wanted to know if Kelli had time today to grab
a quick lunch.

Kelli agreed in a heartbeat. Not only did she hope
to glean wisdom from this successful businesswoman,

but even more, she hoped this would be an entrée to the start of her career. If Cedric had helped Tina, surely Tina would help Cedric's sister. Wasn't that how it worked?

But the lunch appointment at the quaint corner café in Clayton ended with expectations dashed. Tina did want to return the favor, but it didn't reach farther than the lunch itself and a sprinkling of encouragement and advice. As for an actual job, Kelli should call her in three to five years, once she'd gotten great experience elsewhere.

Kelli mulled the disappointment as she walked to her metered parking spot and got in her car. But it didn't take long for her thoughts to change course. She was headed to Brian's for their first "official" collaborating session. She couldn't deny the anticipation she'd felt the last few days. There was nothing sweeter than the sound of melodies in her head again—they were still coming. That she might be able to do something tangible with them was almost too much to grasp. But it was also hard to grasp the thought of working with Brian.

Her phone rang as she started the car. She wondered if it was Brian...or Miles. Strange having them coupled in the same thought.

She pulled out her cell and smiled. "Hi, Miles."

"How did it go?"

"Lunch was good, but she's not looking to hire me."

"That's too bad. I thought for sure it would lead to something."

"Yeah." She shifted into drive.

"What's your next step? Sending off more résumés this afternoon?"

She pulled into a lane. "No, not this afternoon."

"Don't you think you need to? Maybe you should be more aggressive."

She frowned. "You don't think I've been aggressive enough?"

"Well, your first meeting with my parents will go a lot better if you're working someplace, positioned in your career. Shows them you're worthy of their son." He chuckled.

Kelli had no words. Well, she had plenty, but none she could say.

"That last part was supposed to be a joke."

"Right." She pulled to a red light and watched the foot traffic, people leaving restaurants and heading back to work.

"Kelli? I hope you're not getting too discouraged over the job search. You've seemed…distant lately."

"I have?" She pulled into a lane, blowing out a silent breath. She'd hoped it wasn't obvious.

"A little. Not calling as much, not talking as long. I figured it was either the job search or something else. I wondered if you were back in touch with your old boyfriend."

"Brian? Oh, no worries where he's concerned. It's just been so busy with this transition back to life in St. Louis." Was she talking faster than normal? Should she at least tell him she was working with Brian? Why was she inclined to keep it quiet?

"I understand," he said. "It's only normal. But I miss the days when we could spend hours studying in the library on campus and grabbing a meal." He paused. "I miss *you*, Kelli."

"I miss you too, Miles."

"Guess we're finding the new rhythm of our relationship. I'm hoping the melody is just as beautiful."

She stared at the stretch of road before her, taken aback by his analogy. "Me too." If he only knew how melodies figured into her life, into this very day.

She couldn't stop thinking about it as she pulled in front of Brian's house. There was another whole side of her about which Miles knew nothing, the side that held her deepest thoughts, hurts, and dreams. Only one person knew Kelli fully.

Brian's front door opened, and he poked his head out. "Coming in anytime soon?"

Kelli grabbed her purse, change of clothes, and old notepad from the passenger seat, then stepped out. "Hi, Brian."

"Hey. Don't you look cute." He held the door for her, smiling as she walked up. "You didn't have to dress up for our session, you know."

"Ha-ha." She lifted the jeans and shirt she was holding. "Can I use your bathroom?"

When she came out, Brian was standing in the kitchen eating a fast-food sandwich.

"Where's Grandma Howard?"

"Still at church. They've got noonday prayer now, and she likes to make it as often as she can."

"She amazes me. Always on the go." Kelli eyed his food. "So you thought you'd sneak that in while she's gone?"

He popped the last bite into his mouth. "She still gives me a hard time about fast food. Thinks I should eat leftovers every day for lunch." He took a drink of his soda. "How was your lunch?"

She set her clothes on a kitchen chair. "No job leads."

"Yet," he said. "I'm praying for you." He balled up his trash and threw it away. "Ready to get to work?"

Kelli followed him downstairs. "I'm ready. Did that producer send some samples?"

She couldn't believe that all she had to do was call the producer's voice mail and sing the chorus she'd gotten in her head on Sunday, and he'd put together music tracks that fit the melody.

"He e-mailed three. I already listened, and there's one I think is perfect." Brian plopped into his swivel chair. "But I won't say anything. Wanna see what you think."

Brian played the first one, and Kelli stared at the floor as she listened. She liked the beat well enough, but when it got to the chorus, she wasn't sure about it. She sang along anyway, trying to tweak it to make it fit. She looked at Brian and shrugged. "It's okay."

"Here's the next one."

Two seconds in, she was nodding her head. "Ooh, I love this." She looked at Brian. "You hear that string arrangement?"

Brian's feet were propped up on a stool. "The strings are dope."

Kelli heard some ad-libs in her head that she could sing during Brian's verse and tried them out.

"Aww, Kel, that 'oh-oh' thing you just did...on the money."

She sang the chorus, and it dropped perfectly into the musical arrangement. "I don't know what the next sample sounds like, but there's no way it could be better than this one. This is our track."

He smiled. "Exactly. I knew I wouldn't have to bother playing the third."

"So we've got the track and the hook. What about your part?"

Brian turned off the music and pulled his Bible from the desk. "Okay, so we're doing this love letter to the suffering, which is something we all have to go through. Philippians 1:29 says we're called to believe and suffer for Jesus' name." He flipped some pages. "First Peter really rocked me as I studied—the comparison between suffering for doing what's right, which finds favor with God, and suffering because you've done wrong." He looked at Kelli. "I know what the latter feels like. I built my verses around that juxtaposition." He passed a notepad to her.

She raised an eyebrow. "You've got a notepad now?"

"Comes in handy, you know?"

She had to smile.

Kelli looked at the lyrics, lines that spoke of being brought low and treated badly because of something "you knew you shouldn't have done, a wrong move you couldn't outrun." Then they flipped to school and the workplace, standing for Christ, suffering ridicule and rejection. Kelli could hear the chorus kick in. *You're blessed...rejoice...when you suffer...you are blessed...*

She pondered the lyrics more before looking at him. "I have a confession."

Brian looked at her.

"When I first heard you were doing Christian rap, I thought it would be a lot of fluff with a good beat. But I listened to a couple of your songs on iTunes, and working with you now"—she paused—"it's more like theology with a beat. God is really using you."

"You too, Kel." Brian's eyes penetrated. "You're

stepping into what you were always meant to do. Remember how you dreamed of music as a career?"

His question landed deep. She'd dared to dream that dream for a little while, but she didn't dare embrace it again. This was a temporary project. *Brian's* project. She would help him and, in the best of scenarios, might even enjoy it. But her career lay elsewhere.

"I remember," she answered, "but we dream a lot of things in our youth that don't pan out. You were sure you'd be a scientist."

"I still might be—hey, that reminds me," he said suddenly. "This is the last week for that body exhibit at the Science Center. Will you go with me if we get done before too late?"

"I can't, Brian."

"Why not?"

"It would seem like we're jumping back into the way things used to be, and things aren't the way they used to be."

His face fell. "But we're working together. We're becoming friends again. Aren't we?"

"Working together, yes. Friends?" She turned it over in her mind. "On a certain level, I guess. But there's so much water under the bridge. I don't see how it could ever be the friendship it once was."

He turned toward the console. "Guess we couldn't have picked a better day to record *this* love letter." His cell phone rang, and he looked to see who it was. "I need to get this."

Kelli's thoughts lingered around her last statement. Was she as sure as she sounded?

"So you're coming Friday morning?" Brian was saying. "Sounds like a plan. Yeah, we can all ride together... I'm looking forward to it too. It'll be fun. What's that?... Oh, I'll have to tell you about it. I feel like I'm finally rolling on this album." He listened. "I'm not sure. Kelli will be doing the singing, at least most of it."

Kelli's eyebrows lifted. She had the impression she'd be on all of it.

"Kelli," Brian was saying, "the one who gave you that song."

Monica. Interesting.

"We can talk about it... Okay."

Brian hung up, his eyes on the equipment. "We'll lay down the hook first. I think we'll be able to knock the whole song out in a few hours. That'll be two down. I'm pumped."

Kelli nodded. Where was Brian going Friday? Was Monica asking to sing on his album? What did he think about that?

In the past he wouldn't have hesitated to share his life, his schedule, his thoughts. And she wouldn't have hesitated to ask. But hadn't she just told him their friendship wasn't the same? Apparently, he was abiding by that. Also apparent—he had someone else to fill the gap.

Kelli was almost home after six hours in the studio with Brian. They'd indeed finished the song, the process generating one creative idea after another. What they ended up with far surpassed what they'd imagined.

Her phone rang as she turned onto her street, and she slowed to look at it. *Cedric.*

"Hey, I'm almost home," she said.

"I'm on my way to church. We've got a meeting

to talk about the new ministry. And when I talked to Doug earlier, it sounded like there could be an opportunity for you. Can you come up here and talk to him?"

She pulled up to the curb. "What kind of opportunity? And who's Doug?"

"He's Director of Communications at Living Word. Not exactly sure what the opportunity might entail, but you should meet him."

Cedric was all about networking. Granted, it was his line of business, but she hated to get her hopes up for nothing. "Well, okay. I guess I can meet you there."

"We'll be in the main building, second floor. Once you pass the classrooms, you'll see a conference room. Bring your résumé. And, Kelli?"

"Make a good impression."

"Riiight."

Kelli chuckled. Cedric had been drumming that in her head from the time she interviewed for her first job in high school—look the part in any interview situation, even if it wasn't official. She ran into the house and changed back into her skirt, yelling a "Hey!" at Cyd and telling where she was headed. Something yummy awaited on the stove, reminding her she was starving—but for now, a banana would have to hold her.

Kelli pulled into the parking lot at church, surprised to see so many cars until she remembered that the choir rehearsed on Thursday evenings. She drove to the familiar area of the lot. She and her family not only inhabited the same pew but the same parking spaces when they could get them. She spotted Cedric's and Scott's cars near one another and parked by them. In the building, before she took the stairs, she took a peek inside the sanctuary. Logan was at the piano, directing the choir in a song that was building. At its height he cut it off.

"Right there," he said. "Sopranos only until the next measure, then my altos kick back in, *then* my tenors and basses. You almost had it, but I know I heard a few bottom voices in there."

Kelli ducked back out and headed up. She couldn't help but think how nice it would be if Heather still attended Living Word and sang in the choir. But she knew how painful that would be for Dana…

The door to the meeting room stood ajar, and Kelli could see a few people milling about. Cedric and Scott spotted her and introduced her to Doug, Karen the graphic design specialist, and Waylan, who handled web design.

Doug looked to be in his thirties and was a hair shorter than Kelli, with one of those faces that seemed to always be smiling. "Cedric tells me you've been job hunting, looking for something in the area of public relations and communications?"

"Yes, the search has been harder than I anticipated. Most companies simply aren't hiring, and those that are want three- to five-years' experience."

"Been there. Went through the same thing out of school. You just want to scream, 'Somebody, please give me a chance.'"

"Exactly!" Kelli wagged a finger. "Haven't tried the scream yet. Maybe I should."

"Our communications staff is basically Waylan, Karen, and me, and we're overworked. We'd love to hire a full-time communications assistant, but it's currently not in the budget. We can bring someone on board part-time, though." His smile turned apologetic. "Is that something you'd be remotely interested in?"

Kelli's face lit up. "Absolutely. I'd love to be part of the team. That is, if you find me suitable."

"Tell you what. Why don't you sit in on the meeting, get a feel for some of what we do, chip in if you want. Afterward, we'll talk a little more."

Everyone moved to a seat at the oblong table in the middle of the room, pens and pads in front of them, along with coffee cups and water.

Doug spoke first. "We scheduled this meeting to play catch-up. By the looks of things, this ministry for young men has tapped into a felt need. Not only was the first day of sign-ups huge, but we've fielded a lot of calls since from people interested in participating."

"That's incredible," Cedric said. "So what are you thinking we need to do next?"

"Initially, we thought we'd start with the usual—the printed brochures and flyers we gave you, an information page on the church website. But with this kind of interest, we want to ramp it up. Roll out the ministry with a dedicated web presence like we do for our teen ministry. Plus we'd like to shoot a video that'll play on the site's home page."

Cedric was nodding. "I'm tracking with you. Very cool."

"What are you thinking for the video?" Scott asked.

"From what you two have told us," Doug said, "one of the central themes for the ministry is choices. Guys between eighteen and twenty-five are faced with choices that could impact them for the rest of their lives, and the ministry aims to help them make the right ones. Am I right?"

"Exactly," Scott said. "In fact, we're planning to kick it off with a series of speakers who will share their own stories of choices they've made, some good, some bad, that'll hopefully inspire the guys to take the right course."

"Awesome." Doug scribbled some notes. "So the video could feature snippets of those stories, or maybe just one story."

Kelli raised a finger, and Doug nodded.

"You could even think about writing a short script and filming a vignette in addition to that. There's something compelling about seeing a story acted out."

"I like that a lot." Doug wrote something in the margin, then looked at Cedric and Scott. "As the leaders, might make sense for one or both of you to share some of your story in the video."

"That could work," Cedric said. "We're planning to speak to the guys, for sure. As long as you don't think it'll do any damage to have us old dudes on film."

Scott looked hesitant. "I don't know. My wife is still dealing with the residue of my bad choice. Now's not the time to tell her, 'Hey, honey, guess what? It'll be broadcast on video too.'" He shook his head. "Think I'll stick to speaking in closed sessions with the guys."

Doug twirled his pen. "That's totally fine, Scott. We have a lot of options here."

"Have you all considered a ministry logo?" Kelli asked. "I might be weird for noticing things like that, but I saw that the women's ministry and the teen ministry had special logos. Might be an added touch that enhances the kickoff."

Doug looked at Cedric. "Will I have to pay you a finder's fee? I'm keeping this one."

Kelli could feel excitement building within and not just because it looked like she might have a job. Right here in the meeting, she heard another song in her head…a love letter to young men.

Chapter Twenty

Brian and Monica strolled the festival grounds in the Lake of the Ozarks, only a hint of sunlight left in the day. It had been a long one. Monica's tour bus had rolled into St. Louis at ten in the morning, and Brian and his road manager, Nate, hopped aboard for the three-hour trip west. They'd both performed individually at the festival, then wowed the energetic crowd of thousands with the song they recorded for Monica's upcoming album. They ended the evening watching other artists perform and enjoying the vibe among the crowd.

"Ooh, cotton candy!" Monica tugged on his arm, a grin across her face. "Brings back memories. Let's get some."

"Definitely brings back memories." He could hear Kelli squealing about it, back when the carnival would come to town. They'd share a stick, pulling puffs and stuffing them into their mouths, laughing about their lips turning blue. He shook the memory.

It's not about Kelli anymore.

They watched the woman swirl the cotton into a big fluff. Monica happily took it. "You gonna get some?"

"Yeah." He smiled, trying to be happy about it. "I think I will."

They continued strolling through the crowd, licking sticky fingers, stopping at merchandise booths, occasionally signing autographs. Only one more act to go, a popular band, and they'd decided to stay and hear them. The bus would get back into St. Louis late, then keep going to Nashville.

"You must be excited to be done with the album," Brian said. "Feel good about it?"

Monica paused by a guy twisting balloons into animal shapes. "I love it. I think it has just the right mix—a little funk, rock, praise and worship. It's really eclectic. I'll e-mail it to you."

"I was wondering why I hadn't gotten it. Didn't want to chastise you just yet."

She laughed. "You knew it was coming." Her smile faded. "Still can't believe your friend's song didn't make it on there. My producers had found another song that same weekend and thought it was a better fit to round out the album. We'd been battling about other things, so I didn't want to make that a fight too."

"Don't sweat it. It worked out. I'm using the song on my album, a remake of it. Already recorded it."

"Really? Wow. Can't wait to hear it. Can you send it to me?"

Brian's face issued an apology before his words. "Wish I could. We're waiting until we figure out how we want to share the story behind the song. It's…kind of personal."

Monica looked puzzled. "Who's 'we'?"

"Me and Kelli. We recorded it together."

"Oh." She looked away. "And you have a personal story to go with the song? I've never heard you mention a special person in your life."

"She's not… I mean, that's all in the past. She happened to move back to town, and we're working on this album together."

"Oh," she said again. She tried a smile, but it was thin. "Must be why I haven't gotten a call to sing on the album."

"Truthfully? I probably would've called you if it hadn't come together this way. But I've got several songs to go yet." He tried his own smile. "So keep your vocal cords warm."

Monica started walking, and Brian was sure he heard a sigh.

"Monica," he said, coming up behind her, "talk to me. You're upset because I haven't asked you to sing on the album?"

She turned toward him. "I don't know. That might be part of it…feeling like I'm out of the loop."

"Oh my gosh! It's Monica and Alien!"

The girl was probably in her early teens.

"Hey, you guys!" She waved her arms to get her friends' attention. "Come here!"

Brian and Monica looked at one another. The girl hadn't exactly spoken to them, wasn't even looking at them, but they knew they needed to wait right there for her friends.

Five other young teens emerged, all of them giggly, braces shining in the evening spotlights as they smacked on chewing gum.

"Can we get your autographs?" The first girl spoke

for them, but they all produced their programs. "We love you guys. Like, totally. I can't even tell you."

Monica flipped her inner switch and smiled big. "Aww, very cool! You guys are awesome." She whipped out a black marker and signed each, then passed the marker to Brian.

"We appreciate the support." Brian handed their programs back. "We couldn't do what we do without you. Thank you."

"Can we get a picture too?"

"Of course," they both said.

The girls flagged down a woman who'd been hanging back, probably mother to one of them. She had her camera at the ready and took at least three shots.

"Facebook it tonight," one of the girls said.

"And send me copies!" a couple more chorused.

Brian and Monica smiled and waved good-bye, and the mood dialed down quickly again.

She glanced up at him. "We've got about ten minutes before the last band comes on. Can we talk?"

He had a good idea where this was going but no idea what he would say. "Sure."

They walked to the edge of the crowd to claim some quiet space and stood side by side, looking around. Monica finally spoke.

"I don't really have a problem with not singing on your album." Her gaze remained on the crowd. "I think it's the fact that you're working with Kelli."

"Why is that a problem?"

Her gaze fell to the ground. "I guess I liked fancying myself as the main girl in your life, the friend you could talk to and hang out with. And I always kind of hoped that one day…"

Festival noise abounded, but the awkward silence swallowed it whole.

Brian measured his words. "I hadn't thought about it that way, Monica, but you actually have been the main girl in my life for a while now, my closest female friend."

"But..." Monica said.

"I really didn't have a 'but.'"

Monica looked at him now, exasperated. "Brian, do you not get it? We get along so well. You're single, I'm single. We're both in the business. Yet you've never once indicated an interest in me beyond friendship. There *has* to be a 'but.' Either you find me unappealing—"

"Oh, Monica, you know that's not true."

"—or it's Kelli."

"That's not true either. That writers' conference was the first time I'd seen or talked to her in years."

"Doesn't mean your heart hasn't kept a primary spot on reserve for her."

A crease formed in his brow. "I've just been focused on school and music. I haven't had time to think about much else." He paused. "But I value your friendship. Who knows what the future could hold?"

"Can I be honest with you, Brian?"

"You know you can."

"It's hard for me to keep being friends with you, yet having to hide my feelings." She threw up her hands. "I'm falling in love with you."

Brian sucked in a heap of air and tried to blow it out under his breath, to hide his shock. He stared into the dark sky, searching his heart for answers he might've missed. How did he feel about her? Could he see the two of them in a real relationship?

Seemed a given on so many levels. She was beautiful, kind, talented, serious about her faith, and a good friend. And she was interested in him. Did he need special bells to go off to alert him that she was worth pursuing?

And yet…

Was Kelli a factor? How could she be? She'd made it clear they were barely friends.

But what did that matter to his heart?

Maybe Monica knew better than he—his heart *had* held a place for Kelli, no matter how ridiculous that might be. Or maybe he'd been waiting for someone else to fill it, to become all that Kelli had been to him. Did Monica come close to that? Was it even fair to ask? He didn't know. But what he knew was that it wouldn't be fair for Monica to think he felt the same.

His heart sank when he looked at her, her arms folded, wet streaks down her face. He'd never wanted to hurt her. "Monica, you're my friend. That won't change."

"It has to change." She wiped her face with the palm of her hand. "My heart needs to let go, and the only way to do that is to minimize contact."

"But your album's coming out. We've got dates on the calendar to perform that song."

"I know and that's fine. But talking on the phone, being together like this… I can't do it."

"I'm sorry."

"You didn't do anything. I'll be okay."

The band had come onstage and started to play.

"You want to walk over and listen?"

"No. We should go."

Without a word they walked back to the area where the buses were. It would be a long and lonely ride to St. Louis. The next days, weeks, and months would probably be lonely too. Maybe one day his heart would get its act together, find room for someone else.

Or maybe…maybe one day, if a miracle happened, it would welcome the one person it longed for.

Chapter Twenty-One

"So, will you forever be Heather the Adulteress, resigned to hang your head in shame and regret? Is that who you are?"

Heather sat cross-legged on the sofa, bare feet poking out, hair falling forward as she double-checked the verse in her lap. She didn't know this was in there. She was named among a whole host of what she could call "bad actors"—from idolaters and adulterers to thieves and drunkards. She leaned into the page to read again what it said about them. About her. *"And such were some of you; but you were washed, but you were sanctified, but you were justified in the name of the Lord Jesus Christ and in the Spirit of our God."*

"And such *were* some of you…"

Heather looked up at Cyd. "No." Her voice was bare. "That's not who I am. I've been washed…"

She didn't want to, but she broke down, crying through the pain of what she'd been and the joy of what Jesus had given her—the gift of a new identity.

Kelli draped an arm around her, and Cyd came over from the armchair to sit on Heather's other side.

"Sweetie." Cyd handed her some tissues. "I'm so glad you're seeing who you are in Christ, the 'new you' as you like to say."

Heather wasn't looking at her, but she could tell Cyd had a smile in her voice.

"Let's look at your papers and see what you ended up with. You two made quite a list."

Heather dabbed her eyes and took her paper from the coffee table. Cyd had told them to write *I am* at the top of a page, then jot down anything they could spot during the study that made up their new identity. She called it their "new who."

Heather and Kelli had made a contest out of it. She leaned over now to look at Kelli's paper.

"Nope." Kelli hid it. "First let's see who has the most, then we can swap and add the ones the other has."

Heather smiled. "Okay, here's my list. I am…forgiven, loved, redeemed, blessed, a child of God, saved, a witness, an ambassador, protected, accepted, adopted, more than a conqueror, salt and light, free, delivered, a bond servant, an alien and a stranger"—she glanced pointedly at Kelli—"and *a new creation—woo!*"

"Woo-hoo!" Kelli and Cyd sent cheers up.

Kelli was looking at her paper. "You had a few that I didn't catch. I'll just tell the ones I didn't hear you say. I am…a believer, born again—"

"I can't believe I didn't have those!" Heather wrote them down.

Kelli kept going. "—a slave to righteousness, a citizen of heaven, set apart, a living stone, and His workmanship."

Heather shook her head. "This is mind-boggling. Just one of those 'new whos' is enough to get excited about. To know that I'm *all* those things?"

"And more. Those are just the verses we had time to cover." Cyd closed her Bible. "I want you to keep your list close and read over it now and then to get it down deep. The enemy will try to make you feel guilty about your past, and he'll use your own thoughts or he'll use other people. But if you know who you are, he won't succeed. Got it?"

"Got it!" they said.

"Ready to pray?"

"Cyd, first…" Heather could feel the nerves inside. "I don't know how to say this, but…last week at the mall, I noticed the tension between you and Dana, because of me. I just wanted to say I've gotten a lot out of just these two times we've met. I think I'll be fine studying on my own from here."

Cyd's eyes were soft, sympathetic. "Heather, you don't even have a church home. I love your heart, but I'm looking forward to spending more time with you and covering more ground. Discipleship isn't an overnight process."

"I feel so bad, though. What do you do when you've played a part in devastating someone like that? I know I can't go to her and apologize."

"This is one of those hard realities," Cyd said. "You know you're forgiven. You know you're a new creation. But sometimes we still have to deal with the consequences of the past. Honestly? Dana may never like you. And no, I would not advise going to her." Cyd made a face that said it would not be a wise move. "But you can always pray for her. In fact"—she nodded as she thought about it—"that would be awesome."

The suggestion moved Heather. "I like that. I'd like to start right now." Heather thought a moment. "And I have something else. My mother's having a fiftieth birthday party tonight, and I don't really want to go. When she and her friends start drinking…it's a scene I can do without."

Cyd and Kelli were listening. Heather never talked much about her family.

"But the main thing is I want to get her a Bible," Heather said. "I know she'll think it's weird, but I've been praying for her to know Jesus too, and this could be a first step. I guess. I don't know, I'm really nervous about it. Can we pray?"

The front door was ajar, people coming and going as Heather walked up to her mother's house. Her mother had lived in this north St. Louis neighborhood for more than ten years. If nothing else, she'd built a great camaraderie with the neighbors.

"Heather, haven't seen you in a while!"

She turned. "Hi, Mrs. Harris. Good to see you. You're looking quite festive."

"When Diane said she was throwing a seventies party, I got excited. That was my time, you know." The raspy-voiced woman was in her sixties, decked out in polyester bell-bottom pants and a long-sleeve paisley shirt. She flicked her cigarette, and orange-colored ashes fell to the ground. "I still had the clothes, and my daughter found me this wig at some secondhand shop." She fluffed her Afro. "Ain't it nice?"

Heather chuckled. "Just don't stand next to me.

You'll show me up, for sure." The most she'd done to get in costume was wear her widest-legged jeans and a T-shirt with a peace symbol on it.

Heather and Mrs. Harris walked inside the ranch-style home together. The front room had been transformed with tie-dyed sheets over the furniture, but the main action was obviously in the basement. "YMCA" blasted through the floorboards, along with loud voices.

"Hey, I love that song!" Mrs. Harris went straight for the stairs.

Heather headed to the kitchen to drop off her gift bag. Her mother probably wouldn't open gifts until tomorrow. Heather hoped she'd discover this one in just the right mood, quiet and reflective, though she wasn't sure it would make a difference.

She stepped inside the kitchen—and turned right back around. A couple she didn't recognize was leaning against the counter, kissing. They didn't even pause when they heard Heather's footsteps.

She headed to the basement instead, waiting for her eyes to adjust to the disco-ball lighting as she joined the partiers. Donna Summer was playing now, the crowd lively, covering most of the floor space. Heather saw many of her mother's friends as well as neighbors, all of them wearing some form of throwback attire—and almost all of them with a beer bottle or other drink in hand. Finally she spotted her mother, disco dancing in a sparkly minidress and go-go boots, her blond hair styled like Farrah Fawcett's.

Her mother saw her too. "Heather," she called. "You made it. Come here, honey!"

"Happy birthday, Mom," Heather said, giving her a hug.

Her mother stopped dancing and posed. "Not bad for fifty, eh?"

"Not bad at all," her dancing partner said.

Diane smiled and poked him in the chest. "You, sir, are a shameless flatterer. And I love it." She looked at her daughter again. "Heather, honey, let me introduce you. This is Cliff. He's a friend of..." She looked confused. "Who *did* you come with?"

"Mike."

"Oops." Diane laughed, covering her mouth. "He's my *boyfriend*." She glanced around. "I'd better find him before he gets mad at me."

Heather leaned close to her mother. "Mom, what's that smell? Are you letting people smoke that stuff down here?"

"Since when is that a big deal? Don't people use it as medicine these days? Certainly makes *me* feel better."

Heather sighed, ready to leave already.

Diane grabbed a younger guy walking past. "Tim, this is my daughter, the one I was telling you about. Didn't I tell you she's a hottie?"

Heather gave her mother a look. "Mom, please." She turned back to the guy and extended her hand. "Hi, I'm Heather. Nice to meet you."

He lifted her hand and kissed it. "Pleasure's mine. Wanna dance?"

"Um, not right now. But thanks."

Diane tugged on her hand. "What is *with* you? That guy's gorgeous."

Diane had always acted more like a girlfriend than a mother, setting Heather up with guys, handing her mixed drinks as a teen. But it never seemed sad to her until this moment.

"I'm really not feeling my best," Heather said. "Maybe I can come visit with you tomorrow."

"Aww, but I'd hate for you to miss the party—hey, is that a gift for me?"

Heather remembered the bag in her hand. "Oh, I meant to leave it in the kitch—" Why try to explain? "I'll just take it to your room."

"You'll do no such thing. I wanna see my gift. Is it the perfume I like?" Diane took the bag from Heather and stuck her hand beneath the tissue. "What's this?" She lifted it out. "A *Bible*?"

Heather cringed.

Diane burst into laughter. "Hey," she called to those around her, "my daughter gave me a Bible for my birthday." She held it up in the air. "Think she's trying to tell me something?"

People raised their beer bottles and cheered.

"When's the Bible study, Diane?" one of them asked.

Diane thought that was even funnier. "Yeah, I'll let you know," she yelled. She turned to Heather. "So what's the deal? You turn religious on me? You must be conspiring with that brother of yours."

Heather frowned. "Ian? What does he have to do with it?"

"Oh, he tried sending me a Bible a few years ago. Now he just puts Bible verses in birthday cards. Got one today. Haven't even opened it."

"You never told me that," Heather said.

Diane shrugged. "You never asked." She put the Bible back in the bag and handed it to Heather. "No offense, honey, but I would've used the perfume."

Cliff took her hand and got her dancing again.

Heather eased back upstairs, avoiding the eyes of

those in her path, wondering about her half brother. She didn't know him well at all. Diane had given birth to him at nineteen but had no interest in raising him. His paternal grandparents took him first, and when Ian's father married, the father's wife adopted him. Heather remembered a couple of visits here and there when she was younger and school pictures in the mail, but it had been years since she'd seen or heard about him. He was a believer?

She walked down the hall, took the Bible out of the bag, and tucked it inside her mother's nightstand. Then she stopped back in the kitchen, which was deserted now. Out of curiosity, she checked her mother's mail pile. There in the stack was a card with a return address sticker that said *Ian and Becky Engel*. So he was married. She wondered if they had any kids—if she had any nieces or nephews.

Heather wrote down their Illinois address. After all these years, she suddenly had a real desire to know her brother.

Chapter Twenty-Two

Cyd had a groggy understanding that a phone was ringing, but she didn't know how to answer it. When she realized that it wasn't a dream, she reached for her cell from the nightstand and answered, but no one was there.

Cedric rolled over. "Babe, get the phone."

"I'm trying."

Forced to pry her eyes open, she realized it was the landline. Goodness. What would she do when her baby needed her in the middle of the night? Was there a mommy thing that kicked in to help a person get her bearings?

"Hello?"

"Sorry to wake you, Cyd."

She sat up. "Dana?" She saw the time now—6:00 a.m. "Is something wrong?"

"No. Well. Can you meet me before church to talk, maybe at Starbucks?"

"Uh, sure." Cyd worked to gather her faculties.

Until two seconds ago, she wasn't sure what day it was. "What time?"

"Seven thirty?"

Cyd was about to ask why she needed to call so early, but given the climate between them of late, she thought better of it. "That's fine."

They agreed on a Starbucks, and Cyd sat in bed pondering what this could be about, that it couldn't wait till after church. She remembered Heather's heartfelt prayer yesterday. Was God answering already? It would certainly encourage Heather. She'd called last night to say the gift hadn't gone over well, that her mother had laughed. Maybe God was giving *her* a gift by touching Dana's heart. Or maybe Cyd was getting ahead of herself. Dana might have an altogether different issue in mind.

Cyd felt a pull to get up, make coffee, and spend the time before their meeting with God. Whatever it was, depending on how it went, things could end up worse than ever between them.

Cyd pulled the Starbucks door open and saw Dana behind one person in line. She hated the jumpy feeling she now got when she saw her friend, not knowing what to say, how she would be received. Sucking in a big breath, she stepped inside, surprised to see that the place was fairly empty.

She walked up beside her friend. "Good morning."

Dana turned and gave her a slight smile. "Good morning. Thanks for coming."

"No problem."

Their gazes landed on the menu board, as if they needed to survey what was available. Dana moved forward and ordered her usual, a grande nonfat vanilla latte. "I'm taking care of hers too."

"Thanks," Cyd said. She took a step up. "Is it possible to get a decaf mocha latte?" She still wasn't used to thinking of herself as pregnant.

Dana looked surprised. "Decaf? Early in the morning? Never seen you do that."

"I know. I'm…changing things up."

The barista handed them their drinks, and they settled at a small tabletop by the window, each taking a first sip, staring at their cups.

"Okay, so, I pretty much haven't slept well since Maggiano's."

Cyd looked at Dana, waiting for more.

"But last night I really couldn't sleep." Dana was studying her cup. "And it's not just that I couldn't sleep. I felt all weepy inside, like I was grieving." She looked directly at Cyd now. "Like I'd lost my best friend." She sighed. "And for the first time, I talked to God about it, about this…situation. And then I got weepy for real."

"Why?"

"He showed me *me*—and I hadn't even asked Him too!"

Cyd smiled faintly. The Daughters liked to say one of the hardest prayers was, "Lord, show me *me*," because He usually responded with something they wouldn't like.

"Yeah, He'll do that, won't He?"

"I was wrong, Cyd." Dana's brown eyes showed her sorrow. "I let my bitterness toward Heather get in the way of so many things. As if God can't get ahold of her heart? I should be glad she's been changed, but it was like…it was like I wanted to keep hating her, and the only way to do that was to keep believing the worst about her. When you befriended her, I didn't know what to do with that."

"I know. It's been hard for me, too, knowing how you felt. I can totally understand."

"But that doesn't make it right. I'm sorry for giving you a hard time about helping her. I know you. You wouldn't have done it unless you were convinced God wanted you to." She shook her head. "But what really got me about 'me' was thinking I was better than she was. Boy, did it sting when God showed me I'm as much a sinner as she is, that we both need a Savior." She paused. "I was able to forgive her, Cyd, just like you said. I had to call you right after that breakthrough."

"Dana, wow." Cyd got up and embraced her. "I'm so happy for you. I know it was hard. No one should have to go through what you went through. But forgiveness is so huge. What's that old saying? 'We're most like God when we forgive.'"

"Hmm." Dana pondered it. "I love that."

Cyd sat down again. "So…now might be a good time to give you my news."

"What news?"

A huge smile lighted Cyd's face. "I'm pregnant. Cedric and I are going to have a baby."

"What?" Dana covered her mouth and looked around, embarrassed by her own volume. She leaned in and said it again in a whisper. "What? How far along? When did you find out?"

"Not sure how far along because I haven't been to the doctor yet, but I'm guessing six weeks or so. Found out on Monday."

"But we were all at dinner on Tuesday. Why didn't you say anything?"

Cyd gave a light shrug. "I had planned to."

"But I got an attitude and walked out. Wonderful. Ruined your big moment."

"No big deal," Cyd said. "But it would've *really* been a problem if I had to go through this whole pregnancy without Aunt Dana in the mix."

"Oh no, sweetie. We've waited much too long for this. Maybe that's another reason God shook me up, so I'd get a clue about what I was missing out on. *You're having a baby!*"

Dana got up this time to give Cyd a hug, tears springing to her eyes. "All those conversations we had through the years, wondering if God would send you a husband, whether you'd ever have a child. I'm just… wow, wow, wow." She laughed. "You will be an awesome momma."

"Thank you." Cyd had a sigh in her voice as they took their seats. "Pray for me, though. I'm worried about the age thing. Cedric said we need to trust God, and of course he's right. But every time I get a little excited, I get this warning that nothing's guaranteed. Something could go wrong. So I shouldn't get too happy until the baby's actually here."

"Oh, Cyd. I hate that I haven't been praying for you about this. I'm getting the ladies together for a DF prayer-and-praise celebration. We're going to pray over you and the baby and praise God for this blessing He's given you and Cedric. And we're praying those worry thoughts away. This should be a time of joy!"

Now Cyd had tears in her eyes, and a memory

surfaced. "Remember when I was leaving for grad school?"

Dana nodded big. "And you were sad because we'd been together for middle school, high school, and college—"

"And I said it would never be the same, that we'd grow apart."

"And what did I say?" Dana asked.

Cyd smiled. "That I'd been accepted into Harvard, and it should be a time of joy."

Dana nodded again. "And God would take care of the friendship. Seems to me He did."

"To this very day."

Dana eyed her friend suddenly. "Did you eat before you left the house?"

"No."

"You might've been able to go to church with nothing in your stomach in the past, but that's not gonna work now." Dana rose from her seat. "Be right back."

"Where're you going?"

"To get a whole grain bagel. Baby needs nourishment." Dana got back in line.

Cyd rubbed her stomach. This would probably be the longest nine months she'd ever experienced, but she needed to stop thinking she had to hold her breath the entire time. Right now a baby was growing inside of her, a baby God was molding and shaping. Dana was right. She should actually enjoy the process.

But the thought made her a little sad too. She realized that with the pregnancy, she had a slight window into Kelli's pain, her feeling of loss. As she caressed

her own tummy, she prayed right there for Kelli and
for the song she and Brian had recorded, that it would
bring healing and hope to those who would hear it.

Chapter Twenty-Three

Kelli felt strangely glad to see Brian at church. She knew he'd been gone Friday, with Monica—though she didn't know where—but she'd expected to hear from him on Saturday. She'd been looking forward to sharing her newest song idea, the love letter to young men. At the rate they'd been collaborating, they might've been able to knock it out by evening. But he didn't call, and when she texted him after the Bible study with Cyd, she didn't hear back then either, which wasn't like him.

But there he was now in the back of the sanctuary, among the crowd heading to their seats.

"Girl, go get him," Stephanie said. "I don't know why he doesn't just come over here."

"I'm supposed to walk back there?"

"Yes, let him know he's welcome. It's the Christianly thing to do."

Kelli smirked at her. She wasn't opposed to Brian sitting with them, but she didn't want to go out of her way to invite him either. "Looks like I won't have to."

Cyd and Dana had come in and were talking to him.

"Thank God." Phyllis was on Kelli's other side. "I was really praying for those two after that dinner at Maggiano's. Good to see them smiling together."

Cyd and Dana started down the aisle, with Brian in tow. When they got to the pew, everyone stood and did a pew version of musical chairs. Cyd moved in next to Cedric. Dana walked further down to sit next to Scott. And space suddenly appeared between Kelli and Stephanie.

Brian filled it. "Hey."

"Hey."

Brian eyed her. "How was your weekend?"

"Good. How was yours?"

Brian nodded. "Real good, actually."

Kelli wanted to roll her eyes. *Probably spent Saturday with Monica too.* But why should she care?

Logan and the praise and worship team walked out on the platform, and the band launched into the first song. The congregation came to its feet.

Brian leaned over. "I didn't get your text until late last night. Sorry."

"No problem."

It was his album. If he could afford to lose a working day, that was his business. She'd never seen him ignore his phone for long stretches, though. Must've been totally preoccupied.

Brian allowed the worship music to consume him. He didn't whisper another word. With hands raised, he sang the song in a low voice, eyes mostly closed, yet he knew all the words. Kelli told herself to stop peeping at him. She got lost in the praise herself and practically forgot Brian until they sat down for announcements… and fell into an old habit.

Brian started it, asking if she had a pen. He drew a tic-tac-toe board on the back of the program and passed it to her. Without a word, she got another pen and filled in her X in the middle. He did his corner O, and they finished four boards without a winner. Brian drew a fresh board as an announcement was made about the young men's ministry. He paused and looked up front to catch it.

"So the new website will feature real stories of choices young men have made. If you'd like to submit your story for consideration, please send your e-mail to Kelli London at the address in the program."

Brian looked at Kelli with surprise and opened the program they'd been using. "You didn't tell me about this. You're working at the church now?"

"Only part-time, in the mornings. I start Tuesday."

"That should be great experience, Kel. Congrats. And I love what they're doing with this ministry."

She nodded. "I really hope it makes an impact."

They tucked the game away during the rest of the service, focusing on Pastor Lyles's sermon and a moving song afterward by the choir, the one Kelli had heard them practicing Thursday evening.

When the service was over, Brian had his eye on Logan. "I have to ask him if he wrote that song. That was incredible."

"I hadn't thought about that. I'd like to know too."

Kelli and Brian waited as Logan talked with his bass player and drummer.

"Hey! Good to see you guys," he said when he saw them.

"I know you're busy between services," Brian said,

"but had to tell you that song was the bomb. Did you write it?"

"I did. Thanks, man."

"You have a real gift for leading in worship," Kelli said. "I bet you wrote that song from last Sunday, too, based on Psalm 91. Stayed in my head all week."

"You two are embarrassing me. Yes, I wrote it, but… from what I'm hearing, you're putting together some awesome songs yourselves."

Kelli smiled. "Let me guess which little bird told you that. Heather?"

Logan smiled in return. "She did. No specifics, just that it's awesome."

"I'm glad she has you for a friend," Kelli said.

"She's probably a better friend to me than I am to her. And she helps me feed my inner child. We're going to Six Flags after church."

Kelli and Brian gave each other a look.

"What?" Logan asked.

Brian had a gleam in his eye. "We used to be Six Flags fools. When I got my first car, Cedric bought us season passes—"

"Best gift ever," Kelli added.

"—and we'd go even if we only had a couple of hours to ride the Screaming Eagle fifty times."

"Oh, well there you go." Logan lifted his hands. "It's a foursome. Screaming Eagle fools unite."

Brian looked to Kelli. She knew he was remembering her response when he'd asked to go to the Science Center. But this was different. It wouldn't just be her and Brian. She'd have Heather to pal around with as well.

"I think it'll be a lot of fun," she said. "Let's do it."

* * *

Brian was brimming with enthusiasm, ready to thank God already for answered prayer.

Friday night in the Ozarks had been hard, especially because it caused him to think even more about Kelli and what they *didn't* have. He'd felt defeated all the way back to St. Louis, thinking he'd never have the one woman he cared deeply about, due to his own failures.

Somewhere on that road back, though, a radical notion came to him—unplug for several hours Saturday and pray. Pray about Kelli. Pray about the album. First he thought he'd gone mad. He'd been planning to call Kelli first thing and spend the day in the studio. How could he afford to give up a Saturday, given his deadline? But the urge was insistent, so he went with it, thinking by the end of the day—as a nice bonus—the divine quiet would bring a flood of musical inspiration.

He didn't get that flood, but he got some hope, if only a little. Focusing on God all that time and diving deep into Scripture reminded him that he didn't need to feel defeated. Nothing was impossible with God, not even the seeming miracle of knitting his and Kelli's hearts back together.

But he sure hadn't expected movement the next morning—sitting with Kelli and her family, making plans to spend the rest of the day at Six Flags. He was almost afraid to get excited, but how could he not? He couldn't wait to go home, get changed, and meet up with her again.

Kelli hadn't ridden a roller coaster in years. It felt like part of her was reawakening, the carefree side that enjoyed life and made the most of it. She couldn't remember when she'd laughed this hard.

"Heather, seriously, let's ride in the first car this time." They were at the point in line where they had to choose a lane.

"Uh-uh. Girl, I told you... I love roller coasters, but something about the very front makes me nervous. I feel like I'll fall out."

"I'll sit in front with you."

Kelli looked at Brian. They'd been at the park two hours, and thus far the pairing on the rides had been Kelli and Heather, Brian and Logan. Heather had even told Kelli she was glad they came, so it wouldn't seem too much like a "couple thing" between her and Logan.

But Kelli had to sit in front at least once. "Let's do it."

The roller coaster lurched upward with Kelli and Brian in the lead car, pumping their fists and yelling.

Heather and Logan were right behind.

"Truth be told," Heather yelled, "I'm not crazy about the second car either. I like the comfortable middle."

Kelli turned around, smiling. "You'll love the thrill. And don't close your eyes."

At the very top, Kelli and Brian stuck their hands in the air. Kelli laughed when she glanced behind to see that Logan was doing the same, but Heather was holding the bar, eyes shut tight.

Kelli screamed at the top of her lungs when they tipped downward. She and Brian bumped into one another as the car jerked this way and that, taking tight curves and zipping down more hills. It sped through the tunnel and screeched to a stop.

They unbuckled their belts and got out. Kelli goaded Heather. "Totally different experience, right? Admit it."

"I did get a rush." She laughed. "I might be up for trying the first car. After a break. Whew. Was that eight times straight?"

They talked as they strolled to another section of the park, Kelli and Brian now side by side, Heather and Logan just behind. She looked back at Heather. "So I want to hear more about the conversation with your brother. Did you talk about getting together soon?"

"We didn't talk long. When I called, they'd just gotten home from church and were on their way to a barbecue or something. He was so shocked to hear from me, he mostly kept saying, 'I can't believe this.'" Heather was smiling. "We caught up on the past some and said we'd talk again this week. I'm really excited about getting to know him and his family. I've got two nieces and a nephew!"

"It'll be nothing for you to go see them," Logan said. "Normal is only two hours away."

"I love that they're so close," Heather said. "I might pop over there so often I make a pest of myself."

"I doubt that," Kelli said. "Sounds like he was as excited as you were."

"Lemonade!" Logan's shout startled them.

Heather laughed. "Hey, Logan, how would you like some lemonade?"

He wiped his forehead. "I need a bucket. The sun ain't playing today."

The four got in line at the fresh lemonade stand, continuing the banter, when Kelli's phone rang. She glanced at it...and let it go to voice mail.

When it rang again, she remembered she'd told

Miles she'd be available to listen to a draft proposal he'd written for work—but that was yesterday, before the Six Flags opportunity. She faced away from the others and answered. "Miles, hi."

"I'm glad I tried you again. I'd really like your input on this—where are you? Do I hear screaming?"

"I'm, uh, actually at an amusement park. It was just a spur-of-the-moment thing with some friends from church." Kelli moved up with the rest in line, keeping a slight distance.

"An amusement park? So…you're with your girl-friends?"

"Just a group of friends, no big deal." Kelli tried to keep her voice light.

"Sounds fun." He paused. "Wish I could be there with you."

"Yeah. Me too."

"I've been thinking more about that lately, that we need to plan a visit. I think it would be nice to come to St. Louis and see your favorite spots, since I've never been."

"Definitely. Let's plan that." Suddenly, the thought of Miles in St. Louis seemed a little more complicated. Couldn't happen while she and Brian were working on the album, that was for sure.

"I'll let you go," Miles said. "Call me later?"

"Absolutely."

Brian handed her a tall plastic cup of lemonade.

"You didn't have to get that for me. Thank you."

They moved out of line, waiting for Logan and Heather.

"Why didn't you tell me?" he asked.

"Tell you what?" She inserted her straw.

"You have a boyfriend, Kel?"

Her stomach dipped. "Brian, it's really kind of private."

"Private? You can't even tell me yes or no?"

Heather and Logan walked up, but when they saw Kelli's and Brian's faces, kept moving and stopped at a baseball hat kiosk.

Kelli nodded. "Yes, I have a boyfriend."

"So, I say again, why didn't you tell me?"

"There was no need to tell you, Brian. It's none of your business." Kelli felt like she had a split personality, part of her defensive about his questioning her, the other part wishing he hadn't found out.

Brian looked away, wearing that look Kelli knew like the back of her hand. His feelings were hurt.

"You're right." He still wouldn't look at her. "It's none of my business."

Kelli sighed. "I wasn't trying to be mean. I was just—"

He held up his hand. "My fault, Kelli, I shouldn't have asked." He yelled over to Heather and Logan. "Y'all ready?"

The pairings shifted again, Kelli and Heather, Brian and Logan.

Logan had the map out, trying to find the quickest route to the newer wooden roller coaster, when a couple with three children came toward them. They slowed, whispering, and Kelli saw Heather turn slightly away from them.

The woman approached. "Logan? What a surprise to see you here."

"Oh, hey, Sue"—Logan nodded to her husband—"Herb. You guys having fun with the kids?"

"Having a great time. But...can we talk to you a minute?"

"Sure." Logan followed them a few feet.

The couple's faces registered concern, and the more they talked, the more bothered Logan appeared.

"What do you think's going on?" Kelli asked. "Do you know them?"

Heather sighed. "They're in the choir. They're talking about me."

Kelli frowned. "Why?"

Heather gave her a look.

Moments later the family continued on, and Logan returned, staring after them.

"You all right?" Brian asked.

Logan gave a quick shake of his head. "I don't get people. We say we're followers of Christ. We say we believe in forgiveness and redemption. And yet..."

"They said you shouldn't be here with me, didn't they?"

"Let's just say they questioned my judgment. But please don't let it upset you. We're having way too much fun."

"I'm not upset. I'm in too good a mood after talking to Ian and spending time with y'all. And anyway, they think I'm the old Heather, but I know who I am."

"There you go." Kelli high-fived her. "You're not the same. Remember the twins."

Logan arched an eyebrow. "Twins?"

Heather nodded. "Cyd likes to say, 'Nothing like those twins Grace and Mercy.'"

"I like that," Logan said.

Brian sounded a quiet, "Amen."

They began walking slowly again, three of them. Kelli remained in place, listening.

"Girl," Heather said, turning, "I started talking, thinking you were beside me."

Kelli heard her, but she had to get this. Head angled to the side, bobbing, she focused a few seconds more. She looked up finally, into inquisitive faces. "Let me try a melody out on you guys. I only have the first couple lines, but here goes…" She paused to get it again. "His grace and mercy have covered you; you're not the same…"

"Mm, I like that," Heather said. "Sing it again. I want to try something."

Kellie did. "His grace and mercy have covered you; you're not the same…"

Heather added, "No longer bound by what you used to do."

Kelli grinned. "That's why He came."

"So you could make a change, completely new."

Kelli high-fived her again. "And in His name…"

"You are a conqueror, beloved too."

Logan looked incredulous. "Did you two just stand here and put together a chorus on the fly? And you sounded beautiful together."

Kelli looked at Brian, unsure because of the tension between them. "Might be another love letter."

Brian's gaze was contemplative, somewhat distant, but he nodded. "I agree with Logan. It was beautiful. I'm hearing both of you on the chorus too."

Kelli's face lit up. "Brian, really? That would be so perfect, Heather and I singing about God's grace and mercy." She turned to Heather, hands clasped. "You have to do it. No way could those words have come to you like that if you weren't meant to sing them."

Heather stared downward. "I've never felt the presence of God like that, like...He was really doing it." She paused again. "Brian, if you want us both to be on the chorus, I'd be honored." She looked at Kelli, tears cresting. "I agree. It would be so perfect."

Chapter Twenty-Four

Kelli woke up Tuesday morning excited about her new job, but now that she'd been at it for two hours, she was even more enthused. She'd spent the first part of the morning settling into her cubicle, touring the three buildings on the church's property, and familiarizing herself with the various ministries, including their printed brochures and web presence. She had no idea Living Word had so much going on—Bible studies and accompanying DVDs on almost every book of the Bible that shipped to people around the world, tons of active outreaches in the community in addition to ministries within the church, not to mention a music ministry that was gaining more and more outside recognition. All of this meant that the internal and external communications connected with these efforts—web, publications, media, and video—needed to be consistent with Living Word's vision and commitment to biblical integrity.

Now she was digging into her first project, thrilled that it was the newest ministry being birthed at Living Word. She'd been reading through the stories that had come in since Sunday's announcement, amazed at not only the sheer volume, but at the transparency of the men. She flagged particularly poignant ones or those that showcased different walks of life.

The one in front of her was especially moving, a young man who'd started dealing drugs at fourteen after his father died and his mother was herself strung out on drugs. Reminded her somewhat of Brian, whose mother also struggled with addiction. If it weren't for Grandma Howard, who knows? He might've ended up like this guy, living a life of robbing and stealing and violent assault. Someone eventually told this man about Jesus, and he was forever changed. At twenty-nine he now worked in the inner city, sharing the Gospel with guys who were like him. That was definitely one to feature on the website, if not the video.

Kelli sat back a moment, thinking about that video. Doug told her this morning she had a green light to script it. She wondered if a portion should be an interview format, maybe of Cedric, since Scott didn't want to tell his story that way. She could write a list of questions for him to answer on camera, which would then be edited for seamless effect. But she knew she wanted a dramatization as well, and as she read through these stories, she was looking for one to feature. So many possibilities. So much potential impact.

A shadow fell across her desk, and she looked up. "Brian? What are you doing here?"

He got a chair from another seating area and placed it in the cubicle. "I'm here every Tuesday, meeting with the pastor."

"I didn't know that."

His gaze was solemn. "Got a minute?"

Kelli nodded. "I do."

He leaned over, elbows on his thighs. "I talked to Dr. Lyles about something and thought I'd run it by you too, since it involves you."

Kelli turned more toward him.

"The love letter to our baby..." He looked down a moment. "I'd come to the conclusion that I would release the album, the song would be on there, and people could piece together on their own that it's about our love for a baby. But I wouldn't directly address it, and they'd never really know the story." He paused again. "But I feel like God is moving me to do more with the song...to make it the first release on the album and tell the story behind it in some form or fashion."

Kelli took a breath, eyes widening. "I don't even know what to say."

"Yeah, that was my first thought. If I have to be honest, I know what I'm struggling with. I'm not the Christian rapper who came out of a really hard street life. I'm the one with the 'good boy' image. What'll happen if people see this other side of me?" He sighed. "I thought about how people treat Heather, knowing her past. I might lose a lot of support."

"What did Pastor Lyles say?"

"Same thing I knew in my heart but needed to hear—that I can't operate out of fear. I have to do what I feel God's leading me to do. But he said something else—that he thought God would use this in ways I couldn't imagine."

Kelli's heart was beating fast, trying to catch up with what Brian was saying and what it might mean. "So...how much would you tell? About the baby only?

About us?" Her mind flashed to Miles. He didn't know about her past.

"That's why I wanted to talk to you. I wanted to get your thoughts on it, but I also wanted your help. You're the communications person. I wondered if you'd work with me on how to frame the story and through what format."

"Don't you have a management team and PR people to guide you with stuff like this?"

Brian shook his head. "I let my manager go. I have a booking agent and a road manager, and the label does some marketing stuff but a professional publicity team? No. Nothing like that."

"But I'm not a professional either, Brian. I'm just getting started. You need someone with experience to help you with something like this."

"But the story involves you, too, and even though you wouldn't be named publicly, I trust how you'd handle it."

"Won't people guess I'm involved, since I'm singing on the song?"

"Not at all. You'll be on every song. They'll just think you're on the album because I love your voice"— he smiled for the first time since he arrived—"which I do."

Kelli sighed and stared vaguely at the stack of stories on her desk. Stories about choices, some of which caused a great deal of pain, yet God somehow brought beauty from the ash heap. She tapped her pen on the desk as a realization beckoned. This really wasn't about Brian or her. It was about God using them to convey a message. And wasn't that the business she was in?

"Okay," she said.

"Okay what?"

"I think you should do it, and I'll help you—though I have no idea what to do."

"Thanks, Kel. I already feel a lot better about it." He got up. "You're coming this afternoon?"

"I'll be there. Looking forward to working some more on background vocals for the song with Heather and me." They'd started it last evening.

"The part you already did blew me away. I got kind of misty listening."

"So did I, when I heard it back. Made me think of all God's done in just the last month." She held Brian's gaze. "I'm seeing God in a whole new way by working on this album. Thank you, Brian."

"I'm along for the ride, just like you." He got up, lifting the chair. "And we've got awhile to go yet."

Kelli watched him leave, his last words lingering.

Chapter Twenty-Five

Heather couldn't remember a more stressful Thursday. The very first patient showed up several minutes late, throwing off every other appointment, which caused one woman to curse at Heather because she couldn't get in and out quickly enough. One of the hygienists didn't show up at all—citing a babysitting problem, which by now had been such a recurring problem that said babysitter should've been replaced. That threw the office in a tizzy as they sought a temp. Heather had to get impressions for braces, which meant slathering a bunch of goo in the mouth of the patient, but before the goo dried, it ended up back on Heather's lap along with the patient's lunch. And Dr. Henry stepped up his subtle flirtations, standing inches from her face, telling her he preferred the tighter scrub tops she used to wear to work.

She'd never been happier to leave, though even that was a challenge. Her workday was scheduled to end at five. It was now six fifteen. A sigh of frustration, fatigue, and longing escaped as she waited for the elevator—longing because every hour of the day, all she could think was she didn't want to be there. And it wasn't because of the stress at work. It was because of the work she'd done in the studio.

She was singing again, and the experience was like nothing she'd ever known. She'd been in the choir; she'd sung praise songs. But this time it was more than a vocal exercise. It was as if God had kissed her voice, renewed it, coupled her heart and soul with it. She felt close to God as she sang. And when she finished her part last night, the feeling was incredible.

Then she had to wake up and come to this.

The elevator door opened, and Heather rode down to the first floor, her heart heavy as she made her way to the parking garage. She'd said she could do this job the rest of her life if that's what God wanted, and that could very well be the case. What happened this week—singing on a Christian rapper's album—would not be a regular occurrence. Nor would it pay the bills. She could appreciate the experience, but dwelling there was counterproductive. She might never be able to work full-time in music, and that needed to be okay. But it did beg the question, couldn't she have a regular job *and* sing?

She got in her car and started the engine. She'd been shooting up prayers about a church home in the midst of the day's stress. She felt kind of guilty, though. Part of her reason for wanting to find a church home was to sing in a choir. But at least this time, she wasn't looking to sing to get noticed. She just wanted to use the voice God had given her to praise Him.

It'd be nice if God would pick her up and transport her to the exact church she should attend. Just stand her right in front of the building. She'd gone online to check out churches, but when she listened to the sermons, they didn't connect like Pastor Lyles's did, which saddened her. All the time she'd been there, she hadn't appreciated his teaching. But these last two weeks that Kelli had brought her a CD of the sermons, she'd eaten it up. Deep down, she wanted to go back to Living Word. But she couldn't sing in that choir again, not after what happened. And what if she ran into Dana on any given Sunday? She knew the mere sight of her was painful for Dana. She just couldn't do that.

Heather sat in her parking spot. She needed a pep talk to raise her out of this funk, let her know it would be all right. God would lead her to a great church. He would help her to be content with her job once again. And He could even give her another opportunity to sing. Somehow, hearing someone else say it—like Logan or Cyd—made all the difference.

She got out her phone. Logan was at church preparing for choir rehearsal, so she couldn't call him. Scrolling to find Cyd, she smiled when she passed the name *Ian Engel*. One day, she hoped, she and her brother would be close enough for her to call and share her heart. She didn't think it would take long either. He'd called her twice this week to chat, and they were determined to find a weekend soon to visit.

She called Cyd's number but was disappointed when voice mail clicked on. *Oh well.* Heather would probably be fine once she got home and rested from the day. But then again, Cyd only lived five minutes away. She'd told Heather not to hesitate to get in touch if she needed to talk. Maybe she'd pop over and see if she had a quick minute to pray with her.

When Heather got to the house, she saw Cyd's car in

the driveway, Kelli's behind it, and a couple of others in front. Did they have company? But people parked wherever they could around here, so it didn't mean much. Heather pulled in front of the house next door, walked up, and rang the bell.

Her heart froze when the door opened. Dana.

"Um, I'm sorry... I shouldn't have..." Heather turned, wanting the sidewalk to open up and swallow her. She couldn't get to her car fast enough.

"Heather."

Her feet stopped, heart hammering. Did Dana just say her name?

"Did you need to see Cyd?"

Tears spilled from her eyes. Was it the weight of the entire day? Or just this moment? She turned back around in her scrubs. "I did, but it's okay." She barely looked at her.

Dana paused. "Wait."

She closed the screen door and disappeared. Seconds later, Cyd came out.

"Heather, I didn't know you were coming."

She couldn't stop crying. "I'm sorry, Cyd. No one answered when I called, and I should've just gone home."

"It's okay, sweetie." Cyd took her into her arms. "Really. It's okay."

"No, it isn't." Heather wet Cyd's chest. "I know Dana hates seeing me, and I don't blame her. I didn't mean to cause trouble between you two again."

"Sweetie, shh." Cyd stroked her hair. "Listen. God answered your prayer."

Heather took a step back so she could see Cyd's face.

"He touched Dana's heart. She was able to accept us working together, and she forgives you."

Heather couldn't process what Cyd was saying, but her emotions could. Fresh tears wet her face. "But... why? Why would she forgive me?"

"Bottom line? Because God has forgiven her."

Heather shook her head. "It can't be that simple."

"Actually, it kind of is."

Heather stared at her, overwhelmed.

"So, what made you stop by? What's on your mind?"

Heather blinked, trying to rewind ten minutes. "Oh, we can just talk about it next time I see you. I know you're busy."

"Oh!"

Heather made a face. "What?"

"I want to tell you my news." Cyd took a breath, eyes sparkling. "I'm pregnant. That's why people are here, having a celebration get-together for Cedric and me."

"Oh, Cyd! You'll make the best mom ever. I'm so happy for you!"

She grinned. "Thanks. I'm pretty excited myself. But"—the grin was fading—"I wish I could invite you—"

Heather waved away the thought. "It's no problem."

"See you Saturday?"

"You know it. Tell Kelli to call me later tonight if she gets a chance."

"Will do."

Heather drove onto the grounds of Living Word past nine o'clock that night with an eerie feeling. She hadn't been here in ten months. Under the glare of the lampposts, she saw less than a handful of cars in the vast church complex—just as she'd hoped. Choir rehearsal had ended, and everyone was gone. Well. Most everyone. She drove to the lot nearest the main building and spotted the old forest-green Jeep Cherokee. She parked beside it.

Heather hoped the main doors hadn't been locked yet from the outside. The first two she tried wouldn't budge, but the one on the far right let her into the entryway. She rounded the bend to the sanctuary and slowed as she approached a set of double doors propped open.

She could hear the piano playing softly now, and she lingered a moment just inside, watching. Then she made her way down a side aisle, out of Logan's direct sight. He stopped playing and noted something on a sheet—then turned suddenly and saw her.

"Heather…hey. Surprised to see you here." He got up and walked to the edge of the platform. "You haven't been home yet from work?"

She looked down at her apparel. "No. Stopped by Cyd's, then walked the mall, got something to eat."

Logan came down the steps. "And decided to come to Living Word? How did that happen?"

Heather sat in the first pew. "Kelli told me about the new songs the choir's been singing. Made me sad that I don't get to hear them anymore…or sing them. The thought hit me that I could come after choir rehearsal and you could play them for me. That is, if you're not too busy."

He shrugged. "Sure, I can play them if you like. But only if you sing. You were one of my favorite solo voices, you know."

"You never told me that."

"Not something I'd tell you while you were in the choir. But your voice has such depth, a lot of soul."

"Logan, that means a lot coming from you. Thank you."

He motioned her forward. "To the piano we go."

Heather sat next to him at the baby grand and listened as he played the first song, lending his own melodic voice.

When he'd finished the last chords, she stared at him. "That was crazy. You have such a gift for writing worship songs. I loved that."

He simply smiled and began playing it again. "Ready?"

She looked at the music sheet on the stand to get the first words. "Ready."

Their voices blended together, Heather's stumbling at first to find the rhythm, then continuing strong. She had that soaring feeling again, like she was in the zone. At the end, Logan looked at her strangely.

"What?"

"I had no idea the song could sound that good. You're pretty amazing."

She shirked the compliment. "Oh, Logan."

He played the next song and, as before, she joined him on the second go-round, moved by the worship it engendered.

"You're the one who's pretty amazing. I'm glad I stopped by to hear these."

"Me too."

Their gaze lingered, then they looked away.

Heather rose from the bench. "I'd better be going. Need my rest so I can be up early and raring to go for another awesome day at the dental office...she said with fake enthusiasm." Her face turned sheepish. "Sorry. I said I wasn't going to complain about the job."

"Whenever you want to release some steam by hanging out after choir rehearsal and singing your heart out, feel free."

"Careful. I might take you up on that."

With one hand he fingered a few chords. Then he paused and looked up at her. "That's what I was hoping."

Heather smiled, backing away. Then she turned and walked the few steps down the platform and up the aisle, trying to ignore the weird sensation inside. Sure felt like her heart did a skitter. But it wasn't the old "wow, he's handsome" skitter. It seemed to be coming from someplace deeper.

Chapter Twenty-Six

It was Friday, and Brian was starting to panic. So far only three songs had been recorded, and the album was due to the label end of next week. He was thankful he finally knew where he was going with it, but for the last album, he'd recorded ten songs more than needed—way in advance—so people he trusted could listen and tell him which were best to include. Now he was stressing over whether they'd have time to write and record the bare minimum, each of which needed to be good. And added to *that* stress was the fact that he was about to expose his past, which could bring a ton of controversy.

He stared vaguely at the computer screen in the studio. At least his label was on board with what he was doing. It considered itself a ministry with a mission to present the Gospel and a biblical worldview through music. The label owner told Brian, "We've never shied away from letting our artists tell the raw truth about their pasts. It makes the light of Christ shine all the brighter."

He just hoped the public would see it that way.

He brought his focus back to the computer, trying to clear his inbox before Kelli arrived from work. *Kelli.* He hated how often she came to mind, even more so when he was trying not to think about her. After that blow at Six Flags, he told himself to forget all hope that the two of them could be together. Of course she had a boyfriend. What an idiot he'd been to assume otherwise.

He leaned forward when new messages downloaded to his mailbox and let out a groan at the first one. His academic advisor. He skimmed the note, zeroing in on the bottom line. *We need to know by end of next week whether you will continue your studies in the fall or terminate your degree at the master's level.*

Brian's head fell on the desk. He was supposed to know his life's future by next week? If the album turned out well, did that mean God wanted him to focus solely on the music? How would he really know?

He lifted his head with a new thought. Maybe it wasn't the either/or it seemed. He could resume studies in the fall because the album wouldn't release until the end of October, when the semester was half over. Somehow he'd make it work. He'd work double the extra hours in the lab on the days he could, to compensate for concert dates out of town.

And anyway…who said he needed to do tons of concert dates? People who followed his music knew he was a student. Wouldn't they understand he couldn't be on the road much? But his label definitely wouldn't understand. After all, this was a business. Albums cost money. They needed him to get out there and promote it. That might even be in his contract.

Vaguely, he moved his mouse to the next message, concerning possible artwork for the CD cover. They needed feedback today. He went to the next—and the doorbell rang.

Brian sighed, knowing it was Kelli. It wasn't that he no longer enjoyed working with her. It was that he loved it too much. He needed someone to tell him how to shut off his heart. He bounded up the stairs and let her in.

She looked cute as usual in simple white capri pants, her hair gathered in a side ponytail. "Hey," she said.

"Hi, Kelli." He stepped aside as she walked in. "You can go on downstairs. I need to run up and get some notes I had for a song idea, though I confess I'm not jazzed about it."

Brian went to his bedroom, grabbed the notes from his nightstand, and went down to the studio. When he sat in his chair, he saw what he'd left showing on his computer screen—a picture of him and Monica with their arms around one another at last Friday's festival. One of the teen girls had sent the e-mail through his website.

Kelli had her head in her notepad, but he was sure she saw it. Whatever. Didn't matter anyway.

He switched screens on the computer and turned toward her. "I'm really hoping some ideas came to you, 'cause I've been stressing the last couple of days."

She sat back, crossing her legs. "I have two to run by you."

"Excellent. Shoot."

"First one comes from this project I'm working on at church. I've been so impacted by the stories. I think we should do a love letter to young men."

Brian nodded. "Importance of choices, not just living in the now."

"Exactly. Responsibility. Taking the right path. A decision today can affect your life for years to come, not to mention the lives of others."

"Okay. What's the other?"

"The parallel, a love letter to young women. Choices are huge there too. The song would let them know it's okay to be different, to hold on to virtue and modesty, to save sex for marriage. Also encourage them to look closely at the kind of men they're dating."

Brian laughed, but without amusement. "Why do I feel like both these ideas are aimed at slamming me?"

"What?" Kelli frowned. "That's not the aim at all."

"If you're a young man, don't make the choices Brian made, taking your girlfriend to bed, leaving her when she gets pregnant. And if you're a young woman, avoid a guy like Brian at all costs. Absolutely. Let's put that on the album."

Kelli looked confused. "Why are you even going there? We both made choices we regret, but we can take the lessons learned and pass them on."

"So you wish you'd never dated me?" There it was, his heart on his sleeve. He was fighting with everything he had to keep his emotions in check.

Kelli locked eyes with him. Her silence was killing him.

"I'd never say that, Brian."

"No, say what you feel. I'm a big boy. I can take it."

"You were my best friend, a huge part of my life."

"But you wish we had left it at that, right? You wish we never ventured over into dating?"

Kelli shifted in her seat. "It's crossed my mind. If

we hadn't started dating, things wouldn't have gone where they did. We would've saved ourselves a lot of heartache."

He nodded, moving his swivel chair back toward the computer. This was great. He was supposed to somehow get past this and work? Knowing that the woman he loved not only didn't want a future with him but wished they'd never been involved in the past?

Did I just admit in my heart that I still love Kelli?

He ran his hand across his neck. He needed to remove himself and their experiences from the equation. These were good song ideas. He blew out a huge sigh and forced himself to move on. "Okay, any ideas for a hook for these?"

Kelli was staring at her phone. "Excuse me a sec. I need to reply to this."

She got up and walked across the room, facing away from him. "Hi, got your text. You'll be here *tonight*?"

Kelli was talking low, but Brian could hear. So what if he was straining.

"What time?… How long are you staying?… Sunday morning? Miles, why are you springing this on me? I thought we would plan the visit together."

Huh. Miles.

"I'm just saying, I have things to do…"

Brian's head was pounding.

"I understand… I know. You're right… I'll make it work somehow… See you."

Kelli sat back down, then seemed to remember him and looked up. "You asked about the hook?"

"We're not ignoring the elephant in the room, Kelli. Your boyfriend's coming, and you won't be able to work tomorrow or even late today. Right?"

"Wrong. I mean, he's coming, yes. And I might not be able to work late tonight. But I made a commitment to work on this album with you, and that's what I'm going to do. I'll be here tomorrow."

"Does he know you're working on this project?"

She cut her eyes over at him. "You're in my business again, Brian."

So apparently the answer was no.

"Should be an interesting weekend, huh?"

Kelli waited inside the terminal near baggage claim, growing more excited by the minute to see Miles. Most of the afternoon she'd had an attitude with him. Booking a ticket without consulting her? Having to stop work when they'd hit a nice groove?

But once she'd gotten away from the studio, her mind shifted to the reality that he was actually coming. They'd be able to spend some time together. She'd been so busy with Brian, so taken with creating music once again, that her relationship with Miles had admittedly suffered neglect. But her heart fluttered on the drive to the airport—he really did mean a lot to her.

She saw a new wave of passengers descending the escalator and spied Miles among them, overnight bag on his shoulder, handsome in dark blue denim and a polo top. When he saw her, a smile spread on his face, and he opened wide for a hug.

"I can't believe I'm here," he said, arms tight around her. "It's so good to see you."

"I can't believe you're here either." She inhaled his nearness, the feel of her head against his chest, then leaned back, narrowing her eyes at him. "Especially since it was so last minute."

"Still mad at me?"

"I wasn't *mad*." She glanced at baggage claim. "Did you check anything?"

"Nah, I'm good."

She led him out, and he took her hand.

"You can charge and convict me if you want," he said. "I'm guilty. When I saw an opportunity to come see you, I grabbed it." He paused as the automatic doors opened, a little-boy pout on his face. "Aren't you a little glad to see me?"

Kelli smiled. "I'm a lot glad to see you." She shooed the comparisons flitting about in her head—a hair taller than Brian but not as built, every bit as handsome... not that it mattered.

They continued to the parking garage. "It's just that we could've had more time if we'd planned a weekend next month."

"You alluded to that earlier," he said. "What do you have going on this weekend?"

"Oh, we'll talk about it later." She fished her keys out of her purse. "I'm excited you finally get to meet my family. They're at the restaurant now, getting a table."

"What did you tell them about me? That I'm head over heels crazy about you?"

"Ha. Yeah and that you'd be popping the question tonight."

He pulled her to a stop just short of the car. "I'm not joking, Kelli. Do you think I'd drop everything to visit just anybody? Don't you know how much you mean to me?"

She stared into his eyes. "I might have an inkling."

Her heart fluttered again. Maybe this impromptu visit was exactly what they needed.

* * *

Kelli and Miles walked hand in hand down the sidewalk toward one of her favorite pizza places in the Central West End. Every restaurant they passed looked lively, filled with people indoors and out.

"This area has a nice vibe," Miles said. "And the weather tonight is perfect."

They approached the outdoor hostess stand, and Kelli spotted her family waving them over. "There they are," she said.

Everyone at the table rose, and Kelli took Miles around, introducing him to each.

"Nice to meet you all, finally," he said. "Kelli has always had great things to say about her brothers."

Cedric smiled. "Nice to meet you too. And welcome to St. Louis. Kelli says it's your first time."

"Believe it or not," Miles said. "I'm looking forward to Kelli showing me the sights tomorrow."

Kelli hid her reaction. *Didn't I say we'd talk about it?*

As they all took their seats, Miles excused himself to find the restroom.

Kelli knew it was coming—the grilling.

"He thinks you're sightseeing tomorrow?" Stephanie asked. "You haven't told him you're working on this album, have you…with your old flame?" She put her elbow on her chair and sat back. "Might be some fireworks this weekend. I'm…just…sayin'."

"It won't be a big deal. He knows Brian's a thing of the past."

"Mm-hmm," Lindell said. "I'm not sure *I* know that, based on the two of you at church Sunday."

"And don't forget Six Flags," Cedric said.

Kelli ignored them.

"So what's up with dude hopping a plane to St. Louis last minute?" Cedric asked. "You really just found out he was coming this afternoon?"

Kelli nodded. "We've been talking about getting together. He said he realized this morning he didn't have anything on his calendar past noon, so he checked getaway fares on Southwest and decided to come. But…" She lifted the water glass at her place setting. "I think it was spurred by the fact that he called while I was at Six Flags. Even asked who I was with." She took a sip.

"Oh, really?" Stephanie cocked her head. "Did you name Brian?"

"I said a group of friends."

Cedric chuckled. "Dude's antenna went up. He's checking up on you."

"And staking a claim, I'd say," Lindell said.

Cyd laughed. "You guys, cut it out. You've barely met the guy, and you think you've got him figured out."

"So what's the deal, Kel?" Cedric asked, looking to make sure Miles wasn't near. "I know you've been with the guy awhile, but how special is he?"

"Very."

"Really?"

"Yes, really. Brian's not the only person who'll ever be special in my life."

Cedric looked incredulously at the others. "Did I say anything about Brian?"

"You implied it. Just give Miles a chance."

Cedric lifted his hands, grinning. "Absolutely!" He leaned in closer. "He's living right, though…right? 'Cause dude ain't staying at the house otherwise. Cyd told me y'all talked about him taking the sleep sofa."

"He didn't mention booking a hotel, so I figure he needs a place to stay. And it'll be fine. He knows the boundaries I've put up, and he's always respected—"

Stephanie gave her a look, and Kelli clammed up.

Miles took the empty chair next to Kelli and pulled up to the table. Seeing their party complete, the server stopped to take their order. Miles bowed to the recommendations of the others as to which pizzas were good.

Cyd smiled at him when the server had gone. "So you grew up in Dallas, Miles?"

"Yes, in Plano. My parents both work for Texas Instruments, and I've followed in their footsteps, I guess."

"Sounds great," Cedric said. "What do you do for them?"

"Information systems. Your job sounds great too," he added. "VP of an executive search firm? Hopefully I'll move high enough up the ranks in corporate America to use your services one day."

Cedric sipped his Coke. "I have no doubt."

Miles turned to Kelli. "So you finished your first week on the job. Haven't had a chance to ask how it went."

"Real well. I love the project I'm working on, which happens to be for a ministry Cedric had a hand in starting."

"And what's the plan? You'll keep looking for a real PR position while you're doing that?"

Kelli's brow wrinkled. "This *is* a real position, in communications."

"Well, I mean it's part-time, and it's at a church… I'm assuming you still want a position at a boutique PR firm or corporation to start your career."

"Actually, Miles," Cedric said, "just so you know,

Living Word is a church of thousands. Its ministries reach around the globe. The experience Kelli's gaining there is a fabulous start to her career."

"Sounds like a mini-corporation," Miles said. "I didn't realize it was that big."

Even if it weren't... Kelli chewed a piece of ice, slightly irked. She'd seen glimpses of this, Miles measuring a person's worth based on his or her career, but he'd never done it to her. Maybe he just wanted the best for her, what he perceived to be the best anyway.

"Soooo, Miles," Stephanie said, "what do you like to do in your spare time?"

"I'm an admitted workaholic, but when I can, I love to golf."

Lindell leaned forward. "Seriously? I took it up last year. If you're up for it, we can hit the links tomorrow while Kelli's in the studi—*ow*!" He looked at Stephanie, who pretended she didn't have a clue why.

Everyone but Miles was suddenly thirsty.

He looked at her. "That's what you have to do tomorrow? Something in a studio? Is it job related?"

She set her glass down. "It's…another project I'm working on. But I'll definitely explain it all…later." She smiled at him. "Promise."

Kelli and Cyd stood on either side of the sleep sofa mattress, tucking their ends of the blanket. Cyd placed a pillow at the head of the bed.

"I've got another blanket if you need it," Cyd said. "Even when we adjust the A/C, it seems to stay cold in here—Reese, get down." Cyd nudged her off the mattress. "Oh, and I put towels in that chair for you."

"Everything is perfect," Miles said. "You've gone

above and beyond with the hospitality"—he cast a playful glance at Kelli—"especially given this was last minute. Thank you."

"No problem at all," Cyd said. "And you're welcome."

Cedric spoke up. "There's a caveat to all this, though."

Kelli shot a *don't-embarrass-me* look at her brother.

Cedric tipped his head toward the family room doorway. "Those stairs that lead to Kelli's bedroom? They creak. Loudly."

Cyd pushed him toward those stairs. "Come on, Mr. London." She smiled over her shoulder. "Good night, you two."

Kelli heard him mumble, "Just kidding," as they went out the door.

After they'd gone upstairs, she sat on the love seat and took a breath. "So, I said we'd talk later about tomorrow."

Miles joined her. "I was starting to think it was a big mystery. What's the deal with you and the studio?"

"I'm working on an album project, collaborating on some songs."

His surprise showed in his hesitation. "Collaborating how? Like…writing?"

"Writing and also singing."

"When did you get interested in music? I've never heard you talk about writing songs. For that matter, I've never heard you sing."

She almost felt guilty. She never intended to lock away the deep things of her heart from Miles. She was simply avoiding them altogether. "I actually started writing songs in high school. Sang in the church choir too. But in college I put music aside." She shrugged, hoping that would make it no big deal.

He looked intently at her, clearly pondering. "And in the short time you've been back in St. Louis, you've suddenly jumped into an album project? That's huge. How did it happen? And why am I just now hearing about it?"

She sighed inside. Such fat open-ended questions that made it next to impossible to avoid the word *Brian*. "Well...a little hard to explain... The opportunity came about because of Brian. He's the one I'm working with."

"I *knew* you were spending time with him, your... high-school sweetheart."

"I never called him that."

"That's what he was, wasn't he?"

"We were friends—"

"Who dated."

"Eons ago. Now we're just working together on a limited basis."

"I must be missing something." He stroked his chin. "How are you two working on an album? Is he a producer? A singer?"

"He's a Christian rapper."

"A *rapper*? You can't be serious."

Kelli wasn't sure what he meant by that, but she didn't like it. Now that she'd been working with Brian, she saw firsthand the depth of ministry he poured into it. Was Miles minimizing that?

"*Christian* rapper. The lyrics are all about the Gospel, our relationship with Jesus, how to live out the Word of God."

"Okay, whatever..."

Whatever?

"So you're helping him write his raps or what? Are you rapping too?"

"I'm writing the chorus part of the songs—the 'hook'—and singing it as well."

"Sounds like you two are Sonny and Cher."

"Miles, I know you may not get what we're doing, and I do apologize for not telling you sooner, but this has become an important work to me." She hadn't realized how important until the words came out of her mouth. "We're under a deadline and need to work tomorrow."

He retreated into his thoughts. Then, "Why do I feel I'm being played for a fool? You've been working with your old boyfriend all this time but haven't told me. And I'll bet you've been doing more than work. You were at Six Flags together, weren't you?"

"He was among the group of friends, yes."

"You're falling for him again."

"No, I'm not. I didn't tell you because I knew you'd think there was more to it than there is."

Miles stared at her. "I hope you're being straight with me, Kelli. Because if you want to be with Brian, just tell me and I'll back away."

Kelli held his gaze. "I don't want to be with Brian, Miles. I'm here with you. I'm right where I want to be."

Chapter Twenty-Seven

Brian was surprised by how well things were progressing. With Romeo in town, he was sure Kelli would be distracted and want to cut short the session. Instead they started early and had been on a roll, so much so that Kelli had called Cyd and Heather to ask if they could delay the start of Bible study by an hour.

They'd finished the love letters to young men and women and were well on their way with another—one to "the least of these," people devastated by natural disasters. This one was Brian's idea. He'd been rocked by images of Haiti after the earthquake hit, but school obligations had made it hard to respond in a tangible way.

He paused his work on the song to look over at Kelli, who was piecing together a melody at her keyboard—a welcome addition to the studio. She'd decided to keep it, with strong encouragement from her family and Brian. He loved watching her in her element—totally engrossed, creating. Today she reminded him of the high-school Kelli, hair clipped in the back of her head, pieces falling down, face free of makeup, wearing a plain shirt, walking shorts, and flip-flops. She was beautiful.

Kelli paused her playing. "Forgot to tell you," she said. "i'm thinking through an idea for the love letter to our baby."

His heart skipped. That song was such a part of him. "What are you thinking?"

"Your album releases about the same time the Choices ministry kicks off, and we're looking to feature a story for the Choices video. In my mind's eye, I can see you telling your story, with lighting that coincides with the mood. For example, your face would be partially hidden in shadow as you share the choices you made." She used her hands to illustrate. "The scene would switch throughout from you to actors who dramatize what you're sharing, but we'd still hear your voice. Near the end, as you share what God did in your heart and the mercy you found, the light will get brighter and 'I Will Love You' will play. I see a burst of blue sky, the redemptive nature of the story shining."

Brian could see it too as Kelli spoke. The thought of telling his story still brought some trepidation, but what she described stirred his heart. "So you're thinking we'd film the video and use it for the Choices ministry?"

"Right. We can put it on the ministry's website and also on your website, YouTube, and elsewhere. I'll talk to Doug to make sure there wouldn't be a problem."

Brian chewed his lip, nodding. "I like the Choices framework. I'd start the story at the innocence of our friendship, then the choice to go down an intimate path." He looked away for a moment, then at her again. "You were right, Kelli. We should've stayed best friends, nothing more. Then I wouldn't have had an opportunity to hurt you like I did."

Kelli only stared at him, their eyes conveying the history in their souls.

"And then," he continued, "we'd take it through to that final choice I made to walk away from you and our baby." He closed his eyes. Every time he thought he'd felt the last of that pain, it came roaring back again.

Kelli got up and walked over to him. "That wasn't the final choice, Brian. That's not where the video will end. The final choice was turning back to God."

He looked up at her, flicking a tear from his eye. His head fell again.

"I haven't said this yet, Brian, but I forgive you. I do. I forgive you."

A dam broke in his soul and rivers gushed forth, of mercy and even joy. If he and Kelli never had anything more, her forgiveness was a treasure he could hold on to. He stood, and she allowed him to hold her as he wept into her hair. "I'm sorry, Kel. I'm so sorry."

"Brian, I know. You don't have to keep saying it. I forgive you."

"I just wish I had treated you like you deserved to be treated, of supreme value. You know? I wish I had cherished you."

The word traveled from his mouth to the depths of his heart to a loading zone in his brain as he tried to grasp it—*cherished*. He'd said it without thinking. Why was it blazing in his mind now?

"We don't have to keep torturing ourselves about the past, Brian. I'm thankful I finally see that." She backed gently from his embrace and looked at him. "Can we pray together right now that God will use our story, our choices, to affect the choices of many others for the good?"

Brian got on his knees, Kelli with him, and they prayed. And somehow in the midst of their prayers, in the outer reaches of his mind and heart, Brian got a glimpse of that word again—*cherished*—and a plan that was awakening in his heart.

Brian and Logan grabbed a table at Five Guys late Saturday afternoon, waiting for their burgers, settling in for good conversation.

"I'm glad you were free," Brian said. "It was fun hanging out at Six Flags, but I thought it'd be cool to get together one-on-one."

"That was on my mind as well," Logan said. "You beat me to it. Good day in the studio?"

"Awesome day. Mad productive, in more ways than one."

"Can't ask for better than that. I've been praying for you and Kelli as you work on it."

Brian was moved. "Appreciate that, man. That means a lot. I feel like God is answering too."

"I told you, I'm a fan, so these might be selfish prayers. I'm ready to hear some great stuff from you. Comes out in October?"

"Yeah, but if you *really* want to hear it, you can listen before the release—but there's a catch. You'd have to critique it as well. I could use the feedback."

"Seriously? Don't mess with me now." His smile was genuine. "I'm in."

"It'll be good to have your ear." Brian hesitated. "Can I give you something else to pray about?"

"Absolutely."

They looked up as their numbers were called. When they'd gotten their food and sat back down, Brian continued. "The theme of the album is love letters, and the first single is a love letter to our baby."

"Your baby?" Logan leaned in, taking a bite.

"Kelli got pregnant the summer after we graduated from high school, and we, uh…"

Logan nodded. "Got it. I understand."

Brian sighed, hands running down his face. "I've got to get used to talking about this. That's why I need prayer. I'll be doing a video, talking about the choices I made and hopefully steering people to different choices. But it won't be easy."

Logan put his burger down. "Brian, wow, to go public with something like that—"

"Crazy. I know."

Logan shook his head. "That's not what I was about to say. Courageous is what came to mind. So many people have similar stories but never say anything. I've counseled people myself. You bet I'll be praying for you." He lifted his burger. "Things okay with you and Kelli as you work through it?"

"Might be getting to the point where it's becoming okay." Brian stared at the table a second. "To be honest, I wish it could be more, but I don't think I'll get another chance with her after what I did. I walked away from her when she needed me most." He made a face at Logan. "What is it with you, man? I barely know you and I'm unloading my life."

Logan smiled. "I think we get to that point, especially as men. It's hard to find guys you can connect with and be real with, so when you do, it all comes tumbling out." He checked his phone when he heard a notification sound. "Choir member, but it can wait." He looked at Brian. "I hear you. Never know what God might do. Can I add that to the prayer list too?"

"I guess. Her boyfriend's in town this weekend, and I'm the last person she'd want to be with anyway, so... how do you like those odds?"

"I like 'em a lot. Sets the stage for God to do something awesome."

Brian nodded, smiling. "Okay. That's what I needed to hear." He picked up his burger and took a bite.

"Got something I'd like to unload too, if I could."

"Unload away. Hope I can help."

Logan wiped some ketchup from his mouth. "I get approached a lot about pastor of worship positions, and I decided to talk to a church in central Florida. I'm a finalist now, and I've told Pastor Lyles and Chip, our pastor of worship. If they offer me the position, I'm thinking about taking it."

"Really? Why?"

"My mom and dad and most of my mom's family are down there. I came here because it was an opportunity to work with an amazing music ministry—and it's been fabulous—but I don't have family here. Lately I'm kind of sensing a shift within...a longing for relationship as well as ministry at this point in my life."

Brian sipped his drink. "I could be way off base, so feel free to shoot me down, but could this shift have anything to do with Heather? Looks to me like you might be building a relationship with her."

Logan hesitated. "We're still unloading?"

"We're still unloading."

"It very well might have something to do with Heather. I knew her from the choir, but when we reconnected in Indianapolis, it was like God plopped her down in the middle of my life. We connect on a lot of levels."

"Okay... Sounds like there's more..."

Logan sighed. "I don't know. Feels like we're building something, but I'm not sure what." He shrugged. "Maybe just a friendship, which wouldn't be a reason to stay in St. Louis." He thought a moment. "Maybe she was the impetus I needed to show me what was lacking in my life, and my family's really the answer."

"When will you know about the position?"

"Not sure. Month maybe."

"I'll be praying for you, but I've got to admit my own selfishness. I'd hate to see you leave Living Word. I think I'll focus my prayers on something jumping off between you and Heather so you'll have a reason to stay."

Logan laughed. "Kind of funny, isn't it, that Heather and Kelli are together right now? Think they spend any time talking about us?"

"Not if Kelli has anything to do with it."

"Yeah, Heather too. She's been praying *not* to focus her attention on any guys right now."

"Wonderful. We're unloading about them, and I bet right now they're digging into the Bible. How's that for a side-by-side comparison?" Brian shook a fry at him. "We need to get our act together."

"I agree. Next time we'll bring our Bibles and set them on the table as we unload. Then we can feel more spiritual about it."

A thought shot through Brian's mind, and he got a faraway look in his eyes.

"What?" Logan drained his soda to the bottom and shook the ice.

"I have an idea you might be able to help me with."

"You know the drill," Logan said. "Unload."

Heather had a big grin. "Time for open discussion?"

Cyd looked down at her Bible. "I think we covered everything, and you two asked great questions, as usual. So, yep."

"Good." She turned to Kelli. "I want to hear all about Miles."

"What?" Kelli frowned at Heather. "Excuse me, girlfriend. Open discussion is for *you* to bring up *your* issues. Not for you to bring up *my* stuff."

"Aw, come on. The man flew to town to see you, he's sleeping right here on this sofa, and I don't know much about him. I want to hear the scoop. How'd you get together?"

Kelli closed her Bible, reflecting. "We were part of a group of friends that hung out on campus. He and I paired off, started going to movies, eating out, studying together. Basically became a habit—that developed over time."

"And..." Heather leaned dramatically toward her.

Kelli pushed her back, laughing. "And nothing. That's the scoop."

"How do you feel about him now?"

Kelli thought about it. "I'm trying to figure that out. I'd say we're close. He wants our relationship to go deeper, and I pretty much want that too. He means a lot to me. But..."

Heather and Cyd let the word hang, waiting for her.

"I don't know," Kelli continued. "How close could

we really be if I only told him last night about my songwriting?"

Cyd had a focused look about her. "Why didn't you keep him in the loop as things were developing with Monica and then with Brian's album?"

This one was easy. "I was afraid it would open up too much about the past that I wasn't ready to tell," Keili said. "Still not. He only knows the music part."

Cyd angled her head. "But God's done so much in bringing you out of that past. Are you thinking Miles wouldn't understand? What's his spiritual life like?"

"Well…I'm not sure." The realization surprised Kelli. "Neither of us went to church in Austin. He said he was a Christian, and that was good enough for me. But now that you mention it, we don't talk about spiritual stuff."

She pondered that more. Now that she was growing closer to God again, was that a missing dynamic between her and Miles?

Heather hit her on the arm, an inquisitive look on her face. "Here's a test. If you had to make a decision right now to spend the rest of your life on a deserted island with either Miles or Brian, which would you choose?"

Kelli narrowed her eyes at Heather. "What in the world does Brian have to do with this?"

"Just for fun, but you have to be honest. There's a Bible on your lap."

"I hate 'what if' questions that could never happen in reality."

"Which one?"

Kelli imagined herself on the island, frolicking to pass the time. "Understanding the ridiculous nature of the question, I'd…probably have to say"—she tapped her finger on the Bible—"and the answer shall forever remain between the three of us—Brian."

Cyd's eyebrows arched. "Whoa."

Heather sat back and crossed her legs. "As I suspected."

"Meaning?"

"Oh, I don't know. I've never seen you with Miles, so you'll have to take this with a grain of salt—"

"Obviously…"

"—but I *have* seen you with Brian, and there's just something about the two of you."

Kelli sighed big. "So, now that we know I'd choose Brian in a hypothetical situation that will never arise and thus means nothing, let's move to a real-life question for you, Heather." She grinned. "Didn't think you'd escape unscathed, did you?"

"Bring it, sistah."

"In your heart of hearts, could you fall in love with Logan?"

"What? No fair! I haven't focused on Logan like that. How am I supposed to—"

"Yada, yada, yada. Take a moment, think about the times you've spent with him and how you felt. It's not pass or fail. Just answer." Kelli sat back, then said, "Oh, wait." She slid Heather's Bible from the sofa into her lap.

Heather tossed her eyes playfully. "Well…a couple nights ago, I stopped by the church after choir rehearsal, and Logan and I sang some of his songs together."

Kelli's mouth dropped. "I can't believe you hadn't told me yet!"

"I think I've been processing it still. But to answer your question"—she took a deep breath—"yes."

"Wow. No qualifiers?"

"You asked whether I *could*. There are lots of qualifiers as to whether I *would*."

"Still," Kelli said, "I'm impressed. Can I ask—"

"No. One question apiece. You ask another, I'm asking another."

Kelli stood. "Looks like we're done here."

Amid the laughter, Cyd got up and reached for both of their hands. Kelli loved this part, when they could take everything they'd talked about, even the silly stuff, and send it upward. More and more, she was starting to trust that what came back down would be exactly what she needed.

Cyd squeezed their hands in the circle. "So what are we praying about, girls?"

Kelli went first. "The project at work I told y'all about and the album project of course, that God would continue to lead us creatively." She hesitated. "And Miles. He's leaving early tomorrow morning, but this evening we're going to dinner and a movie. Please pray that I'll know in my heart where our relationship stands. Our discussion's really got me thinking."

"What's he been doing today anyway?" Heather asked.

"Thank God for Lindell. He took him golfing earlier, and I guess they got to talking historical Civil War stuff in Missouri. So they did some sightseeing afterward. Miles has been texting me, excited about what he's seeing."

They looked to Heather for her turn.

"Hmm...all the things I shared earlier about job frustration and feeling again like I want to sing. And the trip to my brother's next weekend."

"I'm so excited for you," Kelli said. "Take lots and lots of pictures."

"Might take video too," Heather said. "And one more thing... I guess I'll go ahead and ask for prayer about the Logan situation."

Kelli looked at her. "The Logan situation?"

Heather nodded. "I've tried hard to ignore it, but I do feel my heart slowly gravitating toward him. But I think we're meant to stay strictly friends."

"And if you're not? Maybe we should pray it'll be whatever God wants it to be."

She gave Kelli the eye. "Why are you all in my prayer request, trying to amend it? I didn't hear you say we should pray for your relationship with Brian to be whatever God wants it to be, but did I say anything? Noooo."

Cyd laughed at them. "I wish you two had seen me last fall. The only thing I was certain about was that Cedric and I would *not* be together."

Heather and Kelli looked at each other.

"You don't know what God will do," Cyd continued, "or the timing of it. At your age, I never thought I'd have to wait till forty to meet the man I'd spend my life with."

Heather and Kelli looked at each other again, this time with eyes wide.

"So yes, we'll pray, for God's will and God's timing with *everything*." Cyd smiled. "And for the two of you to be able to accept whatever it is."

Chapter Twenty-Eight

Kelli wanted to be understanding, but she was finding it really hard. Her nerves were frayed, stomach jumpy, same thoughts moving in circles—all because Miles had changed his flight so he could spend more time with her. They were on their way to church.

How could he do this again, just make plans without consulting her?

"Is that the church?" Miles stared ahead. "That's a huge complex."

"It's grown over the years." She pulled into the parking lot, then waited as a policeman directed traffic. "But there are lots of huge churches in Dallas, aren't there?"

"True, but it's not like I visit them. We've never been big churchgoers in my family."

She looked at him. "So…you just read the Bible on your own, then?"

Miles shrugged. "Not really. Why?"

"Just wondering."

When she got the go-ahead, she found a parking

spot, and they got out. Kelli led the way to the building, fighting for a better attitude. Of course he'd want to take a later flight. They hadn't spent much time together yesterday. But that always brought her back to her original vexation, that he should have called before he made plans in the first place.

Stop rehashing, Kelli. You said you were glad he was here. And she was. She just didn't want him to be *here* at Living Word.

They walked inside, through several pockets of conversation, Kelli greeting a couple of people she knew. As they rounded the bend, she saw it, just outside the usual sanctuary door—the very thing she didn't want to happen. Her family was talking to Brian.

She wanted to duck inside a different set of doors, but it was too late. Miles had already begun walking directly to them. He gave polite hugs to Cyd and Stephanie and shook hands with Cedric and Lindell. Then his hand went to the only other guy remaining.

"Hello. Miles Reed."

Brian shook his hand. "Good to meet you, Miles. I'm Brian Howard."

Kelli saw the name register. Miles nodded, letting loose his hand.

She made eye contact with Brian, who acknowledged her, then looked away.

Cedric took Cyd's hand and moved to the door. "We should go in."

As they filed in, Stephanie tapped Kelli and motioned for her to look behind them. Brian was headed to the far side of the sanctuary, back to his old seat.

A little farther down the aisle, Cyd stopped in her tracks. "Is that Hayes?"

"Oh my goodness." Stephanie shielded her eyes to see better, as if the sun were shining. "Phyllis didn't mention he was coming?"

"Knowing Hayes, he decided last minute."

They continued to the pew as the congregation stood for praise and worship. Cedric and Lindell greeted Hayes with warm handshakes, Stephanie and Cyd with big hugs. Kelli shook his hand. "It's nice to see you here," she said.

Hayes gave a thoughtful nod. "It's good to be here."

Phyllis was hugging her friends, and Kelli was sure she had lots she wanted to say. For now, she simply smiled.

Kelli hurriedly introduced Miles to Phyllis and Hayes, then to Dana and Scott. Then she closed her eyes and did her best to focus on worshipping God as a bevy of emotions knocked around inside.

What is wrong with me, Lord? Why am I reacting this way to Miles being here? Help me feel good about it. I pray he gets something out of the service. And Hayes too.

Miles leaned over during announcements. "So that was your old boyfriend?"

Kelli gave a faint nod.

"What's up with him wearing jeans to church?"

The question threw her. She looked around. "Miles, there are lots of people wearing jeans." She saw no need to tell him Brian was serving at the youth picnic after church.

"I have to admit something to you."

Kelli leaned closer to him.

"I figured Brian was with you at Six Flags, and I got a little jealous, knowing you were near him again.

That's what prompted me to come." He paused. "That's also why I wanted to come to church with you, since you mentioned he was a member. You had told me he was into science, so I pictured this dapper guy on his way to making a name for himself."

Kelli bit her tongue. The "better attitude" was growing more elusive.

"But now that I've seen him and know he's a rapper?" He made a face. "I'm no longer worried."

She swallowed hard, glad the choir gave her an escape as she turned his words over in her head. Miles's measuring worth by one's career again was bad enough, but it was more than that. It was the reaction she felt deep within, wanting to defend Brian.

"Actually," she said, unable to bite her tongue, "he's still into science. The jeans are probably more a part of who he is as a lab guy than a rap guy. He's in a bio-chem PhD program at Wash U."

Miles took that in. "Oh."

Much as she tried to focus on the sermon, Kelli couldn't stop thinking about Miles—and Hayes. She stole a couple of glances at Hayes, thinking about things she'd heard Phyllis say, how she'd been praying for him for years. Was that the sort of future she wanted with Miles? Praying for him to have a serious relationship with God? To have a *real* desire to come to church?

The more she thought about it, the clearer her thoughts became. She *would* pray for Miles, that this sermon would speak to him, that he'd find a church home in Dallas. But she needed to pray also for the words to tell him that this would be the last weekend they'd ever spend together.

As the choir sang the last song, Kelli pulled her

purse into her lap and eased her hand inside. She was becoming a pro at clandestine texting. Seconds later she had a reply, just as the service ended.

As they made their way into the aisle, Kelli saw Phyllis and Hayes head to the front, where Pastor Lyles was talking with people. Moments later Pastor Lyles led them off to the side, their heads close together.

"I don't even know what to say," Cedric said. "God is good."

Cyd and Dana both looked ahead. "Seven years of DF prayers," Cyd said.

"How often did we pray for that picture," Dana asked, "for Hayes to be willing to talk to Pastor Lyles?"

The pews were clearing, and their group began moving up the aisle. Kelli spoke with Cedric a moment, then turned to Miles. "We need to talk."

"Here? Can't we talk on the way to the airport?"

"I don't see any reason to delay this." She directed him to an empty pew.

Miles sat, his eyes on Kelli. "I don't like the way this is sounding."

Kelli gazed downward, searching for words. "You've been a special part of my life, Miles…" She brought her eyes to his. "But it's suddenly clear to me that we don't have a lot in common anymore. I wanted to believe we could deepen our relationship, but I honestly just can't see it. And I don't want to pretend with you. I'm sorry."

He said nothing for long seconds. "Well, this is a first. Don't think anyone's ever broken up with me in church. It's about Brian after all, isn't it?"

"No, Miles, it's not. It's about you and me."

He blew out a sigh. "I came all this way to spend time with you, for you to dump me?"

She gave him a knowing eye. "Actually, you came all this way to check up on me. But it worked out for the best." She touched his hand. "I don't see it as dumping you, Miles. You're still my friend. We just don't need to fool ourselves into thinking it can be more."

"'We can still be friends.'" He shook his head, moving his hand. "That's classic, Kelli."

"I meant it, Miles."

"Yeah. Okay." He stood. "So we get to ride to the airport as 'friends'?"

Kelli stood as well. "Actually, I asked Cedric if he and Cyd could take you. They're waiting in the foyer and can get your bag out of my car. If you don't mind."

He hesitated, taking her in. "I prefer it, actually. Take care, Kelli." He started up the aisle without her.

Kelli noticed the pastor, Hayes, and Phyllis still talking in hushed tones. She looked upward, sighing thanks. The conversation with Miles wasn't easy, but it would've only gotten harder with time. She headed to the café area, which was brimming with people enjoying coffee, tea, and fellowship between services. Brian sat at a tall pedestal table, talking with a guy who'd walked up beside him. Kelli slid into the seat on the other side, waiting for them to finish. When they were done, Brian turned to her.

"I was surprised to get your text."

"Why?" She knew why, but she felt like fishing.

"I thought you and Romeo—"

"Miles."

"—would have plans after church."

"He had to catch his flight."

Brian gave a shrug of a nod. "So why'd you want to see me?"

"To give you an invitation."

He glanced at her hands, looking for a piece of paper. "To what?"

"To sit with us each week. I…" Where did the sudden emotion come from? "I don't want you to have to sit alone."

"I appreciate the invite, but what would Ro—uh, Miles think about that?"

"Does it matter?"

Brian simply looked at her.

"I broke up with him. Okay?"

He came forward on his elbows. "And you're telling me, as if it's my business?"

Kelli took a napkin from the table, balled it up, and threw it at him. It sailed far right.

"You never were a good shot."

"You make me sick."

Brian smiled, his eyes penetrating. "I know."

She stared at him a second, memories flooding her soul. She brushed them aside. "So you've got the youth picnic after second service?"

"Yeah, should be fun. We've got lots of games set up outside." His brow crinkled as if an idea hit him. "You should join us."

Kelli narrowed her eyes. "Why?"

"Oh, I don't know…just broke up with your boyfriend, might be a little shaken. Some fun and games would do you good."

"Are you trying to be funny?" Kelli felt nowhere near shaken by the breakup, and she was fairly certain Brian knew that.

"Nope, not trying to be funny at all…although…it

might be true that I'm looking for an excuse to get you to hang with me today."

She couldn't hide the smile in her heart. "You don't need an excuse, Brian. I actually think it'd be fun. I just need to go home and change."

"How about I treat you to breakfast first…which was where I was headed anyway, because I'm starving."

She twisted her mouth as she considered. "Pancake house?"

"Where else? I can drive and bring you back."

Kelli followed him to his car. "I'm surprised you haven't asked me what happened."

"With what?"

"Me and Miles."

He glanced at her. "Would you have told me?"

"Probably not."

He opened her door, and when she got in, he looked down at her. "Is it important?"

"Not really."

He walked around to the driver's side and got in. "Kel, all I really care about is that we're forming a real friendship." He started the engine, then looked at her. "Or am I assuming too much again?"

She returned his gaze, but barely…afraid what her own might reveal. "No. You're not assuming too much."

Chapter Twenty-Nine

Heather pushed her cart down the aisle of Schnuck's, loading up for the week. She'd been grocery shopping on Sundays for months now, but it still felt weird, like she was unplugged. She'd begun thinking this morning that maybe she should be visiting churches rather than testing them out online. But which ones were worth visiting? She always ended up in the same place. Stuck.

Her phone rang, and it took her a minute to find it in her purse. Kelli called every Sunday with news about the service, and Heather was especially eager to hear from her today and find out what had happened with Miles.

She blinked three times to make sure she wasn't seeing things. The name on the caller ID said *Ace*. Heather's heart hammered in her chest. Was it really him? Why? Should she ignore the call?

"H-hello?"

"Hey, beautiful. How've you been?"

His voice was smooth as ever. She closed her eyes,

gripping the handle of the cart. "How have I been? As if you care."

"Listen, I hated what happened. I had planned to spend the weekend with you, remember? I couldn't help that Angela showed up."

"Ace, you slept with me, then put me out. And then sat in that conference the next day acting holier-than-thou. You're a hypocrite."

"You're not judging me, are you now, Heather? You were right in that bed with me."

She didn't know what to say. *I gave my life to Jesus afterward*?

Ace continued. "But seeing you the next day did tear me up. I'm telling you right here and now I'm sorry it had to go down like that."

Heather pressed her lips together. "After all this time? Save it. What do you really want?"

"What I want is to make it up to you."

She pushed her cart further aside and stood against it. "What do you mean?"

"I made you a promise. I said I'd introduce you to some artists and try to help you become a background singer. Didn't I?"

Her heart was still hammering. "Yeah. That's what you said."

"And that's what I meant. Turned out it couldn't happen that weekend, but I haven't forgotten. I've got an opportunity for you."

She needed to tell him she didn't want to hear it and hang up, but her adrenaline was pumping. "What?"

"My band's playing in St. Charles tonight, and Peyton Vine is on the ticket. She told me she's looking for two background singers for her upcoming tour. She said she'd be willing to listen to you."

Heather's hand was shaking on the cart handle. She loved Peyton's music, often imitated her voice. She knew her stats too—from Alabama, a couple years older than Heather, got her start in country music with a gospel twang and moved over to CCM with her last album.

Heather shook her head, trying to make sense of what was happening. "Ace, I drove all the way to Indianapolis based on the last thing you told me. Now I'm supposed to believe this? I don't think so."

"First of all, I wasn't lying last time. Things just didn't work out as planned. And second, what do you have to lose? You don't have to drive far at all. And Peyton *will* be there. You can look it up yourself on the Internet."

"Doesn't mean she agreed to see me."

"Hang on a sec."

Heather stood straight. "What are you doing?"

"I'm getting her on the line."

He clicked over, and Heather blew out a long breath. Was this really happening? Seconds later, she heard Ace and a female talking.

"Heather, you there?"

"I'm here."

"Hi, Heather. This is Peyton Vine."

Either Ace was a psychopath who already had someone on standby to impersonate Peyton, or this was really Peyton Vine. Heather had heard and seen enough interviews to recognize her voice.

"Hi, Peyton," she said. "Pleasure to meet you, sort of."

"Peyton, like I said, Heather doesn't believe you've

agreed to listen to her sing tonight. Would you please confirm?"

"It's true, Heather. I'm looking for background singers to tour with me, and Ace said you're awesome. Honestly, it's not a big burden for me to listen for a few minutes. I'm glad to do it."

Excitement began to course through Heather's veins. "Seriously? You're serious?"

Peyton laughed. "Girl, I'm serious!"

"Thank you so much."

"No problem," Peyton said. "I've got to jump off because I'm about to catch my flight into St. Louis, but I look forward to meeting you."

"You too."

Peyton hung up, leaving Ace and Heather. He made a point of clearing his throat. "You can thank me too."

Her mind was racing. "Thanks, Ace. Really. This is huge. How do I meet up with you all?"

Ace told her the time and location and the name to ask for once she arrived. She'd have backstage access throughout the concert.

"Thanks again, Ace."

"You're welcome. Look forward to seeing you."

Heather could barely push the cart as she thought about the evening ahead. No way could she finish shopping. She had most of what she needed anyway, so she moved to the checkout line and called Kelli as she waited. Voice mail kicked in.

She couldn't call Logan because he was still in second service. Besides, she wasn't sure she wanted to. He'd be worried about her seeing Ace again—understandably—but this wasn't about Ace. This was about Heather finally getting a chance to live her dream. No wonder she'd been feeling the pull to sing of late. God had to be preparing her heart for this, letting her know it was okay to pursue it.

Somehow she got her groceries home and put them away. She double-checked the concert date online just to be sure, rummaged through her closet for the right outfit, and started cooking an early dinner, all while intermittently calling Kelli—where was she?—and playing her entire collection of Peyton Vine tunes.

Late afternoon her phone rang, and she almost broke her neck to get to it. "Kelli—finally! Where have you been?"

"I've been going since this morning. Some things happened with Miles, ended up having breakfast with Brian, then went with him to the youth picnic, so we were playing lots of games and I didn't have my phone. We're headed to the studio now, and I saw you called like a thousand times. What's going on?"

"I totally heard you say something happened with Miles and you spent the day with Brian, and you *know* I'm coming back to all that, but I've got to get this out or I'll burst. I'm auditioning tonight to be a background singer for Peyton Vine!"

"Are you serious?"

Heather laughed. "That's what I said."

"Where?"

"She's doing a concert in St. Charles, and she said she'd listen to me sing. I actually talked to her."

"Okay, girl. Back up. What were you doing on the phone with Peyton Vine?"

Heather hesitated. "I got a call from Ace. But before you say anything, he apologized for what happened in Indy and said he was keeping his promise to help me break into the business. He's the one who set things up with Peyton and got her on the phone."

"Mm-hmm. How do you know it was her?"

"Kelli, have you heard her speak? She has a distinctive voice. I have no doubt. Plus I checked the website, and she's definitely scheduled to be here."

"What's the venue?"

"Webster Family Arena." Heather waited. "Kelli?"

"I'm here." She sighed. "I want to be excited with you, but I just don't know. I have zero respect for Ace. What did he apologize for—putting you out or the fact that he shouldn't have had his mind set on plying you with alcohol and getting you into bed? He's sleazy, and I don't think he'd do this without something in it for himself. If I didn't have to be in the studio, I'd go with you. I think you should get Logan to go."

"If I tell Logan, he'll advise me not to go at all."

"Why would he do that? The opportunity with Peyton might be legit. Logan would just be there to make sure Ace doesn't try anything."

"I'll think about it. I do wish you could go, but will you be praying for me?"

"Of course I'll be praying. Call me *the minute* it's over."

Heather forced herself to take a catnap so she'd be fresh for the evening, but she woke up realizing she'd napped longer than planned. It was six o'clock. She jumped up, showered and dressed, and started the twenty-minute drive to the venue, her phone staring at her from the console. She knew she needed to call Logan, let him know what she was doing, but she didn't feel like being defensive about her plans. She wanted to stay upbeat. Better to tell him afterward, when—she hoped—they'd be celebrating.

The arena was more crowded than she thought it would be. She had to park far from the entrance and hustle to get inside before it started. There were three acts performing, the first a newer band she hadn't heard, but she wanted to be there to experience it all.

At the main door, Heather stood in line with no ticket, anxious about explaining that she should not only get in but receive backstage access. The first woman she spoke with looked skeptical, calling over a security guard. Heather explained again, dropping the name Ace told her to use. The guard mumbled a few words into his walkie-talkie, and next thing she knew he was opening a side door for her. Her heart did a leap as he gave her a badge, then took her down a back elevator and through a long corridor. She ended up in a big room with catered food and a few people scattered at tables, talking over the meal.

Heather felt silly when the guard left her standing there, but seconds later Ace appeared.

"Hey, you made it." He hugged her like they were old friends. "Did you have any problems getting in?"

"No, it was all good." Heather smiled, a little nervous. "Thanks again."

"Absolutely. Come with me."

She followed him back down the hall. He stepped into a room where some others were gathered. She recognized a couple guys as members of his band. Three women were there as well, sitting on the laps of three of the guys. They were watching a monitor of the act performing onstage.

Ace didn't introduce her to anyone. She stood

against the wall next to him. After a few awkward minutes she whispered, "Is there any way I could watch the concert in person?"

"Sure." Ace moved immediately, tapping one of the guys. "Be back, bro."

He led Heather past a bunch of lighting and equipment, through a tunnel area, to a nice spot with a great view of the stage. The band was rocking out, the crowd going crazy.

"Where's Peyton?"

"Probably in her dressing room getting ready. She's on next. She'll listen to you after she performs."

"Cool." But her insides weren't. They were jumping like crazy.

Heather was able to grab an up-close seat during Peyton's performance. She watched every move and noted every song in the set, her eyes following the two background singers more than Peyton. She pictured herself up there, sitting on a stool for the slower songs, handling the dance moves on the faster ones. This was what she was meant to do. She just knew it.

The crowd roared when Peyton finished her encore. Heather eased out and found her way back down the hall, texting Ace.

He came out of the same room. "Good timing. I'm going on in ten; we just finished the prayer. I'll take you to Peyton's dressing room."

Ace knocked on the door, and one of the background singers opened it. Ace seemed to know everyone. Heather couldn't believe it when she was brought face-to-face with Peyton. She was more beautiful close-up than onstage.

"Great to meet you, Heather. So glad you could come."

"The pleasure is entirely mine. I'm grateful for the opportunity."

Ace tapped her shoulder, and Heather turned a moment.

"I need to go," he said, "but stick around when you're done. I'd like to say good-bye."

Peyton got her background singers to help with the impromptu audition. They took her aside and taught her a part to one of Peyton's songs, a song Heather knew well. They practiced it twice, then told Peyton they were ready. Heather's heart was beating out of her chest. Peyton sang the lead, though not full-throated, and Heather joined in with the others. The nerves fell away and she could feel herself in the zone, hitting the notes exactly as she'd hoped.

Near the end Peyton was snapping her fingers, ad-libbing, and Heather was the lone voice remaining with her, feeling the vibe.

When it was over, Peyton grinned. "All right, girl! You go!"

They sang another song, a slower one, and Heather was excited because she'd practiced the background vocals to this one earlier. Might've been wishful thinking, but her sound seemed to complement Peyton's well. Members of Peyton's road team who'd left the room returned and stood near the doorway, watching them. When they were done, a rousing applause ensued.

Heather gestured toward Peyton, adding her own applause, but Peyton bowed to Heather.

"They hear me all the time," Peyton said, smiling. "I don't get applause from them. They're applauding you."

"Wow." Heather got teary-eyed. "I really feel like I'm standing in somebody's dream. Thank you."

The people went their way again, leaving Heather, Peyton, and a handful of others in the room. Peyton handed her a card. "I want you to come to Nashville for the next level of auditions. Can you do that?"

Heather's hand trembled as she took it. "I can be there whenever you need me to be."

"Awesome. That's my manager's card. Give us a call next week. I can't promise anything, but I hope it works out."

"I hope it works out too. Thanks for everything. I'll definitely be in touch."

Heather floated back to her same seat and watched the rest of No Return's performance, but she couldn't have told anyone what they sang. She was in another world, reliving what had just happened, envisioning the future. She could actually be on tour with Peyton Vine in the fall.

A deafening roar went up around her, and Heather looked onstage. The band was gone. Already? She got up, showed her badge to a security guard who'd posted himself by the tunnel, and texted Ace again.

She surveyed her words before she sent it: just coming to say goodbye. She waited in the hall, and after a few minutes, Ace came out.

"How'd it go?"

Heather grinned. "Really well. Peyton said she hopes it works out."

Ace brought his arms around her. "That's good news, girl. I told her you were fabulous. This is just the beginning for you."

"I sure hope so."

She slipped out of his hug, and he grabbed one of her hands.

"I haven't told you yet how nice it is to see you again." He pulled her closer. "I missed you."

She cast her glance downward and shifted her weight to put a little distance between them. "Nice to see you too."

"Come here a minute." He pulled her fingers, guiding her down the hall.

Her heart fell out of rhythm. "Where…where are we going?"

"Right here." He pushed open the door to the dressing room next to the one they'd been in previously. No one else was there.

She backed up in the doorway. "Ace, I've really got to go. It's getting late, and I've got to be at work early."

He gripped her hand still. "I can't keep you long anyway. The bus is leaving shortly."

A sigh of relief shot through her, but she kept on alert. "Still, I've got to—"

"Shh." He put his hand behind her back and brought her to him, kissing her lips before she knew what was happening.

"Ace, no, I—"

He smiled at her, his arms locked around her waist. "Playing shy now? I like that."

He kissed her again, and she forced her head back, trying to wrestle out of his grip. "I don't want to do this."

"Ace!"

Stunned, they both looked down the hall. Logan was striding toward them. Ace's grip loosened, and Heather backed completely away…and ran into Logan's arms.

He stroked her hair. "Are you okay?"

"Logan…" She was trembling, barely able to catch her breath, only now realizing how scared she'd been.

Ace swaggered toward them. "Is this a joke? You're rescuing *her*? Logan, I know you. You can do much better than this."

Logan whispered in her ear. "One minute. Stay right here." He turned. "Ace. I know you too and your fiancée—yes, I heard the news, congrats. I'm thinking *you* can do better than to force yourself on a woman who's clearly telling you no."

"You don't know the facts, my man." He held his chest out, pointing a finger at Heather. "I've already slept with this woman. She was just playing hard to get, one of our little games."

Heather held herself. "That's not true. I was trying to leave."

"You think that justifies your actions? That you've already slept with Heather? How are you living, man? You sat in that workshop claiming to have a right heart. You really need to check yourself."

"Oh, now you're judging me too. I don't need a lecture from the choir boy."

"Let's call it a night, Ace," Logan said. "We'll chalk it up to too many beers. I want you to do one thing for me, though. Delete Heather's contact info from your phone."

Ace glanced at Heather, then back to Logan. "I've always respected you, Logan. You're a stand-up guy. So I'm telling you straight, she's not good enough for you. She's a tramp."

Logan's entire body tensed, and he looked like he might swing at Ace. She'd never seen fire like that in his eyes. He turned instead, took Heather's hand, and led her away. Then he stopped and turned back. "And for the record, Ace, you don't know the facts either. She's a better woman than I deserve."

They walked in silence to Logan's car, his arm around her. She couldn't stop the tears. Whatever she'd learned about the new Heather was gone. She saw herself through Ace's eyes again. The tramp, the one who'd easily gone to bed with him.

They got in the car and sat there. Logan looked angry still, his jaw set as he stared out the window.

Finally he looked at her. "Why, Heather? Why didn't you tell me Ace called you? I *know* what kind of man he is."

She was still crying. "He set it up for Peyton to hear me sing––and she liked my voice, by the way. Since we'd be at an arena, I thought I had nothing to worry about."

He threw his hands up in frustration. "That's why you should've told me. Do you know how much stuff goes down in these backstage areas? Did you know his bus had already left?"

She turned shocked eyes on Logan. "He said the bus was about to leave."

"I saw it pull out after I talked to the band. His road manager stays behind to take him wherever he needs to go. That's how he plays it."

Heather's mind filled with horrible possibilities. If Logan hadn't come… "Did Kelli call you?"

"No, Brian did."

"Brian?"

"Kelli told him while they were in the studio, and he didn't like the sound of it."

"Well, how did you get backstage like that?"

"Doing what I do puts me in touch with a lot of people. If a Christian concert comes to town, I almost always know who'll be working it. In this case, they'd already sent me an access pass."

Her head fell, and she put her hand over her mouth. She thought she might get sick. "Oh, Logan, he could've—"

"It's okay." He reached across, his hand on her back. "It's over now."

She stared into her lap. "I really can't blame Ace. He was right about me."

"No. No." Logan got out of the car, came around, and got her out. "Look at me."

She stood against the car, gazing into his eyes, a half moon hovering above.

"He was wrong. He had no right to touch you without your permission. And he was not right about you. All he knows is the Heather that was crucified with Christ."

Her gaze faltered, and fresh tears fell. "But I'm so ashamed of what I did with him in that hotel."

"Heather, no. That's old. You're not going back there." He tipped her chin up. "His grace and mercy have covered you…"

"Logan…"

"Sing it with me. Come on."

Logan started again, and Heather slowly joined in.

His grace and mercy have covered you,
You're not the same;
No longer bound by what you used to do,
That's why He came—

So you could make a change, completely new;
And in His name
You're a conqueror, beloved too.

Heather exhaled, a faint breeze whispering through her hair, twinkling stars overhead, goose bumps on her arms...and Logan in her sight.

It was as if she were seeing him anew.

He ran a single finger across the sides of her face, erasing the tears. She was sure he could hear her heartbeat, make out its new rhythm. They stood that way for seconds more, taking one another in. Then he reopened her door, helped her inside, and drove her to her car.

Chapter Thirty

It was crunch time.

Brian rolled out of bed extra early Monday morning, raring to go. This was it. All the songs needed to be finished by the end of the week. Before Kelli left the night before, they took a fresh listen to the ones already recorded and were still excited about them. As of now, they had six in the can and two in progress—the love letter to the world and to fellow aliens. They needed four more. Well, as far as Kelli knew. There would actually be thirteen songs on the album. Brian had decided to work on one without her.

They'd mapped out a plan where Kelli would work in the studio every afternoon and evening this week. By God's grace, they would get it done. Brian couldn't believe it, given how much he'd struggled, but it was looking like this album could be better than the first. He hadn't concluded anything about school yet. He was praying for a clear answer by week's end.

He hopped in the shower with a melody in his head that Kelli had been playing last night. He'd caught himself looking at her again as she worked, thanking God that she was there, that they were connecting again. That they were friends. Sunday was the best day he'd had in recent memory, just being together and acting goofy at the picnic. She was a gift. Someone to be cherished.

Something about that word—*cherished*—put everything else on pause and beckoned him whenever it came to mind. He wasn't even sure of the full extent of its meaning, but he'd keep squeezing it until he was.

Brian got dressed and peeked into his grandmother's room. She usually beat him out of bed, but it was his habit to check on her. The room was empty. Probably on her morning walk. Maybe she'd be back shortly and they could have their cereal together before he went down to the studio.

He came down the stairs and entered the kitchen— "Grandma!"

She lay on the floor by the kitchen table, a broken bowl of oatmeal beside her. He ran to her side, shaking, heart constricted, afraid of what he'd find. He got on the floor beside her and felt her face.

"Grandma, wake up. Come on." He felt her heart, put his fingers to her wrist. She didn't seem to be breathing. "Come on. We haven't talked yet this morning. You know how we do." He stroked her hair. "Grandma, please wake up!"

The tears flowed as he pulled his cell phone from his belt clip and called 911. Then he called Kelli.

Brian sat with her on the floor, her head in his lap, singing "A Mighty Fortress Is Our God," her favorite hymn, and stroking her hair. She was gone. He knew she was gone. Why hadn't he heard the bowl break?

Had he been in the shower? What if he'd found her sooner?

He heard the ambulance coming, but he couldn't separate himself. Would he be able to hold her again? The finality of the moment was more than he could bear.

The banging on the door forced him to move. He placed her head gently on the floor. When he opened the door, he discovered not only the paramedics but a slew of neighbors wanting to know what was wrong. He let the paramedics in, asking the neighbors to please wait. He needed some time.

Brian found the paramedics hovered over her in the kitchen. He hung back, staring at a picture of the two of them on the counter.

"Sir, she's already gone. Had she been suffering from anything?"

"She's been the picture of health. Only thing she complained of recently was headaches. She'd been taking pain relievers, but I told her she might want to go to the doctor."

"We'll know more when we get her to the hospital, but could've been a brain aneurysm."

Brian rode in the ambulance to the hospital, answering Kelli's texts the whole way.

how is she?
do they know what happened?
how are you?

The last one he couldn't answer. He was too numb to know.

He sat with his head down in the waiting room, trying to pray, though unsure what to ask, trying to wait, though unsure what he was waiting for.

The tears started again. He was thankful she'd lived a vibrant life, thankful she hadn't suffered a debilitating illness. But he wished he could've said goodbye. A few minutes earlier and he would've seen her, laughed with her.

He heard someone approaching and looked up. "Hey, Kel."

Without a word Kelli sat in the chair beside him, clutching his hand, sharing his tears. She was the only one on earth who knew exactly what his grandmother meant to him.

"I loved her, Brian. She was like my own grandmother, always so good to me."

"She loved you too. She thought you were special." He shook his head. "Had the nerve to tell me I'd never find anyone better."

"When did she say that?"

He glanced down. "Last week."

Kelli held his hand. "She was the special one. I can just see the ruckus she's causing in heaven right now. Probably asking for the VIP tour." She shook her head. "It's so hard to believe she's gone. She was just in the studio with us last night." Kelli smiled. "She was digging those new songs, wasn't she?"

Brian smiled too. "I'm glad she got to hear them." He'd let her hear everything but the love letter to their baby. No way had he been ready to reveal that to her. "She did seem to like them, didn't she?"

Brian and Kelli looked up as the doctor came toward them. Brian stood.

"Mr. Howard, preliminary tests reveal that your grandmother indeed suffered a cerebral aneurysm, and when she fell, she broke her hip, compounding the injury."

"Do you think she died instantly?" Brian asked.

"I do. I don't believe she suffered."

Brian took in his words, trying to find in them a sliver of comfort. "What happens now?"

"Our administrative assistant will guide you through the necessary paperwork. She should be out momentarily to help you. Our sincerest condolences to you and your family."

When they were alone again, Brian sighed. "I don't even know what to do when I leave here. Am I supposed to go straight to the funeral home? Do I go home? But how can I do that? They just took her body from the kitchen."

"Brian," Kelli said, "I just got a text from Cyd. They said for us to come over when we're done."

Brian took a breath and nodded. "That would be good."

Brian hadn't expected to see so many people at Cyd and Cedric's home. He didn't expect Cedric, for one. But he'd apparently left work when he'd gotten word. Stephanie was there, saying Lindell would arrive after his last appointment. Phyllis and her toddler had walked over, Dana had come, and even Logan and Pastor Lyles were there. Pastor Lyles couldn't stay long, but he prayed with Brian and said they'd talk more at their scheduled meeting the next day, if Brian still felt up to coming.

A day filled with lively conversation served him

well—the lively activity probably more so. After school let out, Phyllis's boys came over and showed off some raps they'd written, infused with what they'd learned about God. That alone would have picked up his spirits.

By early evening Scott had brought his kids, and Lindell and Hayes had joined them, all of which contributed to an impromptu, braggadocio game of flag football with the guys—and Reese.

Brian was surprised how good he felt afterward, especially since it was followed by good food, which had been flowing in all day. By nightfall, with kids needing to get ready for school in the morning, Dana's and Phyllis's families had left, and it was only Kelli's remaining, plus Logan...and Heather, who'd wanted to be there for Brian. Once Dana had gone, Kelli let her know it was okay to come over.

Kelli sat on the floor of the family room, petting Reese. "You know you'll have to do this all over again at your house for your family and Grandma Howard's friends."

"Yep, I know." Brian had grown wistful again as they sat around sharing stories about the past. "We'll gather there after the funeral. I just couldn't handle it today."

"Do you know what you want to do about funeral arrangements?" Cedric asked.

"I thought we'd try to have the funeral Thursday or at least the viewing Thursday and the funeral on Friday, but my great-aunts say the funeral needs to be Saturday so family can get off work and get to town. There's so much to think about I'm getting a headache."

"I hesitate to ask, then," Logan said, "but have you told the label you need an extension?"

Brian looked defeated. "This is already my third. If I miss it, everything's thrown off." He sighed. "And yet, I don't see how I can make the deadline either. Today is gone. The rest of the week'll be filled with nonstop calls and visits, plus preparing for the funeral. And creatively it's next to impossible. My mind's in a totally different place. I can't even remember the melody that was in my head this morning." He let his head fall back and hit the cushion. "I can't believe this is all happening right now."

"I think we can do this."

Cyd turned surprised eyes to Stephanie. "We? You know your way around a studio?"

"I'm serious." Stephanie scooted forward. "Brian, you're trying to carry everything on your shoulders. All you need to do is set up the funeral arrangements—and you should go with your family's wishes. A Saturday funeral gives you all week to work. You and Kelli can do what you do in the studio, and if you'll let me, I'll set up a base of operations upstairs in your house. I'll handle the calls, visits, all that. Matter of fact, if you give me some names and numbers, I'll start a phone chain in your family. I'll call Aunt Suzie May or whoever with the arrangements, tell her to call her people, then they can call their people, and so on."

Brian was overwhelmed. "You'd do all that?"

Stephanie smirked. "That's nothing. Cyd'll help if I need it. Right?" She glanced at her sister. "See? We got this."

He was trying to think it through. "I'm still afraid I'll get in the studio and be too depressed to work."

"I could see that," Lindell said, "but God is able."

Brian looked at him. "You said that so simply."

"I'm a simple kind of guy." Lindell smiled. "From what I've seen, you weren't trying to make it happen on your own anyway. Haven't you been relying on God all along?"

"Trying to."

"Okay, so now you'll *really* be relying on God."

"With some added prayer power," Cyd said. She nodded with a smile. "I'll get a whole slew of folk prayin'."

"Didn't I tell you?" Stephanie asked. "We got this."

"However I can help," Logan said, "I'm there."

"Me too," Heather said.

Brian looked at each of them. "I don't know what I would do without all of you. I'll never be able to thank you enough."

"Just give me a shout-out in the CD liner notes, and we're good."

Brian's heart smiled. "You got it, Steph."

Brian might've thought initially he would have to carry everything on his shoulders, but for the remainder of the week, he had no doubt—he was the one being carried. From the ease with which he was able to set up arrangements with the funeral home and his grandmother's church, to Stephanie's efficient handling of the casseroles and bread pudding dishes— not to mention efficient handling of his family, which wasn't easy—Brian knew prayers were being answered in a huge way.

But nowhere was it more apparent than in the studio. Even the producer had to be feeling the effects of the prayers. He sent music tracks that blew him and Kelli away, more than they needed, two of which inspired lyrics on the spot. And Kelli was able to work from morning to night. When Doug at Living Word learned what happened, he told her to devote the week to the album. Next week, he said, she could work full days to make up the time.

But while they were rolling, there were only so many working hours in a day. It took, at minimum, several hours to write and record. Kelli's vocals alone took a long while, since the lead and several layers of background were recorded on different tracks. They tried not to stress about the clock, but by the end of the week, they had to admit Friday had shown its face much too soon.

Kelli and Brian sat looking at one another, waiting for a final burst of inspiration. Only one more song to go.

Brian groaned. "There's no one left to write a love letter to."

"'Course there is. We're just not thinking of it. And anyway, do we have to have twelve songs? What'll happen if you turn in eleven?"

"Originally I was shooting for fifteen. When the love letter idea came, it was so clear to me that there would be twelve letters to different segments of people. At least… I thought it was clear. If nothing comes soon, eleven it'll be."

They both sighed, Bibles in their laps, leafing, waiting.

"Hey!" Stephanie called from upstairs. "Y'all want some of this peach cobbler somebody just brought? It is slammin'."

Kelli frowned at the stairway. "It's still morning, Steph."

Brian looked at Kelli like she was crazy. "Can you bring mine with milk, please?"

Stephanie brought the slice and a glass of milk, setting it down on the computer table.

"Thanks, Steph."

"No problem. How's it going?"

Kelli aimed her pencil at Stephanie. "Let me ask you a question."

Stephanie waited.

"If you got a love letter from God, what would you want it to say?"

"Hmm…" Stephanie flipped her eyes upward as she thought. "If I got a love letter from God…"

Brian and Kelli gave one another the eye. *Well, it couldn't hurt.*

"I'd love for God to tell me I don't need skinnier hips or thighs or a different nose or thinner lips to measure up. That I'm fine just like I am, thank you very much—Spanx and all."

"So…" Brian couldn't believe God was dropping the answer like this. "You'd want Him to reassure you that you're fearfully and wonderfully made."

"Exactly!"

Brian looked at Kelli. Kelli looked at Brian.

"Stephanie?" he asked.

"Yes?"

"You just totally earned that shout-out in the CD."

"Well, shoot, I thought I was doing that upstairs. What's the next level? Royalties?"

At 1:42 Saturday morning, Brian had his finger on the Send button. He looked at the faces in the studio. "Should I do it?"

"Do it!"

He clicked it, and the songs hurled into cyberspace, off to the label for mixing. He fell back in his chair.

Applause and cheers went up in the room. Heather and Logan had joined them early in the evening, lending an ear, providing helpful critique on the last songs, boosting Brian and Kelli as fatigue from a long week set in.

Kelli collapsed on the floor with a squawky groan. "I have no voice."

Heather smiled down at her. "You sound cute like that, all hoarse-like."

"You're such a trooper, Kel." Brian's neck hung over the chair. "I'll get you some tea."

"You don't have any energy yourself," Kelli said, "and don't worry about it anyway. I'm just gonna head home and get some rest…as soon as I can get up."

"The viewing's at ten, right?" Logan asked.

"Right." Brian's own voice sounded deep and throaty. "Funeral immediately following." He made himself get up, comfortable as he was, and stretched. "Well, it's done. Hallelujah. I'm really excited. Good night."

Logan laughed. "You're too tired to celebrate now, but after you get some rest, you'll be pumped. I'm pumped myself. It's unbelievable the way it came together."

"Beautiful." Heather's eyes showed admiration. "I can't believe you just got the idea for that last one. The way you sang that chorus, Kelli…*fearfully, wonderfully*…fire!"

Kelli stretched out further on the floor. "I need

somebody to light a fire under me, or I'll fall asleep right here."

Logan one-handed her to her feet.

The four trudged upstairs, Brian looking back at Logan and Heather. "Y'all hung in there with us tonight. Definitely appreciate you."

"I just feel bad that I won't be at the funeral tomorrow," Heather said.

Brian shook his head. "Don't give it another thought. The visit with your brother is long overdue." He looked at her again. "You're having quite the week, aren't you?"

Heather smiled. "I guess you could say that. I still can't believe I was in Nashville yesterday auditioning for Peyton Vine's tour." She paused. "I didn't realize how many others would be there, though. And they could sing their faces off."

"I'm not worried," Kelli said. "You can sing your face off yourself. I think God's got something special for you."

"I couldn't have said it better myself," Logan said.

Heather and Logan said their good-byes and headed to Logan's car. Brian walked Kelli to hers.

"So how do you feel?" Kelli asked. "I noticed you haven't said much about your decision. Pretty big deal to leave the PhD program."

"I haven't had time to dwell on how I feel yet, and maybe that was for the best." He shrugged. "They needed my decision today, and I couldn't continue unless my heart was really in it." He sighed. "I had a peace about it, and Grandma had a lot to do with that. The night before she died, she said I was putting my heart and soul into those songs. I don't know if I could say that about science. I find it interesting, might even love it. But my heart and soul?" He looked at Kelli. "This week in particular, I've really felt that I'm called to do this music ministry, at least for now."

"I can see why," Kelli said. "I never thought I would enjoy this process as much as I have. And seeing it culminate in something that could really touch people's hearts... It's incredible. Thank you, Brian."

"'Thank you, Brian'? If it weren't for you, there wouldn't have been an album. You were my inspiration."

"Oh, you would've had an album. It was all God."

"But God used *you*."

Kelli allowed their gaze to linger. Then, "I really wish you well with it. I know you will touch a lot of lives."

"We."

"Well." Kelli's eyes grazed the ground, then she brought them back to Brian.

His heart pounded as he looked at her. So much he felt. So much he wanted to say.

He took a step back. "Get some rest, okay?"

"Okay."

He stood on the sidewalk and watched her drive away.

Chapter Thirty-One

Heather surveyed the scene around her, amazed. More than two hundred teen girls and guys were jumping to the beat like a pogo stick as the band rocked out in worship. The song was clearly a crowd favorite.

Heather leaned over to her brother, talking above the music. "Are they always this fired up? They've got me wanting to jump up and down."

"Go for it!"

Ian led the way, jumping while singing with the rest. *Are you living unashamed? Yes! Yes! Do you wanna praise His name? Yes! Yes!*

The resemblance between them was still uncanny to her. Same blond coloring, lean build, even the same nose and thick eyebrows.

Heather joined him, laughing more than singing. Becky pointed at them across the room with a big grin. She'd been jumping the whole time, surrounded by the girls she taught in her small group.

Heather loved Ian and Becky's hearts for these teens. Ian was the youth pastor, and from the time she'd ar-

rived yesterday morning, it had been clear that kids
were his life, starting with his own. Meghan, Han-
nah, and Riley were all under ten still, full of nonstop
energy, and Ian had no problem engaging their every
impulse. Meanwhile, their home had an open door, literally. Heather lost count of the number of teens who
popped in during the course of the day, mostly just to
hang out for a while. Ian lived within walking distance
of the church—a purposeful move, he'd told her—so
they could be a vibrant part of the neighborhood from
which the church drew most of its members.

The band moved to a slower worship song, and
Heather was impressed once again with these teens
and their worship. They didn't seem embarrassed to
raise their hands. They seemed truly focused on God.
Heather wondered how much Ian had to do with culti-
vating the spirit in the room.

She raised her own hands, thanking God for the
weekend. It had exceeded her every expectation. Her
brother and sister-in-law had embraced her as if they'd
known her all her life and rejoiced when she told them
of her newfound faith. The kids loved on her as well,
excited to have an aunt to play with and even to sing
with. They had a blast at the piano as the kids played
the songs they'd been learning, and Heather chimed in
with vocals. Turned out Ian could sing too—though he
was quick to say he wasn't as good as Heather—and
they had fun singing together out of the kids' hymn
book. She'd already told them she planned to be a fre-
quent visitor.

When church ended, the whole family took her to
lunch. It was hard saying good-bye back at the house.
Becky hugged her first, her warmth enveloping

Heather like an old blanket. "So you're coming back next weekend, right?"

Heather laughed. "Don't know if it'll be that soon. But I sure will miss y'all. I feel like I'm part of the family already."

"You *are* family, girl," Becky said. Her brown eyes sparkled. "Now that we've all found one another, we don't want to miss a beat. Come again soon…and stay longer."

Heather smiled. "I will."

"Thought I'd tell you," Ian said, smiling, "the band needs a female vocalist for youth worship." He added quickly, "I know you're excited about this opportunity you might have with Peyton Vine, and we're just small potatoes here in Normal, Illinois. But I thought I'd put that bug in your ear."

It had only been three days, but Heather had hoped to hear from Peyton by now. She'd been checking her phone all weekend to see if she'd missed any calls.

"I can tell you one thing," she said. "Small-potatoes Normal sure ain't normal." She smiled. "Normal knows how to worship. I loved visiting your church."

"We loved having you," Ian said. "Will you tell Diane you visited?"

Heather thought a moment. "Not yet. I mentioned we'd gotten back in touch, and she changed the subject pretty quickly. I think deep down she wishes she'd done more to get to know you when you were younger. She doesn't know what to do with you now."

"I get the feeling she may feel guilty, too, but I wish she wouldn't. I grew up a happy kid. I'll just keep praying for her."

"Me too," Heather said. She hugged her brother. "I love you."

"I love you too." Ian looked her in the eye. "God's got awesome plans for you, Heather. Just you wait and see."

Chapter Thirty-Two

The wind had definitely gone out of Kelli's sails.

After working so intensely with Brian on the album, she'd hardly seen him the last three weeks. After the funeral he'd had successive weekend concert dates around the country, and during the week he'd been busy with one thing or another related to the album release. They'd gotten together for the taping of the Choices video—which left everyone on the set speechless—but he pretty much disappeared again when it was over. After the fun days at Six Flags and the youth picnic, she'd thought they'd fall into a routine of spending time together like the old days. Now she found herself feeling deflated.

And downright sad.

"Heather, you're actually moving?"

They were back at the Cheesecake Factory, just the two of them.

Heather sliced into her strawberry cheesecake. "I know. I'm sad and elated at the same time. You're the best friend I've ever had. But it's not like we'll never talk."

"I know I should be thrilled for you—and I am—but it's happening so quickly."

"I would've been moving right about now anyway, if the Peyton Vine thing had come through."

Kelli looked at her. "I'm still bummed about that. I had such high hopes."

"Well, you know it took me awhile to get over it. I could see myself on that stage with her. But it was like God had a cushion ready for my fall—Ian and Becky and their kids."

"That's for sure." Kelli forked up some chocolate mousse cheesecake. "And a spot on the youth worship team."

"You know what's funny?" Heather asked. "After singing with a nationally known choir at Living Word and auditioning for Peyton Vine, I never would've thought I'd end up in youth worship at a much smaller church in Normal, Illinois. And yet, I'm excited."

Kelli smiled at her. "We've been praying for a church home for you. Didn't know God would give you family to boot." She gave a dramatic sigh. "So when do you leave?"

"Stop that."

Kelli laughed.

"I'm giving myself about two weeks."

"Two weeks?" Kelli set her fork down and leaned back on the cushion. "Wow." She came forward again suddenly. "What about the album release party? You'll come back for that, won't you? It's a Saturday, October 28th. The album releases the following Tuesday."

"I hope so. But I know one thing. I'm downloading my copy on iTunes when the clock strikes midnight."

"You'll already have your copy."

"I'm buying it anyway, for support."

The server refreshed Kelli's decaf, and she added cream and sugar. She glanced up at Heather. "Have you told Logan?"

Heather's eyes went to her cheesecake. "He knew it was a possibility, but I only told the church yes this afternoon." She looked up. "It's Thursday, though."

"I think it's so cute that you two still sing together after choir rehearsal."

"Yeah." Heather glanced downward. "I'll definitely miss that."

"What about Logan? Think you'll miss him?"

She angled her head downward. "He's my closest friend besides you. But we could've been separated either way. He's still waiting to hear from that church in Florida." She sighed. "We'll have the phone, e-mail, and all that."

"Won't be the same, though."

"No. Won't be the same." Heather pushed the remains aside. "I'm stuffed. So what about you and Brian? How are things?"

Kelli raised a brow. "There is no 'me and Brian.'"

"From what I could see, you two had gotten kind of close by the time the album wrapped."

Kelli shrugged. "Might've seemed that way because of the pressure of the deadline, but now that it's passed, we're each doing our own thing."

Heather eyed her. "How do you feel about that?"

"You had to go digging, didn't you?"

"I try to do my part."

Kelli took another sip of coffee. "Not sure how I feel about it. I went from hating him to tolerating him…"

"To enjoying him again?"

Kelli gave a reluctant nod. "Crazy, huh?"

"No. You'd be crazy if you didn't. Everybody loves that guy."

"Kind of like everybody loves Logan?"

"Touché." Heather gave a slight smile. "Funny how Brian and Logan have become good friends, isn't it? Think they ever sit around talking about us?"

"Those two?" Kelli shook her head. "Music and sports."

The moment Heather saw him, her heart let her know—she would miss Logan more than she knew. She slow-walked the aisle, listening to him play, watching the movement of his fingers, hearing his heart. He poured so much of himself into his music, into this ministry. Had she ever told him how much she admired that?

She sat by him on the bench, and their smiles and shoulder bumps said hello. When he reached the end of the song, he started into their favorite chorus.

He sang the first line. *"His grace and mercy have covered you, you're not the same…"*

She sang the next line with him, but she couldn't continue. Emotion filled her lungs.

He paused. "You okay?"

She touched his arm. "Please. Keep playing."

The words took her through her moments with Logan, from the Indy hotel to the family arena to every other time she'd ever seen him—each one a demonstration of his special care of her.

He turned toward her when he finished. "You're moving to Illinois, aren't you?"

She nodded, staring at the piano. They sat in silence.

He looked at her again. "It'll be awesome…getting to know your family, leading those kids in worship."

"Yeah, except they'll probably be leading me."

"So." He cleared his throat. "When do you leave?"

"About two weeks."

Silence swallowed the seconds again.

"I'll miss you, Heather."

She met his gaze, fresh tears on her lids. "I'll miss you too. Thank you, Logan, for everything you've done for me. You've been an amazing friend." She added quickly, "Not that this is good-bye—I mean, it's good-bye in some ways, but it doesn't mean our friendship has to end. I really hope… I hope it continues."

"Me too."

"You don't sound too confident."

"I'm a realist. It's not easy to maintain a friendship across the miles. But I do hope it can continue."

Why did Heather feel like her heart was breaking? They were just friends, for goodness' sake. But she couldn't stop crying.

Logan put an arm around her shoulder, and she leaned into him, allowing her head to find his chest. "Normal's not far," she said, "and besides, we'll have the next two weeks together."

He nodded against her hair. "And we have right now."

She reached for his hand and clung to it, remembering Cyd's words a few weeks ago about accepting God's will and God's timing. She really did feel He was leading her to go to Normal, but she also couldn't imagine life without Logan. Was it just a matter of timing? Or was this more of a good-bye than she was ready to admit?

Chapter Thirty-Three

The activity center at Living Word had played host to every kind of youth event, special ministry event, big-name speaker event, and even a music concert, but none had been anything like this. That's the story Brian kept hearing as he waited in a room down the hall. His album release party had packed the place as never before.

He looked up as the door opened and Jackson, a church volunteer, came in looking official—clipboard, cell phone, and walkie-talkie—ready to give his update. The room they were in had grown crowded too. Initially it was just a few people who would pray with Brian beforehand, including his friends who'd flown in from Atlanta. But as word leaked where he was, more and more people had filtered through the loose security system, all to wish him well.

The group grew quiet as Jackson lifted his hands to get their attention. "We're supposed to start in ten minutes, but the line is still stretched across the parking lot. We moved most of the tables out to make room, so we should be able to accommodate everyone. Just a matter of getting them inside in an orderly fashion. I think we'll be ready in twenty."

As the noise and mingling ratcheted up again, two people from Brian's label pulled Jackson aside to talk, and the three of them left. Logan walked over and took a seat beside Brian, who hadn't strayed far from his current posture since he'd arrived—elbows on the table, head resting in clasped hands, shooting up intermittent prayers. So much was riding on this night.

In a matter of minutes he would premiere an album he'd been excited about when first completed, but over the last two months had begun to wonder whether it was too hastily done and not up to par. Plus, he would premiere a video that revealed his darkest secret and receive instant feedback—the good, the bad, and the ugly. And that was only part of the weight he was carrying.

Logan eyed him. "How's it going? You ready?"

Brian blew out a breath. "I don't know if I could ever be ready. Tonight could go so many ways." He glanced toward the door. "Kelli's not even here yet. What am I supposed to make of that?"

Logan glanced that way himself. "You know she'll be here. But you would've made things easier for yourself if you hadn't pulled back from communicating with her."

"I've talked to her."

"About the video, stuff related to the album…"

"I know." Brian had already been second-guessing himself. "I felt like I had to be sure I wasn't running on emotion. I needed the space to pray and be sure"—he winced—"if that makes sense." He sighed. "I'm about to make a fool of myself in front of everybody."

Logan smiled at him. "But if it works out…what a moment."

"That doesn't exactly make me feel better."

Phyllis and Hayes's son Cole brought over a paper plate with two slices of sausage and mushroom pizza. Surprised, Brian looked and saw Hayes had come in with a carryout box.

"Thank you, buddy, I appreciate that," Brian told Cole. Then he called over to Hayes with a smile. "I thought it was settled. I told you I was fine with pepperoni and mushroom."

Pizza delivery had botched the order.

"It was the least I could do," Hayes said. "You should have your favorite on your big night. You deserve it."

Brian looked at him, at a loss for words. "Thank you," he said.

He took a bite, turning back to Logan. "Have you talked to Heather? How's that going?"

"Talked to her last night. She really wishes she could be here. But she's committed to that youth group, and they've got a retreat this weekend."

Brian kept eyeing him. "That's not what I was asking about. Unload, brother."

Logan clasped his hands behind his head. "It's weird. She's been gone, what, a month and a half? I feel more drawn to her now than when she was here. Can't wait to talk to her to find out how she's doing or to tell her about a song I wrote." He paused, a smile lighting his face. "Sometimes on Thursdays, she likes me to play a song for her over the phone."

"Pretty special stuff, man."

"Pretty scary stuff."

"Why scary? You thought a woman would *never* capture your heart?"

Logan narrowed his gaze, tilting his head a little. "I don't think I've wanted to step back and analyze it, but maybe that's it. She's captured my heart."

Brian paused before another bite. "Did it really take 'analysis' for you to see that?"

"You got a point. I almost wish that Florida position had come through. Then I would've been gone anyway. Being here without her is hard."

"Dude. She's two hours away. Not like you can't make a road trip."

Logan seemed to ponder that. "Maybe I should. I'd love to meet her family."

The door opened again and Brian looked, hoping it was Kelli. But Stephanie and Lindell breezed in, a look of bewilderment in Stephanie's eyes.

"What in the world?" she asked, looking back at the door after it closed. She and Lindell headed for Brian. "Two girls saw us headed down the hall," she told him, "and one of them whispered, 'I bet they know where Alien is.' They started following us!"

Lindell laughed. "I told them you'd be in the activity center shortly, but they said it was so crowded that this was the only chance they'd get to see you up close. For what it's worth, they said they're camping outside the door till you come out."

"I forget you're so popular," Stephanie said. "They're wearing shirts that say *I'm an alien too...not of this world*. What's up with that? You've got *shirts*?"

Brian shrugged. He found much of this hard to believe himself. "The label put those out with the first album." He stood. "I'll probably never get used to peo-

ple wanting to meet me. I'll go say hello." He popped
the last bit of pizza into his mouth.

Brian opened the door and stepped out to the sound
of gasps. He thought it funny that on Sundays he never
got this kind of reaction. But news of the release party
had been promoted through his website and other online sites, plus an e-blast for those who had signed
up to get news through the label. Fans had gotten the
word and come out, some of them driving hours, from
what he'd heard.

He smiled, shaking their hands. "Good to see y'all.
Thanks so much for showing up to support the new
project."

"I can't believe you actually came out," one of the
girls said, beaming. She looked at her friend. "He's
even cuter in person."

The friend nodded hard, eyes wide. "We can't wait to
hear the new music. Oh, and can you sign our shirts?"
She handed him a marker and turned her shoulder toward him.

"Sure can." He signed *Alien* and *Phil. 3:20* on both
and handed back the marker. "After you hear the songs,
you have to let me know what you think."

"Really? We'd love to."

Brian's eyes lifted beyond them. Kelli and her
mother were headed his way.

Vaguely he saw the girls depart. He was excited Mrs.
London had come to town, but mostly he couldn't take
his eyes off Kelli. She wore dark-colored pants, a top
and jacket with a slight silver shimmer, high-heeled
boots, and her hair was full and curly. He was glad she
considered this a special night for herself as well be-

cause it was. Her first work on an album. It meant the world to him to share this with her.

He walked the few steps to meet them and hugged Kelli's mom. "Mrs. London, I haven't seen you in so long. I'm so glad you could make it. And you look great."

"I wouldn't have missed it. I'm so overjoyed for Kelli—and you, young man"—Francine held his shoulders—"I'm so proud of you. I'm not surprised at all that you've got a music ministry. You were always special."

"Thank you, Mrs. London." He wondered if Kelli had told her about the video. She'd probably retract her view of him once she saw it. "And I don't know if I've ever really thanked you for giving me a second home growing up. It made a huge difference in my life."

"You made a huge difference in our lives too, Brian. You introduced us to the Lord—you and Grandma Howard, that is. I was so sorry to hear about her passing."

Brian held her words. "I appreciated the flowers you sent." He turned to Kelli. "Hey. You look beautiful."

She smiled, but it seemed distant. "Thanks."

Yep, I'm about to make a fool of myself.

"They say we should be ready to start soon. There are a few refreshments—"

He heard heels clacking down the hall and looked up. *Monica?* What was she doing here?

With an entourage of three she came toward them, looking glamorous in a long sparkly tunic, leggings, and extra-high heels. She spread her arms as she neared Brian.

"I'm so happy for you!" she exclaimed, hugging him.

He backed up a step. "I thought you couldn't come."

"I wasn't sure at first, then I wanted to surprise you. Did it work?"

"Yeah, I'd say it did." He saw Kelli and Mrs. London moving toward the door and stepped toward them. "You remember Kelli, don't you? And this is her mom."

Monica flashed a smile and greeted them. "Great work on the album," she told Kelli. "I was impressed, especially given this was your first collaboration."

Kelli exchanged a glance with Brian. "So you've already heard it?"

"Of course," Monica said.

Brian clarified. "She's heard *most* of the songs."

Monica looked perturbed. "I thought you sent all the songs. Anyway, Demetrius and Yolanda are on their way. We thought it'd be fun to spend some time together afterward, maybe go to dinner, like we've done for our other release parties. What do you think?"

"I'm not sure, Monica," Brian said. "I appreciate all of you coming, but I doubt it'll work tonight."

Monica's eyes flickered Kelli's way. "Okay. Just let us know."

They all entered the room together, and a small uproar ensued when people saw Monica. The last thing he wanted was for the evening to take on a "Brian and Monica" feel, but that's exactly what was happening, as he heard people assuming she'd sung on his album.

When everyone had moved to the activity center, he looked around for Kelli. She'd melded into the crowd, standing with her family, watching as if she too were waiting to hear the music for the first time. When Brian got the signal it was time to start, he gladly took the stage to get things going.

The extended roars and applause overwhelmed him.

Brian raised his hands, keeping Kelli in his line of vision. When the crowd quieted, he shook his head at them. "Y'all really came out, didn't you?"

They cheered again.

"You don't know how much I appreciate your support," he said, "but I have to admit I'm a little nervous." He paused, taking them in. "This project means so much to me. It's intensely personal, and I'm so close to it that I have no idea how anyone else will feel about it." He smiled. "But I hope you like it."

"We'll *love* it," someone yelled, joined by other shout-outs.

"You might've noticed the big screens mounted on either side of the room." Brian pointed to them. "We're also premiering a video tonight. We held this celebration here at Living Word because while the video features the first song that'll be released *on Tuesday*"—he waited while they cheered again—"it's also part of a ministry for young men that kicks off this week at our church. It's called 'Choices,' and…well, I think you'll see why I say this album is intensely personal."

He lowered his mic and waited as the lights dimmed and his face appeared on-screen, then he walked down the steps and stood with Kelli.

"Every good and perfect gift is from above, coming down from the Father," Brian was saying on-screen, his face shadowed, a soft piano playing. "And I saw that big-time in my own life, from the grandmother God gave me, from the mother and father who gave me life…and from the best friend he gave me in high school—Kelli London."

Cedric and Lindell turned to Kelli, stunned, along with Cyd and Stephanie. None of them knew Kelli had decided to go public with her part in the story. Brian had been stunned himself when he saw the final script. But she said she felt God prodding her to be transparent, to let go of needless shame, in order to touch others. Still, it clearly wasn't easy for her.

Brian clasped her hand, sure her heart was beating as hard as his.

"Kelli was the best friend I could've asked for," on-screen Brian was saying. "We shared a love of school, basketball, and music. In fact, Kelli was into music way more than I was. She wrote songs and she could sing, and I was sure one day she'd be a big star. I was the science nerd, and even though she didn't love it, she'd indulge me with fifty trips a month to the Science Center—and I'm only exaggerating a little."

The crowd giggled as young actors on-screen were shown inside the Science Center, wrestling a dinosaur.

"After two years of close friendship, we began dating, and it was innocent enough…for a while." The video showed a young couple walking through the hallways at school, holding hands. "But at the end of high school, I made a choice. Instead of keeping purity in the forefront of my mind, I wanted our relationship to go 'deeper.' Guess you could say we both did. And one day, we acted on that.

"I misused God's good and perfect gift."

The music turned a little ominous as the couple on-screen entered a bedroom, the door closing behind them. Brian took a peek behind him at Mrs. London. Her eyes were riveted to the screen.

On-screen Brian was walking down a lonely sidewalk at night. "Three weeks later, I learned she was pregnant. I spent some time thinking about what I should do." He looked at the camera. "Know what I came up with? I decided to follow up that first bad choice with a terrible choice. I walked away from Kelli and our baby. I wasn't even with her when she went to the clinic."

Brian could feel the stares around him. His stare was on the screen as he tried to hold it together. Kelli was wiping tears.

"My choice was all about me. I'd done my grand-mother proud. I was headed for college, first in my family, ready for a career in science, maybe a Nobel Prize. I didn't want to be weighed down. But when I got to college, I *was* weighed down—with guilt. I couldn't believe what I'd done to Kelli, to our baby—to God. I had sinned against Him, and I could barely stand the sight of myself."

The video showed a man anguished at his bedside, on his knees. "It was there in college, in the middle of the night, that I pleaded for forgiveness, and my life changed forever. I saw God in ways I'd never really seen Him, as a God of great mercy and grace. I re-committed my life to Him, and He led me down paths I never could've imagined…including this path of min-istry through music."

Brian walked through a field of grass, with blue sky overhead. "But there was still a problem, a choice need-ing to be made. As hard as it would be, I needed to find Kelli and tell her how sorry I was. Seven years after I'd walked out on her, I did find her—and trust me, it was hard." He looked into the camera again. "But remember what I said about grace and mercy? Took some time but she forgave me, and something happened beyond my wildest dreams. She became my co-collaborator on my second album, called *Love Letters*.

"But something even greater than that happened. Together we wrote a song for our baby, and it's the first release from the album—'I Will Love You.' We only ask you to do one thing as you listen. Think about the most important people in your life, and make the choice to love them hard now, while they're with you."

The song began playing, and on-screen, different images appeared of parents with their babies and children, couples, friends enjoying life, and back to babies.

By the end of the song, Brian had taken the stage again. As the lights came up, he was rocked by what he saw—people in tears across the room. He lifted the microphone. "I'd like to introduce my friend and co-collaborator on this album, Kelli London."

The room thundered louder than it had initially for Brian. Kelli made her way to the stage, and Brian took her into his arms. For long seconds they held one another, the crowd never once letting up. Finally, they turned to face everyone and waited another long while until the noise died down.

Brian sighed into the microphone. "Well. What did you think?"

He and Kelli looked at one another and smiled when the crowd erupted again. Brian held up his hand. "I am so blown away by your response. God showed up in a big way on that song, didn't He?" Brian paused while a few whistles sounded. "But wait, that's just one song on the album. We've got twelve, and each one is a love letter. Volunteers are passing through the crowd right now to give you a handout so you can read what each love letter is about as the song plays."

He held up a copy of the CD. "And of course, we've got the CD available here tonight. I love this artwork on the cover, but I especially love what it says at the top: *Alien, featuring Kelli London.*"

Kelli leaned over to take a look. "I hadn't seen that. You put my name on the cover?"

He smiled at her, then addressed the crowd. "Kelli and I would love to meet you. We'll be over at the signing table."

She whispered as they walked down the steps. "I'm signing too?"

Brian took her hand. "Of course you are."

Mrs. London was one of the first people they saw in the crowd. He couldn't read her expression.

She looked from Kelli to Brian, then back to Kelli. "Why am I just hearing this tonight? Why didn't you tell me, Kelli? I would've been there for you."

"I know." Kelli barely made eye contact. "There are a lot of things I should've done. I'm sorry."

"I'm sorry, too, Mrs. London. I wasn't the person you thought I was."

She stared them both down, shaking her head, then pulled them into a hug. "Pretty smart, Kelli, letting me find out through that video. Who could stay mad after watching that? It was too powerful." She looked at them again. "Brian, you made some wrong choices— we all do—but you're still the thoughtful young man you always were." She noticed a line growing behind them. She gave them the eye. "We'll talk more later, all right?"

Kelli and Brian glanced at one another. "All right," they said.

Monica approached them next, her eyes teary.

"Brian, I see why you didn't let me hear that particular song until now." She glanced at Kelli. "I knew you two had a history, but I didn't know it ran that deep. That was so moving. I could only praise God as I listened."

Brian was grateful for this first bit of feedback. "I appreciate that, Monica. It wasn't easy to tell that story."

"But it'll impact so many. I know it will." She looked at Kelli. "I loved that song when you played it for me, but I see now why it wasn't meant to be. You two were meant to do it together." She paused. "Actually, you were meant to do this whole album together. What a beautiful story."

Kelli smiled, hanging on to Brian's hand. "Thank you, Monica. That means a lot to me."

Brian spotted the teen girls whose shirts he had signed, waiting behind Monica. He pulled Kelli forward and introduced her to them.

The smiley giggles were gone. One of them was crying.

Kelli let Brian's hand go and hugged her. "What's wrong?"

"I'm eighteen," she said, "and I made the same choice last year." Her chest heaved. "I know God forgives me, but I couldn't forgive myself. I grew up in a good Christian family, and they don't even know. I felt so alone, like I was the only one who had done something like this." She looked at Brian. "Thank you. I loved you before, but I *really* love you now. That video was so freeing for me, just to be able to focus on God's grace and mercy."

Kelli smiled. "That's the song that's playing right now. His grace and mercy have covered you." She tugged on the girl's hand. "It took me a long time to believe that, so I'm telling you now—believe it. Okay?"

The girl nodded, fresh tears spilling. "Can I dedicate that same love song to my baby?"

Kelli glanced at Brian, her own tears welling, and he knew what she was thinking. She couldn't believe the song was already providing comfort to someone else.

"Oh, absolutely you can," Kelli said.

For the next hour, they heard similar stories from people in the signing line. Many, though, simply shared how moved they were by the video and song. Brian and Kelli sat side by side, marveling at the reactions, focusing on each individual. But although Brian was encouraged, he wasn't totally relieved. This was a highly supportive crowd. What would happen Tuesday when the song was officially released? What would the masses say? What would they think of him?

Brian's ear was tuned to the sequence of the songs. When the last track neared the end, he told Kelli they needed to wrap it up and head back to the stage. As soon as the crowd saw them up there, they howled as if they hadn't seen them all night.

"Does that mean you liked *Love Letters*?" Brian asked.

As they yelled affirmation, Brian looked at Kelli. "Can you believe this? All those hours, all that prayer."

Kelli smiled. "God is faithful."

Brian faced the crowd again. "Now that you've had a chance to hear all the songs, for the rest of the evening—"

"Hey! Wait!"

He turned. Logan was coming up the stairs.

"Ladies and gentlemen," Brian said, "one minute,

please. This is Logan Duncan, our assistant worship pastor here at Living Word."

The crowd gave Logan a shout-out, especially the ladies.

Logan whispered in Brian's ear.

"You're saying they haven't heard all the songs?" Brian's jaw dropped as he listened. He checked the back of the CD. "There's a hidden bonus track on *my* album?"

He stared at Kelli with a look of shock. A second later he had his arm around Logan with a wide grin.

"Okay, I have a confession to make, everybody," he said. "You heard twelve love letters—a love letter to our baby, to the world, to those who are suffering, to young men and young women, to the least of these, to fellow aliens"—he waited as they cheered—"to the fearfully and wonderfully made, and so on." He paused. "But there's one love letter you haven't heard yet—my love letter to Kelli."

Gasps and choruses of "Aww…" sounded from the crowd.

Kelli's hand went to her chest as she looked at Brian.

"You all heard what I put her through, how I misused God's good and perfect gift…when I should've cherished her, as God does. My friend here, Logan, did the song with me, and I'm dedicating it to Kelli. We're about to perform it live. It's called 'Cherished.'"

Chapter Thirty-Four

As a chair was brought onstage for Kelli, she didn't even try to hold back her emotion. Brian had written a love song for her? And included it on his album for the world to hear? She couldn't keep her hands still as she sat. These last few weeks, she'd begun to wonder if he cared about her—even as her own feelings grew, though she'd barely admitted it to herself. It was too much to process.

As she focused on the first lines of the song, as the melody entered her soul, she couldn't keep it together. It was absolutely beautiful, Logan crooning the chorus that let her know she was cherished.

Brian rapped the verses partially facing the crowd but mostly facing her. She stared at him through her tears, hanging on every word, words penned specifically for her. He'd written them in such a way that a listener could think of them as God's love, but Brian had already said it…this was dedicated from him to her.

Logan sang the last part of the song, and when it ended, he hugged her and left the stage. Kelli was about to stand, but Brian motioned for her to remain where she was. He lowered himself to one knee, and the crowd went wild.

"Brian…" she said. It was all she could say.

He reached inside his jacket, pulled out a velvet box, and opened it. Kelli closed her eyes, trying to grasp what was happening.

"Can I please have quiet?" Brian asked the crowd.

Suddenly one could hear a pin drop.

"Kelli London…"

She opened her eyes again, and they locked immediately with Brian's.

"…you are the best friend I could ever ask for, the best collaborator I could ever work with, and the only woman I want to spend my forever with on this earth. I love you, Kelli. Will you marry me?"

Marry him? He was asking her right here to *marry* him?

Someone eased onstage to hand her a microphone. She held it, her eyes sweeping the crowd. It was so *quiet*, everyone awaiting her answer. She gulped, looking at Brian again.

"I honestly doubt there's anyone else on this earth I'd rather spend my life with, Brian…" She gazed downward and finally brought her eyes back up to meet his again. "But a short while ago, we weren't even speaking. I'm not saying no. I just need time…to wrap my mind around this, around us…to be…sure."

Low murmurs sounded throughout the crowd as Brian closed the velvet box and stood, avoiding her gaze. Kelli wished the crowd would all disappear, that she could talk to him further, alone. She was moved to her very core by what he'd done, and she hated to do this to him. But they'd barely been in touch lately. What was he thinking?

She rose from the chair and turned to leave the stage, but when she glanced at Brian, she couldn't. She took his hand and led him center stage.

"This evening has been so incredible," she said, speaking into the mic. "Your presence, your enthusiasm, your feedback on the songs—all of it far surpassed our expectations. But please, I don't want you to leave with the impression that my response just now is any reflection on Brian. In fact, my admiration of him just went through the roof. It's just, to me, marriage is a lifelong commitment, and I need to be sure of my own heart."

Kelli gripped his hand still. "I want you to leave knowing that this man is the real deal. He loves the Lord, and he loves this music ministry. He didn't tell you this, but he recently gave up a personal ambition to attain a PhD in biochemistry because he felt this was God's calling on his life." She turned toward him. "Brian Howard, to me, you are the most special guy on the planet—and we could even say you're out of this world."

Brian and Kelli embraced, and the crowd whistled and cheered again. Their music played over the speakers as they left the stage and people began leaving. They took more pictures and heard more stories, but Kelli still couldn't wait to get him alone. They needed to talk.

That moment came hours later as Kelli and Brian stole away to an all-night diner. They placed their order, handed the menus to the server, and stared at one another across a small booth.

"Brian," she began, "what were you thinking, asking me to marry you like that? It's not like we'd been seeing one another. For all I knew, you were dating Monica."

"Monica?" Brian looked hurt, frustrated. "I told her months ago that I couldn't pursue a relationship with her...because of you."

"Well, how would I know that? You weren't pursuing a relationship with me either."

Brian sighed. "I went about things the wrong way— obviously. After spending so much time together on this album, I knew, Kelli. I knew I wanted to spend my life with you. But I thought if I pursued you outright, if I told you I'd fallen in love with you all over again, you'd turn and run. So I asked God to pursue you for me."

"What?"

"Well, deep down, I kind of thought you might be falling for me again too. But I thought you'd be afraid to trust me, given what I did. So I prayed for God to knit our hearts together again. And I don't know... when 'Cherished' came together the way it did, I got excited about this idea of surprising you with the song and a proposal in front of everyone—which I *thought* was from God." He sighed again. "I made such a fool of myself."

Kelli reached for his hand across the table. "Your prayer was answered, though."

"Which one?"

"For God to pursue me for you and knit our hearts together. Even though we haven't talked much the last couple of months, I couldn't stop thinking about you." She stared into his eyes, wondering how much of her heart to reveal. She decided to trust him with it. "It became clear to me that...I'd fallen in love with you again."

Emotion filled Brian's eyes. "When you didn't say it onstage, I thought..."

"I don't know why I couldn't say it. Part of me was still holding back, I guess. But I do, Brian. I love you. I wonder if I ever really stopped."

He grabbed her other hand, and they lingered that way a few moments. "So what now?" he asked finally. He glanced at his coat pocket with a sheepish look. "I've still got this ring."

Kelli smiled. "I'm excited, actually. I'm looking forward to enjoying our friendship again, enjoying *you* again...allowing our love to grow." She squeezed his hand. "I think we'll know what to do about that ring in God's time."

Brian looked at her. "I felt so low on that stage. I wanted to be celebrating our engagement tonight." He paused. "But I feel like we're celebrating something just as special—our love. And that's a gift I thought we'd never have again. I'm thankful, Kel."

"Me too."

He got the sheepish look again. "God's time?"

"God's time."

He sighed. "But I've never been crazy about those 'wait on God' verses."

Chapter Thirty-Five

Kelli and Brian stood on the front step looking down the street, an April breeze whipping through the trees. Kelli rubbed her arms against the slight chill. "Didn't he say they were leaving an hour ago? What could be taking so long?"

Brian shrugged. "Traffic, maybe?"

"On a Sunday afternoon?"

The front door opened, and Stephanie stepped out. "They're not here yet?"

Kelli and Brian shook their heads.

"Wait, I see something." Kelli took a few steps down the front walk to get a better view. "It's them!"

As they got closer to the house, Stephanie chuckled. "Cedric driving that big SUV is so funny to me. I'm still shocked he gave up the convertible." She opened the door and yelled inside, "They're here!"

Lindell, Francine London, and Cyd's parents, Bruce and Claudia, showed their excited faces.

Cedric parked in the driveway and got out. "I think

we saw each and every one of you this morning. Why didn't anyone tell us you were headed over here?"

"It's called a surprise, silly," Stephanie said.

Cedric had a big smile. "You got me. Momma, you said you were on your way back to Little Rock."

Francine hugged him. "We wanted to capture this moment. The three of you coming home for the first time. Now help your family out of the car."

"Oh." Cedric pulled the door handle, where Cyd was comfortably ensconced in the back, her head leaning over the car seat in the middle.

"Let me help you, babe," Cedric said. When Cyd was slow to move, he added with a smile, "He'll be okay without you for a minute."

Cyd turned and took Cedric's hand. Kelli was amused when Cyd's face showed surprise. Was she just now noticing them?

Cyd waved for the video camera in Lindell's hands as she stepped out, then turned to her parents. "Mom and Dad, you were with us at the hospital a little while ago. How'd you beat us over here?"

"Cedric must've been like Bruce when you were born," Claudia said. "I think he drove five miles an hour on the trip home from the hospital, worried something might happen to you."

"Scariest ride of my life." Cedric was on a knee in the back, trying to unhook the infant seat. "This little guy's whole life is in my hands."

"Wait till you're ready to give *him* the keys," Bruce said. "You'll be a nervous wreck."

"I'm on day three, Dad," Cedric said. "I can't see anywhere beyond that."

Everyone gathered around the car to get a fresh look at the baby as Cedric lifted the seat out.

"Look at him," Stephanie said. "He's squinting at the sun. Is that the cutest thing or what?"

Lindell moved closer to film the baby's face. "Welcome home, Chase Kyle London. Wave at the camera."

"Cover him up better, babe," Cyd said. "It's a little windy out here."

Cedric pulled the blanket up more as they moved into the house. Reese jumped on him, then tried to jump on the infant seat to get a gander at this bundle claiming all the attention.

"Uh-oh," Cedric said. "How do we get Reese to calm down around the baby?"

"We didn't think it through yet," Cyd said. "For now, she needs to go in the kitchen." She bent down and rubbed her fur. "Sorry, little sweetie."

"Come on, Reese," Kelli said. She gated the dog and joined the others in the family room.

Cyd had taken Chase out of his seat, and he was nestled against her in the overstuffed chair. She let out a huge happy sigh, looking at Cedric, who sat on the floor beside her. "I think it's finally sinking in. I'm a mom. You're a dad. We have a baby."

Cedric looked overwhelmed. "A healthy baby. I'll never forget the moment he came into the world. I didn't think it would affect me like that. A baby's birth—the whole process, really—is an absolute miracle."

Kelli and Brian glanced at one another on the love seat. Without a word, they knew what was on each other's mind.

Francine was beaming, standing over the baby. "And

I think it's finally sinking in that I'm a grandma, after all these years!"

"Tell me about it," Claudia said. "Now we've got someone to spoil to our hearts' content."

"Ma," Cyd said, "you already bought more clothes than this boy could possibly wear, more toys than he'll ever have time to play with—"

"Cyd." Cedric patted her knee. "Don't even try to fight it. They've waited this long. Let them have at it."

"Now that's the spirit, son." Francine brought her hands together in a big clap. "And by the way, I haven't unloaded my trunk yet. I need one of you boys to go get those gifts. Might take two of you."

Cedric shook his head.

Kelli's phone dinged, letting her know she had a text. She got her phone from the coffee table, read the message, and smiled. "Heather says she's coming Wednesday. She can't wait to see the baby."

"Mm-hmm," Stephanie said. "That's not all she can't wait to see."

"That's probably true," Kelli said, sitting back down. "Last time she visited, I hardly got any time with her— and she was staying here with us. Seems like the move only made her and Logan grow closer."

"I miss her," Cyd said. "Tell her we're thrilled she's coming."

Kelli typed out a response, then looked up again. "Cyd, can I hold the baby? I didn't get a chance at the hospital."

"Of course. Here."

Cedric lifted him gingerly from his mother's arms. He stretched his little body, as if wondering why the interruption. "Come on, little man. Let's go see your Aunt Kel."

Kelli grinned as he placed the baby in her arms. "Everything is so tiny. I can see why you were nervous, Cedric. You feel like something will break." She traced his little eyebrows, handled his little fingers. "It's definitely a miracle"—she spoke almost to herself—"the way God forms all these parts."

Brian moved closer to get a better look. "He's beautiful." He put his arm around Kelli and spoke in a low tone. "It's not easy, is it?"

Hearing him say it brought tears to her eyes. "No. It isn't." She looked to see if anyone else was listening, but they were all engaged in their own conversations. She looked at Brian. "I wonder if ours was a boy or a girl."

"Don't do that to yourself, Kel."

"I'm not. I was just…wondering." She thought a moment. "I guess the baby's always in my mind, though, because that's the song people want to hear."

"Still amazes me. That song has brought healing to a lot of people."

Kelli had been going on the road with Brian, mostly to churches that invited them. During the concert, they always took the time to share their story, and the grace and mercy of God. They each had a box of letters and printed e-mails that people had sent, sharing their own stories.

Chase yawned and opened his eyes.

"He's so precious," Kelli said. She held him in her lap so she could look directly at him. Never had her heart been so moved. "I pray God blesses us with a whole house full of children," she said.

"That would be—" He looked at her. "Wait. What did you say?"

"I said I pray God blesses us—"

"I know what you said. I mean, what are you saying? You said *us*—as in, together?"

Kelli smiled. "What I'm saying is I couldn't be more sure...that is, if you're still sure."

He shook his head as if shaking loose cobwebs. "Kelli, I'm not assuming I understand anything here. Are you telling me you're ready to say yes to my proposal? You'll marry me?"

"Still got the ring?"

"Kel, humor me. I just need to hear one word. I'll even get back on my knees."

"Oh, don't do that."

Brian knelt before the love seat, and suddenly everyone stopped talking. Lindell grabbed the video camera.

Brian took a breath. "Kelli London, will you marry me?"

Kelli looked into his eyes, those beautiful brown eyes. "Yes, Brian. I'll marry you."

He gazed into her eyes, and she knew he was choking back emotion.

"Kelli, I promise you," he said, "I will love and cherish you for the rest of my days."

Cheers rang throughout the room.

"Hey, Brian," Cedric said, "don't know if you know this, but the vows usually come later, at the ceremony." He walked over to him. "Congrats, man. You've got a special girl there."

Brian stood and hugged him. "Don't I know it."

Lindell stopped filming and hugged him too. "I couldn't be happier for you two." He looked down at

Kelli. "But that was brutal, sis, making him wait all this time."

"You leave my baby girl alone," Francine said. "It's a woman's prerogative to take as long as she needs. They've got the rest of their lives to enjoy one another." She looked over at Kelli, eyes dancing. "That being said, I was wondering what was taking you so long, sweetheart."

Kelli laughed, gently stroking the baby's thin hair. "So I'm the bad guy, huh?"

"Not at all," Brian said, sitting next to her again. "God did a lot over these months. For one thing, I didn't think it was possible to love you this much more."

"Aww." Stephanie smiled from the sofa. "And can I mention that neither of you lovebirds has thanked me?"

Kelli looked her way. "For?"

"For bringing the two of you back together after all those years. If I hadn't approached Brian at that conference for help with Monica and then asked to use his laptop, you wouldn't have recorded your song on there, he never would have known about it, and you wouldn't have worked on the album together. Shoot, I'm responsible for that album too."

Brian laughed. "You know, there's some truth to that. This is one of those *It's a Wonderful Life* moments. What would our lives be like without Stephanie?"

"Hmph." Stephanie curled her legs behind her. "A few of y'all would be in trouble. I'm just sayin'."

Cyd reached for the pillow behind her and threw it at her.

Brian laughed again, shaking his head. "I really do love y'all. You're the closest family I have. I'll even claim the fearfully and wonderfully made ones who have to wear Spanx."

"Oh! Did you really go there?"

The room exploded in banter.

Kelli brought the baby to her bosom, cuddling him closer, inhaling the sweet smell that made her heart ache. For years she'd thought her dreams had turned to dust—dreams of music, dreams of a future with Brian. God had brought the dreams back, but in ways she never could have imagined...out of a pain she never would have thought she could endure. Would she have dreamed those dreams, had she known?

She still had dreams, like the babies she hoped she and Brian would have. But what she wanted more than dreams was God's purpose and plan, the things He'd mapped out before time began...for her—and Brian.

Kelli looked at him now, in animated conversation with her family, and smiled. She couldn't wait to tell him—she would love and cherish him too, all the rest of her days.

* * * * *

Acknowledgments

I am so thankful for the ways in which God shows us He cherishes us. With respect to this book, His love and care were shown through the people He sent to aid in the process of writing and getting it into your hands. I'm indebted to the following people:

To my editors, Amanda Bostic and L.B. Norton— you are invaluable, insightful, and plain fantastic to work with. Amanda, thank you for being a sounding board when I had little more than a rough idea for the book, and helping me flesh it out. You are always there, and I'm so thankful for your friendship, not to mention your brilliant editing skills. ☺ L.B., thank you for your knack in taking a completed manuscript and zeroing in on the exact things needed to make it better. And I'll tell ya, I'm going to get that destination wedding yet!

To my publisher, Allen Arnold—you are an "exceedingly abundant" blessing. Thank you for being available, thoughtful, creative, and prayerful. You're an amazing leader, and I'm so grateful for your support.

To Katie Bond, Eric Mullet, Becky Monds, Kristen Vasgaard, and Ashley Schneider—your talent and creativity amaze me. Thank you for your energy, your ideas, and the immense work you put into Thomas Nelson Fiction. Love those roundtable discussions!

To singer/songwriters Nicole C. Mullen, Alex Williams, and Tony "prof. t" Tolbert; Christian rapper Travis "Thi'sl" Tyler; and Artist Manager Gessie Thompson—your know-how, experiences, and anecdotes about the business were invaluable to this book. Thank you so much for letting me pick your brain about something I've loved since I can remember—music!

To my literary agent, Tina Jacobson—thank you for believing in me from the start and encouraging me every step of the way since. To Tami Heim and Shannon Litton—thank you for that *aha!* moment of seeing what God had been building in my ministry and helping to shape it. And Tami, always thankful for the long talks at the Heim B&B. ☺ To Gessie Thompson—thank you for being not only a partner in ministry, but a true sister in Christ and accountability partner.

To the *cherished* members of my prayer team—I can't thank you enough for praying me through the writing of this book and tons more. Thank you for allowing me to be vulnerable and transparent, and always responding with love and encouragement.

To my mother, Edna J. Cash, who's so much more than a mom—thank you for being a personal intercessor and having the discernment to see what God is doing in my life. Your love and wisdom are priceless. To my dad and stepmom, Earl and Joyce Cash—so thankful for your enthusiastic support and encouragement, which have never wavered. I'm a blessed daughter!

To Bill, Quentin, and Cameron—you see me in the good moments and the not-so-good, when life is hectic, deadlines are looming, and patience is wearing… and you love me right through it. I thank God for you. I *cherish* you. I'm privileged to live life with you.

To the God I *cherish*, because He first *cherished* me—without You, Lord, I can do nothing. Thank You for Your grace and strength. Thank You for Your faithfulness. Thank You for moving me to pen a story that highlights the breadth of Your forgiveness and the depth of Your unconditional love.

To the readers—thank you from the bottom of my heart. Your support fuels this ministry. Your notes of encouragement fuel my passion and energy. I thank God for you and I pray for you, that He would meet you as you read, speak to your heart, and draw you close. May you be keenly aware of how much He *cherishes* you!

Dear Reader,

I don't know what could be greater than to live a life of faith and to be called a woman of faith. It doesn't mean we've got it all together. It doesn't mean we won't fail. It simply means we wake up every day with a profound sense that we need the Lord. Every minute. In everything.

Even more, I hope you've seen in *Cherished* that it doesn't matter where you've been. Indeed, strong faith is often built upon brokenness and humiliation. But often, we need the help of other women to build us up, to let us know we can move beyond the hurt and the pain—to encourage us that we, too, can be true women of faith. Kelli and Heather had Cyd. And you can find that same encouragement in real life, through a weekend with Women of Faith.

At a Women of Faith conference, you get the real deal. The women on the platform will tell you the truth about where they've been—their struggles, failures, and disappointments. And they will tell you how a loving God swooped in and showed them how much He cherished them. Each time I've heard a speaker—or a musical artist—share her testimony from that stage, my heart has filled with praise for God. And my own faith has been strengthened.

I hope you'll grab a few of your girlfriends and experience this life-changing weekend together. You will leave inspired. And like Kelli and Heather, you will know that His grace and mercy have covered you, that He cherishes you, and that you can daily walk as a great woman of faith.

Kim

Questions for Discussion

1. A central message of *Cherished* is that you are cherished by God and nothing can separate you from His love. Do you believe that deep in your heart?

2. It was hard for Kelli to consider what God might want to do in her life, because of her past. Is there anything in your past that you feel "disqualifies" you from being used by God? Has the book caused you to see that differently?

3. The women in Daughters' Fellowship have a "DF check" from Proverbs 3:5–6. If one of them is trying to figure out what to do, they ask themselves whether they're leaning on their own understanding or acknowledging and trusting God? Do you tend to be a "leaner" or an "acknowledger"?

4. The tagline of the Songwriters' Summit asked, "What were you made to do?" Ephesians 2:10 says, "For we are His workmanship, created in Christ Jesus for good works, which God prepared beforehand, that we should walk in them." Do you believe God has a plan for your life, something you were made to do? Have you asked Him what that is? Do you believe you're walking in those plans?

5. Stephanie charged Kelli to believe that "all things are possible," from Mark 9:23. Do you tend to

place limits on what God can do through you, or do you believe that all things are possible through Christ?

6. Heather came to the end of herself after the incident with Ace and was propelled to the foot of the cross. Has there been a painful circumstance in your life that caused you to see Christ more clearly?

7. Heather had a change of heart, such that she wanted to get to know Jesus above all else in her life. Do you have a hunger to walk with Jesus and know Him better? Do you take the time to pursue Him?

8. Brian wasn't sure of God's plan for his life, but was willing to go whichever way the Lord led. Are you willing to ask and follow God's will for your life?

9. In the "Heart of a Psalmist" session, the panel discussed how to keep a right heart in the business they were in. How do you keep a right heart before God?

10. If you are in a group setting, statistics say that 1 out of 4 of you have had an abortion. Without anyone having to openly divulge this, take a moment in your group to pray for complete healing for those women. If you are alone and the book has uncovered emotional pain from an abortion, please pray to God for healing and seek help, if necessary. God's arms are open.

11. Ephesians 4:32 says, "And be kind to one another, tender-hearted, forgiving each other, just as God in Christ also has forgiven you." Dana had difficulty forgiving Heather for what she'd done, and Kelli had difficulty forgiving Brian. Is there someone in your life whom you find hard to forgive? Have you sought God's grace to help?

12. Do you have any unlikely friendships, such as Kelli and Heather's, that sprung up as a result of God's work in your life and heart?

13. What character did you identify with most in the book?

14. What aspect of *Cherished* spoke most to your heart?

About the Author

Kim Cash Tate is the author of *Faithful, Heavenly Places,* and the memoir *More Christian than African American.* A former practicing attorney, she is also the founder of Colored in Christ Ministries. She and her husband have two children.